Under the Apple Blossoms

A Lake Harriet Novel

Under the Apple Blossoms
A Lake Harriet Novel
Copyright 2020 © Deanna Lynn Sletten

ISBN – 13: 978-1-941212-50-9

Cover Designer: Deborah Bradseth of Tugboat Design

Novels by Deanna Lynn Sletten

The Women of Great Heron Lake

Miss Etta

Night Music

One Wrong Turn

Finding Libbie

Maggie's Turn

Walking Sam

As the Snow Fell

Chasing Bailey

Destination Wedding

Summer of the Loon

Sara's Promise

Memories

Widow, Virgin, Whore

Kiss a Cowboy

A Kiss for Colt

Kissing Carly

Outlaw Heroes

Under the Apple Blossoms

A Lake Harriet Novel

DEANNA LYNN SLETTEN

Chapter One

Debbie Adams's leg muscles strained as she pedaled her bicycle through her neighborhood toward the trails at Lake Harriet. It was the second week in March, and snow still edged the sidewalks and covered lawns, and the temperature was a chilly forty-one degrees. Despite the weather, she couldn't put off exercise any longer. Rain or snow, cold or heat, she had to lose ten pounds by early summer.

Debbie glanced up at the gray sky and frowned, then looked into the blanket-lined basket attached to the handlebars. Nestled under the fleece was her sweet little dog, Chloe.

"The weatherman promised sunshine today," Debbie complained. "Why are they always wrong?"

Chloe snuggled deeper into the blanket and only stared at Debbie.

"I know, I know. It's cold. But I have to start sometime," Debbie said. She probably shouldn't have brought her little Maltese along for the ride, but Chloe went everywhere with her. The fluffy white dog was her companion at home, at her shop, Deb's Bridal Boutique, and just about everywhere else she went. But dragging her out on this ridiculous attempt to burn calories riding a bike may have been a foolish idea. *It's definitely feeling like a stupid idea,* Debbie thought as her thigh muscles burned. *I should have bought an exercise bike instead and stayed inside the warmth of my house.* But she knew that hadn't been an option. She earned enough from her business to keep a roof over her head and pay for necessities, but not for extravagant items like exercise equipment. That's why she now found herself on her twenty-year-old bike, pedaling through the wet and sometimes icy streets.

By the time she reached the path around the still-frozen lake, her face stung from the crisp air, and her muscles burned. She was bundled up in sweats, a bulky jacket, gloves, and a stocking cap that covered her thick, sandy-blond hair. But her face felt like a frozen popsicle, and her blue eyes watered.

"We've made it this far," she said determinedly, glancing down at Chloe. "We can make it around the lake." She grit her teeth. "Maybe." As Debbie looked up again, she saw something coming right at her. The bike hit an icy patch and slid, and she screamed as she lost control and the bike hit the ground.

* * *

Marc Bennett stared in horror as he watched the bundled-up person on the rickety bicycle nearly run into him. He quickly darted out of the way, tugging Bernie's leash hard so the dog wouldn't get hit either. Marc had been running along the path with Bernie as he did most days throughout the year, his earbuds blaring music. When he'd glanced up, there was the bike, nearly on top of him.

The bike hit an icy spot and slid out of control, causing the rider and bicycle to skid and fall near a bush at the edge of the trail. Marc instantly ran into action, hurrying toward the person lying on the sidewalk.

"I'm so sorry! Are you okay? I didn't see you coming at me," he blurted out, kneeling beside the person. He heard a groan, then the bundle of clothing turned its head, and big, watery blue eyes fringed in thick lashes stared up at him. Marc was stunned for a moment. They were the most beautiful, expressive eyes he'd ever seen. He hadn't been expecting the bundle of clothes to be a woman.

She groaned again.

Marc flew into action. "I'm so sorry. Let me help you up." He reached for her arm.

The woman slowly unfolded and got to her knees. It was at that moment that Bernie decided to help too.

"Ack!" she yelled. "What's that? A bear?" She fell back against the ground again.

Marc chuckled. "Bernie? No, he's a dog. He's a Bernese Mountain Dog, so he's big." Marc reached for the woman's arms. He grabbed a handful of her coat and helped pull her up to her feet. Well, at least he thought she was on her feet. Her entire height only came up to his chest.

The woman stared at her bike in dismay. "The tire's bent!" she cried, sounding exasperated. "How will I ever ride it home?"

"I'm sure we can fix it," Marc said optimistically, although he didn't really believe he could. *She needs a new bicycle. This one's shot.*

The woman stared up at him, tears freezing on her cheeks. His first instinct was to wrap his arms around her padded body and comfort her, but he refrained from doing so. That might make matters worse. Suddenly, he saw her eyes grow wide with terror.

"Chloe! Oh, my God! I forgot about Chloe!" she screamed.

She fell to her knees again and pulled at the blanket inside the basket on the bike.

"Chloe? Who's that?" Marc asked, trying to understand what she was looking for.

"My dog! She was in the basket. The fall would have killed her!" She crawled around the wet sidewalk, searching for her dog. "Chloe! Chloe!" she called frantically.

Marc began searching too. He wasn't sure what kind of dog he was looking for. He ran to the other side of the bush, followed by Bernie. As the big dog stuck his nose into the bush, a high-pitched bark came from inside it. Bernie pushed in deeper.

"Stop him! He's hurting my dog!" the women yelled. She reached inside and pulled out a small puff of fur. Glaring at Marc, she hugged her dog close. "Your dog tried to kill Chloe!"

Marc stared at her in disbelief. "Dog? That's a dog?"

The woman stood up taller, well, at least as tall as she could, and glowered at him. "Of course she's a dog. What else would she be?"

The situation was so ridiculous that laughter overcame Marc. "I'm sorry, lady. But *that's* a puffball." He pointed to Bernie. "*This* is a dog."

What little of the woman's face he could see between the scarf and the stocking cap turned red with anger. "No. *He's* a monster. And he was attacking poor Chloe!"

Marc sobered. "Bernie is big, but he wouldn't hurt a fly, let alone your little powder puff. He's a gentle giant." To prove Marc's point, Bernie sat there innocently watching them.

The woman looked as if she were going to argue with him, but then her face crumpled, and tears began to fall again. "I knew I shouldn't have tried biking today. It's all useless. I'm never going to lose weight anyway. And now my bike's ruined and I almost killed my dog. I give up." She sulked over to a bench beside the trail and sat as best she could in all the clothes she was wearing.

Marc watched, his heart going out to her. He followed her to the bench. "It wasn't a bad idea; it's just a little early to be on this trail with a bike. Wait another month, and the ice will be gone."

"I don't have a month!" she wailed, hugging her dog tighter. "I need to lose weight now! For once in my life, I want to look good for a friend's wedding. I'm always the short, chubby one around all the tall, slender girls. I'm tired of being fat." She rubbed away her tears with the sleeve of her jacket.

Marc sat down beside her. "There's nothing you can do about being the short one," he said, giving her a friendly smile. "And, well, I can't tell with all the clothes you're wearing, but I'm sure you're not fat. You're probably just out of shape. A little muscle-toning and you'll feel better."

The woman stopped crying and stared at him, looking insulted. "You don't know anything about me."

"I'm sorry. I'm not trying to insult you." He reached into the pocket of his sleek workout jacket and pulled out a business card. "I'm a trainer at a gym. I work with people, helping them get into shape." He handed her the card.

"Oh." She stared at it. "Fit in 20. Isn't that a big chain of gyms around the Twin Cities?"

Marc grinned. "Yes, it is. I mainly work at the one on the Nicolette Mall. It's not too far from here."

She stared at the card again as she hugged Chloe. Marc saw the dog's eyes watching him, and it made him smile. He reached out his gloved hand. "I'm Marc Bennett. And I'm sorry I made you fall down."

Debbie shook his hand. "I'm Debbie. Debbie Adams. I'm sorry I almost ran into you."

He smiled wider, and she gave him a slight grin.

"It's nice to meet you, Debbie."

She nodded, then glanced toward her bike. "I'd better start pushing that home. It's going to take a while." She stood and walked toward the bike.

"My car is just across the street. Why don't you let me drive you and your bike home? Do you live nearby?"

She eyed him suspiciously. "It's a few blocks away, but I'll be fine."

Marc picked up the bike, and Debbie placed Chloe into the basket, fluffing the blanket around her. The dog stared at her with worried eyes.

"I won't drop you again. I promise," Debbie told Chloe. She took the handlebars from Marc and pushed the bike a few steps. The tire wobbled and turned with difficulty.

"Please let me help you," Marc said. "I promise, I'm not a serial killer. I'll drive you home, safe and sound."

Debbie stared up at him and looked as if she'd dissolve into tears again. "Okay. Thank you."

Marc smiled and took ahold of the bike, leading her to his car with Bernie following dutifully behind them.

Chapter Two

Debbie sat in the passenger side of Marc's large-sized SUV, giving him a sideways glance. She couldn't believe she'd allowed a complete stranger to drive her home. Her mother, if she were alive, would have had a coronary. But he didn't seem like a bad man. She'd felt like she could trust him.

Isn't that what every victim thinks?

She would've had to been blind not to notice how tall and muscular Marc was. His running pants and jacket fit him perfectly and the outline of his muscles showed through it. But he wasn't overly muscular, like a bodybuilder. He was just right for his build. And his face looked kind; in fact, it had a chiseled model look about it. His brown hair had highlights of chestnut running through it and his eyes sparkled when he smiled. She could actually see the gold flecks in them. Debbie was almost certain he wasn't a murderer.

Almost.

The bear-dog sat in the backseat, staring kindly at her. At least she thought it looked kindly. Maybe he was sizing Chloe up for his next meal. Debbie hugged her dog closer.

"Is this your house?" Marc asked, smiling over at her.

"Yes. The white bungalow," she replied. Marc pulled over in

front of it.

"This looks like a nice neighborhood," he commented, putting the car in park.

"It is." Her heart warmed as it always did when she was home. She loved her neighborhood and her wonderful neighbors. It was a friendly place where they all knew each other and helped each other out.

She moved to open the door but then wasn't quite sure where the handle was.

"Oh. Here." He reached over her and pulled on the handle. "It's like they try to hide them these days."

Her heart stopped a moment at his nearness, and she got a whiff of his musky cologne. *He wore cologne when he ran?* She hadn't even showered yet.

Marc was out of the car and pulling her bike from the back end before she could even get out of the passenger seat. Yet another problem with being shorter than everyone else—she had to jump out of the SUV because her legs didn't reach the ground.

"Let me help you," Marc said, coming up beside her and offering his hand.

Still grasping Chloe in one arm, Debbie took his hand and let him help her down. *Definitely not a serial killer. He's too polite.* They both stood there still holding hands; Marc with the bike leaning against his legs and Debbie clutching Chloe. Then they suddenly spoke at once.

"Well, thanks for the ride," she said.

"Where would you like me to put the bike?" he asked.

They stared at each other, and for the first time since meeting, Debbie laughed. It made Marc smile wider.

"If you don't mind, you can slide the bike in the garage," she said, pulling her hand away from his and pointing toward the one-stall garage attached to her house. She reached into her pocket, lifted out the automatic door opener, and hit the button.

"Great." He pushed the bike awkwardly with its crooked wheel into the garage as she followed him. "You know, I'd be happy to take this to a repair shop and have it fixed for you."

"That's okay," she said with a sigh. "It's old. I really should buy a new bike if I want to ride."

He pushed it up beside her little yellow 2009 Volkswagen Beetle, being careful not to scratch the paint. "Cute car," he said, turning and grinning at her. "It suits you."

His words startled her. "Why? Because I'm short?"

He chuckled. "No. Because it's cute. Like you."

"Oh." Debbie hadn't expected a compliment. Cute? The way she was bundled up in all her winter clothes? He must be teasing her.

Marc walked closer to her. "If you're serious about exercising, come visit me at the gym. I work most evenings. I'd be happy to show you around and help you get started."

"Thanks," she said. "But to tell the truth, I can't afford a gym membership. And I'm not the type of person who'd use it anyway."

His thick brows shot up. "What type of person would that be?"

She shrugged. "You know. Those girls with blond ponytails and long, lean legs who wear those cute, tight exercise outfits. I'd be too self-conscious to go to a place like that."

He studied her a moment, then gave her a wry smile. "I promise you, not everyone who comes to the gym looks like you imagine. They're just regular people who want to get into shape. Tall, short, round, skinny, you name it. All sizes. You don't have to wear anything fancy, either. A T-shirt, sweatshirt, and sweatpants or shorts are fine."

Debbie bit her lip. She desperately wanted to get into shape. She wanted to look nice in the bridesmaid dress her friend had picked out. They were going to the Bahamas for a destination wedding, and for once, she would like to look as good as everyone else. But the cost of a gym still made her hesitate.

"The first session is on me," Marc offered, his straight, white teeth showing as he smiled.

On him? All kinds of ideas rolled around inside her head until she realized he'd meant it was free.

"Well…" she hesitated.

"Great! I'll see you one night this week," he said, not giving her a chance to decline. "Nice meeting you, Deb." He smiled and waved, then headed down the driveway to his car.

Debbie turned and watched as he drove away. "Now what did I get myself into?" she asked Chloe, who was still in her arms. Sighing, Debbie walked into the garage and headed inside the house.

* * *

That evening, Debbie sat curled up on her sofa in front of the gas fireplace with Chloe lying on the blanket beside her. She stared at the business card in her hand. **Fit in 20 Fitness Center,** it stated on the top. The name **Marc Bennett, Fitness Instructor** was underneath. A simple white card with black embossed lettering and a small picture of barbells on the bottom. The back had the address and phone number. It looked non-threatening. Yet, the thought of going to a gym to work out terrified her.

Debbie sighed. Even though she owned a business where she interacted with customers every day, deep down inside she was a shy person. Growing up as an only child with a single mother, she'd spent most of her time, when not in school, around grown-ups in her mother's bridal shop. She'd learned early on to be quiet and polite. She hadn't been popular in school or had a large group of friends. She'd been the soft-spoken girl in the back corner who made good grades and the other kids only talked to her if they needed help with math or English homework. Otherwise, she'd been invisible.

And even now, at the age of thirty-two, she still felt invisible. She did have more friends now, mostly the people in her neighborhood, and she had a reputation for having exquisite taste in wedding gowns and bridesmaid dresses. But deep down, she was still the shy, chubby girl from high school who hadn't dated or attended dances or proms.

"You're a beautiful girl—you just have to get out of your comfort zone," her mother, Gladys, had told her all through school and even into adulthood. "You don't think highly enough of yourself, and you should. You're pretty and smart and just as good as everyone else."

Of course, that was her mother talking. Her mother *had* to say she was smart and pretty. But no matter how many times her mother told her that, Debbie never truly believed her.

Debbie smiled when she thought of her mother. Gladys had never let her size—and she'd been a rather large woman—or the fact that she was a single mother keep her from putting herself out there. The bridal boutique had been the perfect place for Gladys to shine. Her taste in gowns and her deft fingers at sewing alterations had grown her business quickly. She'd always worn colorful dresses and high-heeled shoes, and lots of rings and necklaces. Her curly red hair had been pulled up in a chignon most days with curls popping out all over, but she'd looked incredible. People fell in love with her the moment they walked inside the little shop and felt welcomed.

Debbie wished she had half her mother's personality and style. She did okay, though, and people still frequented the shop because she'd learned how to treat clients with the same care as her mother had. But it wasn't the same. Even now, five years after her mother had passed away from cancer, Debbie's heart still ached with the loss of her vivacious presence.

Standing, Debbie walked past the island and into the kitchen to make a cup of tea. Her little bungalow had been purchased and decorated with antiques by her mother. It had been a proud day for Gladys when she'd been able to buy the small home for her and her daughter. Debbie had grown up in the two-bedroom home filled with love and an array of old furnishing that her mother had found in second-hand stores and antique shops. The distressed oak table and chairs that were hand-rubbed until they shone, the grandfather clock that stood regally in the living room, and the roll-top desk in Debbie's room. So many finds from their weekend excursions all over the Twin Cities. Her mother had taught her the difference between old and antique, and when to refinish a find and when not to. The result had been a home full of well-loved furniture that made each room feel warm and inviting.

Taking her teacup—a china cup found at an estate sale, of course—Debbie returned to her spot on the sofa. "Well, what do you think, Chloe? Should I get out of my comfort zone and go to the gym?"

The little dog glanced up but had no advice.

Debbie sighed again. "I'll see how I feel tomorrow after work." But deep down inside, she knew she had to push herself to go. Maybe it wouldn't be so terrible after all.

Chapter Three

Marc walked into the Fit in 20 Fitness Center at four o'clock Tuesday afternoon. He was in an especially good mood, although he wasn't exactly sure why. All day long he'd thought about the bundled-up woman with the big, blue eyes he'd nearly been run over by in the park. He wondered if she'd come into the gym tonight—or ever. He hoped she would. She'd seemed like a sweet woman, even if she'd been a little on the shy, nervous side. And that dog! That little puffball of fur she carried with her had been hilarious. But hey—any woman who loved dogs was great in his book. Just thinking about Debbie again made him smile.

"Hey, boss. What are you grinning about? Do you have a hot date tonight?" Kyle Giffard, the manager of this branch of Fit in 20, called over to Marc from the front desk.

Marc's smile faded as he walked up to Kyle. The guy was good at his job, but sometimes he rubbed Marc the wrong way. Kyle was thirty years old, in great shape, and considered himself a ladies' man. Marc wasn't a fan of men who were players. Marc was a one-woman kind of guy. Well, when he was in a relationship, which he no longer was.

"No hot dates tonight," he told Kyle, stopping at the desk. "I'm not interested in getting involved with anyone right now."

Kyle laughed. "Right. A guy who looks like you and owns a string of fitness centers all over the cities won't be single long. You mark my words."

Marc winced. He hated when Kyle referenced his money. True, Marc owned the chain of fitness centers and had done very well for himself, but he never bragged about his success. Most people who came to this center didn't even realize that Marc was the owner. He liked working with clients, helping them meet their fitness goals. It was a good feeling. And he preferred it if people didn't know who he really was.

"Speaking of hot dates," Kyle whispered, elbowing Marc in the side. "Here comes Mandy. She's looking pretty smokin' tonight, don't you think?"

Mandy was a tall, slender woman with long blond hair that she pulled up into a ponytail for work. Her legs went on for miles, and she had a pretty face. She was sweet, too, and didn't deserve being talked about behind her back by Kyle.

"She works here, Kyle. Don't talk about her like that, or I'll have a lawsuit on my hands, and you'll be out of a job," Marc said sternly.

Kyle ignored him. "How's it going tonight, Mandy?" he called out to her.

Mandy walked past Kyle and smiled over at Marc. She wore a dove-gray, form-fitting tank top and a pair of body-hugging yoga pants that stopped below her knees. She taught the spin, yoga, and aerobics classes and organized the schedules of the other trainers as well. Marc held her in high regard as both a great fitness instructor and a good worker.

"Hi, Marc," she said, stopping in front of him, her back to Kyle. "I was wondering if we could talk about hiring a new part-time instructor. Katie's school schedule is too busy this semester to work until summer."

"Sure," Marc said. "I have some applications left over from the last time we hired. We could sift through those." He turned and led the way to his office in the back room.

"Yeah. You two go and 'work' while I hold down the fort," Kyle said, making air quotes for the word work. No one laughed at his joke except him.

Marc returned to the main floor after handing the applications over to Mandy. He trusted her judgment in hiring a new instructor, but he hadn't wanted to spend too much time alone with her in the office. Despite his anger at Kyle for making his crude joke, Marc did get a vibe from Mandy that she was interested in him. He liked Mandy as an employee, but Marc wasn't in the market for a girlfriend. He'd been hurt pretty badly by his last relationship, and the wounds weren't completely healed. Plus, he didn't like dating women who worked at the center. It got messy, and the last thing Marc needed was a lawsuit against him if a relationship went bad. That wasn't exactly good for business.

Marc smiled and nodded at some of the regular customers who came in for a quick run on one of the treadmills or a turn on an elliptical. A group of women of all ages was forming outside the classroom where they offered twenty-minute sessions of yoga, aerobics, and spin classes. It was five-thirty, and the place was humming with activity as people left work and tried to get in a quick workout before going home or out to dinner.

As Marc was helping a new customer learn how to operate one of the treadmills, he noticed a woman walking in wearing a light-blue sweatshirt and sweatpants. Her hair was pulled up in a ponytail, and she looked a bit unsure of herself. He smiled broadly. She'd come after all.

"Debbie. Hi. You made it," he greeted her after nearly tripping over himself to get to the entryway. He was afraid she'd change her mind and bolt before he got there. And he'd been right. Debbie had just turned around to leave when he caught up to her.

She turned and smiled sheepishly. "Hi. I didn't see you and thought you might not be here."

"Thought or hoped?" he teased.

Debbie blushed. "Maybe a little of both." Apprehension practically seeped off of her. Marc quickly took charge so she wouldn't escape.

"Let me show you around," he offered, placing his arm familiarly around her shoulders and guiding her toward the gym area.

"Hey, boss," Kyle called over from the desk. "New customer? I'd be happy to help her sign up."

Marc quickly waved Kyle away. "I'll take care of it," he called back, walking swiftly past the desk. The last thing he wanted was for Kyle to scare Debbie away. For some unknown reason, Marc felt protective of her. Maybe it was because he'd saved her after she'd fallen off her bike. Or because her blue eyes always seemed ready to panic. Whatever the reason, he didn't want Kyle near her.

Like a big brother, Marc thought. Well, it sounded good.

"Here are our workout machines," he said, stopping next to a treadmill that wasn't in use. "Our gym is based on the idea that busy people can fit a quick workout into their lives. That's why it's called Fit in 20. Clients come in and do twenty-minutes on one of the machines or take a twenty-minute spin, yoga, or aerobics class, and they're done. Of course, you can work out longer, and take as many classes as you'd like with a monthly membership, but we specialize in the quick workout."

Debbie glanced around, seemingly in a daze. "The machines look complicated," she said.

"They aren't, I promise you. In fact, I was just teaching that nice woman over there how to operate the treadmill and now look at her. She's using it like a pro." He pointed to a middle-aged woman who looked like she was enjoying her walk. Televisions were on all over the gym to entertain clients while they exercised.

Marc still saw apprehension on Debbie's face. He directed her to the classroom, where a yoga class was in session with Mandy leading it. They watched through the window as the group of women of all ages and sizes moved to the calming music.

"I could never do yoga," Debbie said, shaking her head. "I'm not that coordinated."

Marc looked at her. "What do you mean? You're coordinated. You can ride a bike."

She raised her brows and stared at him. "And you saw how well that turned out."

Her response was so deadpan, it was hilarious. Marc let out a howl of laughter that made the room full of women turn and stare at him. He quickly covered his mouth and turned away. "Sorry," he said to Debbie. "But you're funny."

A small smile appeared on her full lips. "I'm just telling the truth."

Marc grinned back. He liked her smile.

"Why don't I assign you a locker in the women's changing room and you can put on your workout clothes so we can get started," he offered.

Debbie's smile dropped. She looked down at her sweats. "I'm wearing my workout clothes."

"Oh. Well, I mean, I figured you must have a T-shirt and shorts on under the sweats. It gets hot when you work out," Marc said.

"I thought you said I could wear anything I wanted to," she said defensively.

"Of course. Yes, you can. I just thought..." he hesitated, seeing her grow more uncomfortable and unsure of herself with every word he uttered. He'd better be careful, or he'd scare her away. And that was the last thing he wanted to do.

* * *

Debbie felt more self-conscious by the second. What had she been thinking, coming to a place like this to work out? She didn't belong here.

"What you're wearing is fine," Marc said quickly, trying to recover from his remark about her sweats. Debbie eyed him, wondering if he meant what he said. She was no delicate flower, but she was always fearful of looking foolish. She didn't know why she second-guessed herself—she just always had. And glancing around the gym, she saw that her oversized sweats did not fit in with all the spandex.

"Maybe I should go," she said, already backing away toward the door.

"Please, don't go," Marc said. Then his expression grew determined. "You said you wanted to get in shape, and I want to help you. Stay at least for one twenty-minute session and see if you like it. Okay?"

Debbie sighed. He was right. She did want to get in shape and lose weight. She had to get over her self-consciousness and make herself stay. "Okay. Thanks."

He grinned. "Don't thank me yet. I haven't done anything."

You talked me into staying, she thought. *That's something.*

He led her to a treadmill. "Hop on. I'll show you how it

works. This one has an incline you can set at any level. I'll have you walk for ten minutes, and then we'll do some strengthening exercises."

Debbie stepped up on the treadmill. It was huge! Especially since she was shorter than the average person. Marc showed her how to turn it on, speed it up, and raise the incline. *Incline, right! I'll be lucky to last ten minutes walking on a flat surface,* she thought.

He started the machine and set it at a slow pace. "Just until you warm up," he said.

Debbie clung to the front handles and walked. It wasn't too bad. She could keep up at this pace.

"Where's your puffball dog tonight?" Marc asked, still standing beside the machine.

Debbie narrowed her eyes. "Where's that bear dog of yours?"

He snorted a laugh that startled Debbie. "I didn't bring Bernie to work tonight, but I usually do. He's a gentle giant. And he loves hanging out wherever I am."

She smiled. A guy who loved his dog that much couldn't be all bad. "I didn't bring Chloe along because I wasn't sure she'd be allowed inside here. But she usually goes everywhere with me. She hangs out at work with me, and all the customers love her."

His brows rose. "Where do you work?"

"I own a bridal shop not far from my home. Deb's Bridal Boutique. My mom opened it years ago, and I've taken it over since she passed away."

"Oh, I'm sorry about your mother. But that's cool that you own a shop. It's nice being your own boss."

Debbie shrugged. "Sometimes. Yeah." He had hit the button that made the treadmill go faster and her breathing became heavier.

"Are you doing okay?" he asked, eyeing her.

"Yeah," she said between breaths. "I'm fine." He hit the incline button, and it rose slightly. Debbie started to breathe even faster. And she was getting hot. Really hot, and not in a good way. The sweats were too heavy to be climbing Mount Everest in.

"Am I done yet?" she asked, looking at the timer on the machine.

"Five minutes to go," he said cheerfully.

She glared at him.

As Debbie sweated and panted on the treadmill, a tall, leggy blonde came over to talk with Marc. The woman was gorgeous. Debbie recognized her as the yoga instructor. She couldn't believe this woman had just finished twenty minutes of yoga and didn't have one bead of perspiration on her body. And here Debbie was, sweating like a pig.

The woman smiled over at Debbie in a kind way, then headed back to the classroom. She had a body like a dancer and wore a cute exercise outfit. She was everything Debbie wasn't.

"I...thought...you...said...this...place...wasn't...full...of... long...lean...blondes," Debbie said between puffs of breath.

Marc looked puzzled a moment then seemed to understand what she'd said. "Oh, Mandy? She's an instructor here. Her *job* is to be fit. If you look around, though, most of the people here are average size and weight. Regular people just wanting to lose weight or get in shape."

She gazed at him a moment, taking in his well-defined arms and long, lean body. He was wearing workout pants and a form-fitting T-shirt with the gym's logo on it. There was nothing average about him. "You mean they're fat like me?"

Marc's expression turned serious. He hit the stop button, and she thankfully came to a halt. "You're not fat. I can't tell exactly what you look like under those baggy sweats, but I can see you aren't overweight. Stop calling yourself that." He waved for her to follow him across the room to a weight machine that looked like a torture device.

Debbie dutifully followed him feeling bad for having upset him. He was just trying to help her, and she wasn't cooperating very well.

"Let's work on toning your muscles," he said, gesturing for her to sit on the bench. "Back up to the wall and take ahold of these grips." He pointed, and she did as she was told.

"Now, pull down, and I'll add just enough weight so you have to work without straining," Marc said. He slowly changed the tension. "Tell me when it's hard to pull but not too difficult."

Debbie wanted to yell 'stop' immediately, but she didn't want to be a wimp. She kept pulling long after the tension was tighter than she could take. Setting her mind to work hard, she pulled, but instead, her body lifted up. She let go and dropped down onto the padded bench.

Marc gave her a little grin. "I guess that's too tight." He took the tension down a little, and she was able to pull down again. After a few pulls, he had her change directions, and she pulled until her arm muscles burned. Still, she didn't complain. She didn't know why, but she didn't want Marc upset with her again. After all, he was helping her at no cost, and she should appreciate it. She didn't want him to think she was ungrateful. And if she were honest with herself, she didn't want to disappoint herself, either.

After a time, Marc had her stop. "Let's do a couple of stretches, and then your torture is complete," he said, a teasing tone in his voice.

She eyed him. "You're enjoying this, aren't you?"

"Me? Of course not." He had her sit on the floor and stretch out her legs in front of her. "Bend down as far as you comfortably can. Now, pull your toes up a little, hold it, then let go again. You don't want your muscles to tighten up tonight and get a Charlie horse. Those are painful."

Debbie stretched the way he showed her. She was no longer out of breath, and she actually felt good. Maybe exercising here wasn't so bad after all.

"Will you tell me why you're in such a hurry to lose weight? The other day it sounded like you had some event you were getting ready for," Marc said, looking at her curiously.

"I have a couple of weddings I'm going to this spring and summer, and one is in the Bahamas. I'm a bridesmaid, and the dresses the bride chose are very form-fitting. I just wanted to lose this fat, er, ah, I mean tighten up a little, so I look good in the dress."

Marc sat back, bracing himself with his hands behind him on the floor. "Toning up and getting healthy is great. But you have to stop thinking you're fat. You're not, and I'm not just *saying* that to be nice. You're short, and I'm guessing you're curvy, and that can affect the way clothes fit on you. But you shouldn't let that make you feel fat. I'll bet you already look great in that dress."

Debbie watched him as he spoke, and she could tell he was sincere about what he was saying. If anyone else had said that to her, she would have argued with them. But not Marc. He meant what he'd said, and it made her want to believe him.

Marc jumped up in one smooth motion and offered her his hand. She took it, and he pulled her up. "See. Light as a feather," he said with a wink.

Was he teasing her?

"Thank you for helping me tonight," Debbie said, straightening her clothes and suddenly feeling self-conscious about how her hair was falling out of its ponytail. She smoothed her hands over it but to no avail. Her thick hair curled when she sweated, and she was sure she had a frizzy mess on her head right now.

"I was happy to do it," he said. "And I'd like to be able to help you tone up for your events. We could do this three times a week, and you'd be ready by summer."

Debbie's shoulders sagged. "Thanks for the offer, but I can't afford a gym membership or to pay a personal trainer."

"But I haven't even told you the price yet," Marc said. "Ten dollars a month and you can use the gym and all the equipment as much as you want. Plus, you can join in on any of the fitness classes." He leaned in closer and said in a quieter voice, "And I won't charge you a cent to help you get fit. That's what I'm here for."

His eyes sparkled, and Debbie felt weak at the knees. Well, it was that, or else the treadmill had done it, she wasn't sure. Seeing Marc three days a week sounded great, but she just couldn't. Ten dollars a month didn't sound bad to Debbie, but it was still more money than she should spend on her tight budget. "Thanks. I'll think about it," she said softly.

He nodded, and she thought he might try to talk her into the membership, but all he said was, "That sounds good."

Debbie thanked him again and walked out the door. Before the automatic doors swooshed shut, she heard the guy behind the desk call out to Marc.

"Hey, boss. You're losing your touch. You didn't close the deal."

Debbie's heart sank. She'd thought Marc was being sincere about helping her, but he'd only been trying to sell her a membership. Disappointed, she got in her little Volkswagen Bug and drove home.

Chapter Four

Debbie opened the shop at nine the next morning and started her typical day, but all she could think about was her workout the night before. With Marc. And each time she thought of him, she sighed.

He's not interested in you, you idiot. He was just trying to sell a membership.

This thought disappointed her. Debbie had thought she'd seen something in his eyes that said he was interested in her. The way he smiled at her and how the gold flecks in his eyes twinkled when he teased. But she should have known that a guy as handsome as Marc wouldn't even look twice at her.

"He's probably dating that leggy blonde," she muttered under her breath.

"What leggy blonde?" a voice said, coming up behind her.

Debbie jumped. "Sheesh. You startled me."

Lindsay laughed. "Good morning to you, too. Now, who's the leggy blonde?"

Debbie shook her head. Lindsay Weaver had been working at the shop part-time since she was sixteen when Debbie's mother hired her. She was a vivacious girl, tall and slender with short, dark hair and lively blue eyes. Basically, she was everything Debbie wasn't. But Debbie adored her like a younger sister. When Lindsay left home at eighteen, she'd moved into the apartment on the second floor of the shop and had been renting it ever since. In truth, it was part of her pay, but Debbie didn't think of it that way. She liked knowing that someone lived in this old Victorian house, keeping it fresh and alive. Houses needed people and Lindsay was the perfect person to care for the home.

"The leggy blonde at the fitness center," Debbie said. "Everyone is a leggy blonde except me."

Lindsay laughed. "I'm not. Neither are Kristen, Mallory, or Lisa," she said, naming off Debbie's neighbors who were also her friends. "Well, scratch Lisa. She is a leggy blonde, but she's sweet and doesn't think of herself that way."

Debbie rolled her eyes. "I meant the women at the fitness center. I felt like a lump around them."

"Ah. So you went after all. Good for you. Didn't you like it there?" Lindsay asked.

"It was okay. I felt like I didn't belong there, though. I'll always be the short, chubby girl no matter what. I should just accept that."

Lindsay crossed her arms and stared at her.

"What?" Debbie asked, but she knew what was coming.

"Your mom always told you not to put yourself down and since she's no longer with us, then I'm saying it. You're not fat. You're not chubby. You're curvy and adorable. And sweet. And you help women find the perfect wedding dress for their special day. So stop putting yourself down."

"I know. I know. I'll try harder," Debbie said, feeling contrite again like she had last night when she'd upset Marc.

"You know, if you'd wear clothes that weren't so big and baggy, you'd see for yourself that you look amazing," Lindsay added.

Debbie looked down at her outfit. She was wearing a loose blouse tucked into a full skirt and a pair of high heels. She was comfortable, well, except for the heels. But she liked how tall she looked in high shoes. "What's wrong with my outfit?"

Lindsay sighed. "Nothing. But if you'd wear clothes that hugged your curves better, you might feel sexier. You could wear a bright T-shirt with that black skirt you're wearing and a wide belt, and you'd look incredible."

"Sexier? I run a bridal boutique, not a lingerie shop," Debbie protested. She studied Lindsay, who had a bohemian style of dressing. She wore brightly colored T-shirts with long, flowing skirts and ankle boots. She always looked cute. But there was no way Debbie could pull off a look like that.

The bell above the door jingled and a customer came in, thankfully, ending their conversation. For the rest of the morning, Debbie helped women try on dresses and pick out veils, shoes, and even tiaras, as they prepared for their special day. Debbie didn't mind the work—she felt very competent at it—but after years of doing this, sometimes she wondered if there was something more out there for her. She'd gone to college and earned a communications and marketing degree and had also dabbled in graphic arts, and she enjoyed working on the marketing side of the shop. But the money was in selling gowns, so that was what she did.

Around noon, the UPS driver dropped off several boxes, and Lindsay went through them. She brought out a dress and showed it to Debbie. "Your bridesmaid dress for the Bahama wedding is here."

Debbie stared at it in horror. It looked so tiny. It was a dark rose color covered in filmy chiffon with a tight, satin, low-cut bodice and a full skirt. Precisely the type of dress that looked terrible on a short, curvy woman.

"You'd better try it on to make sure it fits," Lindsay said, handing it to Debbie. "I bet it'll look great on you."

Debbie's brows shot up. "I'll bet it doesn't."

"The sample dress we have looked good," Lindsay protested.

"But that was black. Black hides all sins."

Lindsay placed her hands on her hips. "Try it on. You have to anyway, so you might as well get it over with."

Since there were no customers in the store, Debbie had no excuses left. She went into one of the curtained dressing rooms, undressed, and carefully pulled on the tiny dress. Gritting her teeth, she turned and looked into the full-length mirror. Ugh! It was as bad as she'd imagined. The dress clung to every part of her body that she didn't want to bring attention too. Her bust spilled over in it, and her waist looked thick. It didn't help that she was short-waisted. Even a corset wouldn't trim down her waistline.

"Come out and let me see," Lindsay said.

"No!"

Lindsay pushed the curtain aside and looked anyway. Her eyes grew wide. "Wow!"

Debbie grimaced. "I know! It's awful! I look like a huge strawberry."

"You look beautiful." A male voice said from behind Lindsay, and both women turned and gaped. Marc stood there looking windswept and handsome in jeans, a blue sweater, and a trim winter jacket.

Debbie's mouth dropped open, and she quickly clamped it shut. "What are you doing here?"

Marc smiled. "Hi to you, too. Is that the bridesmaid dress you were so worried about wearing? You look great in it."

Debbie suddenly remembered the dress and quickly grabbed for the curtain, pulling it closed.

Lindsay spoke up, and Debbie heard her from the dressing room. "She'll be out in a minute. I'm Lindsay, Debbie's assistant."

Marc shook her hand. "I'm Marc. Debbie's would-be trainer if I can talk her into coming back to the gym."

"She'd be crazy if she didn't take you up on it," Lindsay said. The bell on the door jingled, and Lindsay excused herself to assist the woman who'd walked in.

On the other side of the curtain, Debbie fumed. She couldn't believe Marc had seen her in that awful dress. He was just being polite by telling her she looked beautiful in that dress. She knew it wasn't true. Debbie dressed hurriedly, then forced herself to slow down and check that her clothes were on correctly and her hair wasn't mussed. She'd put her long hair into a French braid today, as she usually did to keep it out of her face at work. She smoothed down a few loose strands with her hand, took a deep breath, and walked out of the dressing room. Marc was across the room, admiring an antique glass display case.

"I'm sorry you saw that awful dress," she said, walking up to him. "Now you know why I'm desperate to lose weight."

He turned to face her. "No, I don't understand. You looked amazing in that dress."

Debbie didn't know how to respond. She wasn't used to compliments from good-looking men. Actually, she wasn't used to attention from men at all. "That's nice of you to say. But I still need to tone up, as you say. I really want to look good in that dress."

His expression softened. "Then you should come back to the gym. Now that I've seen you in the dress, I know what you should work on. Not that you need to," he added. "But if it makes you feel more confident, then that's a good thing."

"Is that why you came here today? To sell me a gym membership?" Debbie asked.

Marc looked surprised. "Uh, no. Not completely. I came because you left so quickly last night. And, well, to be honest, I've felt a little responsible for helping you since the day you fell down in the park. You were so upset that day that I really want to help you."

Debbie frowned. *Great. I'm such a loser that good-looking guys are taking pity on me.*

"What's that frown for?" Marc asked. "Did I say something wrong?"

She shook her head. "No. Well, kind of. But it's nice that you want to help. I'll think about it, okay?"

He smiled at her, and her heart almost melted. He had such a warm, infectious smile.

"I was noticing your display case." He pointed to the glass cabinet that held jewelry, decorative hair combs for veils, and tiaras. "It's beautiful. Is it an antique?"

Debbie walked over to it and ran her hand lovingly over the glass. It was framed in dark walnut wood and locked in the back with an old-fashioned skeleton key. "Yes, it is. My mother found it in an old department store that was closing its doors. I believe it's from the 1920s."

"It's incredible. So much history," he said, admiring it. "Are the armoire over there, and the cabinet across the room also antiques? They're beautiful."

"Yes, they are." Debbie was amazed he'd even noticed them. "My mom loved antiques. We used to scour estate sales and antique stores on weekends, searching for pieces we could afford. My house is full of antiques."

Marc's eyes lit up. "Really? So you have an eye for antique furniture too?"

Debbie shrugged. "I suppose. I know a good piece when I see one and whether or not it's overpriced."

Marc's eyes sparkled. "Can I steal you away for an hour? There's something I'd like you to see."

"What?"

"Please. I mean, if you can get away from the shop for a little while," he said hopefully.

"Sure. Go head," Lindsay said, coming up to them. "We're not busy, and you have no appointments with brides today. So you have no excuse."

Debbie hesitated. What on earth could this man want to show her? Her mind went into the gutter for a moment, and then she pulled herself out. Surely not *that!*

Lindsay had gone into the back room and came out with Debbie's coat and purse. "Run along. Have fun," she said cheerfully.

Debbie glared at her. Lindsay was being too helpful. But now Debbie didn't have a choice. "Okay. But just for a little while," she told Marc. He grinned, took her hand, and led her out of the shop.

Chapter Five

"Let's take my car," Marc offered, leading her to his SUV that was parked right outside the shop. He opened the door for her, waited for her to step up inside, and then carefully closed it.

"I only live a few blocks away," he offered as he started the car.

"We're going to your house?" Debbie asked, sounding a little terrified.

"Yes. I want to show you something. I might have a business proposition for you."

Debbie's eyes grew wide, and he almost laughed out loud. He hadn't tried to make it sound illicit, but it had.

"Don't look scared," he said. "I mean this in the most platonic way." He grinned.

Her face grew pinched. "I'm not scared. I knew that's how you meant it."

Marc forced himself not to laugh. He didn't want to insult her any more than he already had. As Marc drove the few blocks to his house, he thought about how quickly the day had changed for him. He hadn't meant to seek out Debbie's bridal shop and go there. But he had, on impulse, on the pretense that he wanted to talk her into continuing coming to the gym. When he'd told her he'd felt responsible for her, he'd meant it. Ever since that day at the park, he'd wanted to help her. He just couldn't explain why. She seemed like a perfectly capable woman, but then, other times, she was so timid and self-conscious. It was sweet, actually, but it made him want to help her even more. Now, he was the one who needed her help.

Marc parked on the curb across from Lake Harriet Park. He noticed that Debbie was glancing around, looking confused.

"You live here?" she asked.

He ran around to her side of the car and opened the door. "Yes, I do. Right up there." He pointed to a house that sat on the hill, overlooking the lake. It couldn't be considered anything other than a mansion.

"Here?" she asked, looking stunned.

"Yep. Let's go up." He followed her up the brick stairway that led to the yard and across the pavers to the front door. The house was a Tudor style made of stucco with bricks outlining the windows. It had been built in 1920 when the very wealthy had built homes by the lake. Admittedly, rich people still lived in these houses, but age had softened their look, and mature trees and bushes hid them away from prying eyes—mostly.

Marc took out a key and opened the oversized wooden door that was rounded at the top. They walked inside the foyer onto black and white marble tile, and Debbie stopped short.

"Did you kill that?" Lying on the beautiful marble was a leopard rug with a ferocious head and glass eyes staring at them.

"No, it's fake," Marc said. "Now you can understand why I need your help. Come see the rest of the décor."

He showed Debbie into the living room, and she gasped. "Uh, this is nice," she said, trying to hide her initial reaction.

Marc laughed. "No, it's not. It's all wrong for this house. All the furniture in this house is wrong. Feel free to express your real thoughts."

Debbie shifted uncomfortably. "Well, it's very modern for a Tudor home." She was obviously still trying to be polite.

"You can say that again," Marc said. "The white sofa and leopard chairs are too much. As are the glass tables. And that furry, white rug under the coffee table. I mean, in an ultra-modern house, this might be fine, but not here. There should be natural colors with rich wood antique tables. And look at that painting over the mantel. It looks like a three-year-old splattered paint on a canvas."

Debbie's eyes followed to where he was pointing, and she grimaced. "It's a beautiful fireplace, though."

"It is," he agreed. "But everything else in this house isn't my style."

He watched as she raised her eyes to the overhead light. Then she turned and looked at the chandelier in the entryway. "Are the lights original to the house?"

Marc beamed. "Yes, they are. They were gas lights that were converted to electric. Aren't they beautiful?"

Her brows lifted as she looked at him. "They are. But if you love antiques so much, why did you decorate this way?"

"I didn't. My ex-fiancé did. I fell in love with this house and bought it before we were engaged. She hated it. So she did everything she could to modernize it. At the time, I didn't really mind, but I wouldn't let her touch the lights throughout the house. Or the woodwork." He pointed to the polished oak wainscoting along the bottom of the walls and on the staircase in the foyer. The handrail was also oak and curled up the stairs.

Suddenly, a deep bark came from the back of the house, and Bernie came running into the foyer as best he could on the marble floor. He slipped and slid, looking comical as he tried to get to Debbie. The dog stopped in time right in front of her so he didn't knock her down.

She laughed. "He's a clumsy bear, isn't he?"

"Ah, poor Bernie," Marc said, rubbing him behind the ears. "These wood and tile floors are tough for him to run on."

"Hi, Bernie," Debbie said, reaching down to pet his head. She wasn't much taller than the dog was when he was sitting down, but Marc knew better than to comment on that.

Marc took Debbie on a tour of the house—all three floors— and each room looked worse than the last. The kitchen at the back of the house was the nicest room. It had been remodeled in a traditional style with dark cabinets and gleaming quartz countertops. It was large, with two sinks and two stoves and an island that seated eight. Attached was a family room, and large windows surrounded the area, looking out to the back yard.

"How'd you manage to keep this so nice?" she asked Marc.

"Alyssa didn't cook," he said with a sly grin.

Debbie walked to the back windows. "Your yard is huge. And beautiful."

"Thanks. Come on out and see it." He opened the French doors that led out to a wide, wooden deck. Bernie trotted behind them onto the deck.

Debbie glanced around, taking in the view. There was a tall, wood fence surrounding the property, but it was mostly hidden with shrubs and trees. There were at least a dozen trees all around the yard and lawn. To the right was a pool, but it was still covered for winter.

"I'll bet this is beautiful in the summer," she said, looking impressed.

"It is," he said proudly. "But Alyssa and my gardener hated it."

"Why?"

"See all those trees? They're varieties of crabapple trees, so they all bloom in the spring. It's a fantasy of pink and white flowers everywhere during the month of May."

She looked up at him. "That sounds gorgeous. Why didn't they like it?"

"Because by the end of May, all the petals fall off and make a mess of the lawn and pool." He laughed. "But the trees are so beautiful when they bloom that I don't care about the mess. It's worth it."

"I'd love to see it when it blooms," Debbie said, her eyes bright.

"You definitely can," he told her. They went inside again and walked from the kitchen into the dining room, which had a lot of silver and glass like the living room. "So, what do you think?" he asked her.

She stared at him blankly. "About what?"

"The house. Well, more specifically, the furniture."

Debbie paused. "Well…"

"Don't be nice. Be honest," he said.

"I'm not sure what you want me to say. If you don't like the décor, then you should change it."

"You're exactly right. That's what I want to do. The question is, are you willing to help me?" Marc asked.

"Me?"

"Yes. You. I think this place needs carefully chosen antique furniture, rugs, and accessories. But I don't have the faintest idea of how to choose antiques. You do. Would you help me?"

Debbie seemed to be sideswiped by the suggestion. "That's a lot of furniture," she said, sounding unsure. "And I don't think you get the concept of antiques. Picking antiques takes years of scouring through shops, second-hand stores, and going to estate sales to find the perfect items that call out to you. It's falling in love with a piece so much, you have to have it. It's about making a space your own, not just going to a store and picking up everything in sight. Finding the right antiques for your home is personal."

Marc frowned. "Wow. I never thought of it like that. I just figured we'd shop together for a few weekends, and you could help me pick up items."

"Well, you *can* do that, but it's not the same. Don't you want to love everything you put in the house?"

His frown turned into a smile. "I don't have to *love* it all—compared to what the house has now, *liking* the stuff would be fine with me." He turned serious. "I'll make a deal with you. If you help me find pieces that will make this house feel like a home, then I'll give you a gym membership for free plus be your personal trainer. Does that sound like an even trade?"

She didn't look convinced, so he added, "And I'll even go with you to that wedding in the Bahamas as your date – I mean if you don't already have a plus one. Not to sound conceited, but I'll bet that'll surprise your friends."

Debbie's face dropped. "You mean, I'm so pathetic that you think I can't even get my own date?"

"Oh, geez. No. I didn't mean it that way," he said, instantly sorry he'd offered. "But you were so upset about the trip that I thought it might be fun to have someone along who thinks you're amazing." He stopped, realizing again he'd put his foot in his mouth.

"You think I'm amazing?" she asked.

He nodded. "I like you. We sort of clicked, don't you think? Listen, I'll do or not do anything you want me to, just please say that you'll help me buy antiques for this house. Please?"

Debbie hesitated as she glanced around. Marc almost thought she was going to decline when she finally answered. "Okay. Sure. It might be fun. Except," Debbie paused.

"Except what?"

"You realize it could be quite expensive." She bit her lip.

Marc waved his hand through the air. "That's not a problem. Money is no object."

Her brows rose. "Being a fitness trainer must pay a lot of money."

Marc realized that Debbie still didn't know who he was. "Uh, well, to be honest with you, I'm not just a fitness trainer. I own the fitness center."

"Oh." He could tell the wheels were turning in her head. "I thought Fit in 20 was a chain of centers owned by one person. It's in the advertisements on television." She stopped and stared at him, her eyes growing wide. "Oh, wow. I don't know why I didn't put it all together before. Marc from Fit in 20. You're that Marc. You look different in the ads on TV."

"Guilty as charged. And yes, I look a little deranged on the TV commercials. But yeah, I own them all."

She frowned. "Why didn't you tell me that the other night. Here I thought you were an employee trying to sell me a membership."

"If you'd known I was the owner, would you have come at all?"

"I don't know, maybe," Debbie said. Her shoulders sagged. "Or, probably not. I would have been too intimidated."

He smiled warmly. "I'm sorry I wasn't completely honest. But I was sincere when I said you weren't overweight and today when I said you looked great in that dress. But if *you* don't feel that way about yourself, then I'm happy to help you get in shape. Do we have a deal?" he asked, hopefully.

She shrugged. "Sure. Why not? It might be fun shopping for antiques. I've missed doing that since my mother died."

His smile grew brighter. "Great! So when do you want to start?"

* * *

That evening after Debbie had gone home, she wondered what she'd gotten herself into. "I'll be spending most days and evenings with Marc," she told Chloe as they snuggled on her bed watching television.

Chloe looked at her as if that didn't sound like a problem.

"Well, yeah, he's good looking," Debbie said in response to her dog's stare. "And he seems like a nice guy. But his only interest in me is my knowledge of antiques—nothing more."

The dog snuggled deeper into the puffy, white down comforter and stared at the Hallmark movie they were watching.

Debbie rolled her eyes. "I can't even get your attention for more than a few seconds. Imagine how much I'll bore Marc." She picked up her phone and scrolled through a list of antique stores in their area. She also checked for any local estate sales. There was one good auction on Sunday over in St. Paul and a few stores open on Monday. Since her store was closed Sundays and Mondays, those were the only days she could shop with Marc. They'd also decided she'd come to Fit in 20 on Monday, Wednesday, and Friday nights to work out. Marc had said he was working on an all-over fitness plan for her.

"He's going to kill me," she told Chloe. "Or, at the very least, injure me."

Debbie laid back on her pillow and thought back through the day's events. She was still wary of Marc's compliment about how good she'd looked in the puffy, strawberry dress. He was just being nice, she was sure. Yet, he'd told her again at his house that he'd thought she'd looked amazing in the dress. Amazing! That from a guy who worked with tall, slender, women. And that house of his. Talk about amazing. It was beautiful, minus the terrible decorating. She smiled when she thought of how his eyes had lit up when he'd learned she was knowledgeable about antiques. He'd been genuinely pleased. She wished his eyes would light up like that over her.

"What?" she blurted out, startling Chloe. The dog stood and looked around, ready to pounce. "Sorry, sweetie," Debbie said, smoothing the dog's silky fur. "I was just thinking stupid thoughts."

Chloe gave her an irritated glance then snuggled back into the comforter.

"I've been watching too many of these romantic movies," Debbie muttered to herself.

A text buzzed her phone, and she glanced at it. Her friend— well, her old high school friend she never really saw anymore yet was somehow in her wedding—Felicia was reminding her to make her plane reservations for the Bahamas. *"I will, soon."* Debbie texted back. She sighed. Debbie had put off making the reservation so she could pay down her credit card first. This trip was going to cost her a lot of money, but she really wanted to go. More for the vacation than for the wedding. She hadn't had a vacation in years, and when her friend had invited her, she'd jumped at it.

"But now I'm going as a fluffy, plump strawberry," Debbie said.

She wondered if Marc had been serious about going with her and being her plus one. That would be incredible. She could see her friends from high school now, staring with their mouths open at the gorgeous hunk on Debbie's arm. They'd be shocked. Or maybe they wouldn't believe it. Chubby Debbie hooking a hunk. Yeah, she couldn't believe it either.

She scrunched down deeper into the bed and pulled Chloe into a hug. "But I can dream, can't I," she asked her best friend.

Chloe stayed silent.

Chapter Six

The next day Debbie stayed busy at work, trying not to think about exercising or antiquing with Marc. It was hard, though. Every time she looked at the display case in the shop, she'd think about how his eyes had lit up with excitement over the piece of furniture. So she did her best not to look that way. It didn't help that Lindsay knew about her deal with Marc and kept reminding her.

"Aren't you excited about going shopping with Mr. Delicious?" Lindsay asked, excitedly. "Maybe he'll even buy you lunch or dinner. Or both!"

Debbie rolled her eyes when her employee brought it up. "It's not like that. Stop reminding me." But Lindsay would just smile knowingly as she went about her work.

That afternoon, Lisa Evans came in for a fitting of her wedding dress. Lisa lived two houses down from Debbie in their neighborhood, but would soon be moving into the large Victorian on the corner next door to Debbie. Her husband-to-be, Avery McKinnon, had bought the bigger home for them because they wanted to remain in the neighborhood they loved so much. Lisa had an adorable daughter from her first marriage, Abby, who was almost three years old. Abby was going to be the flower girl at the wedding.

"Where's Abby today?" Debbie asked, hugging Lisa while Lindsay went to the back room to bring out her gown.

"Avery is watching her," Lisa said. She was still wearing her work scrubs, having just come from her job as a school nurse. "He picked her up from day care for me so I could stop by here. He was going to bring her to the new house and let her help paint her bedroom."

"Oh, my. That's dangerous," Debbie said, laughing.

Lisa laughed. "I'm sure he'll paint over it when she's not around. But he likes letting her help him."

"You have a winner there," Debbie said, and she meant it. Even though Avery had acted like a grumpy hermit the first year he lived in their neighborhood, he'd turned out to be a great guy.

"Yeah, I'm lucky," Lisa said, beaming.

Chloe had settled herself in a tufted chair, and Lisa went over to pet her. "Hey, Chole. You have to come visit Bailey again soon."

The little white dog lifted her head and seemed to smile at the mention of Bailey. He was Lisa's energetic Border Collie. All the neighborhood dogs got along well.

Lindsay set Lisa up in a dressing room, and soon she came out with her gown on. Lisa had chosen a simple dress in ecru with a sleeveless lace bodice and long, flowing skirt. Tiny pearl buttons lined down the back of the bodice.

"Oh, it's stunning," Debbie cooed, clapping her hands in delight. Lisa was tall and slender, and the dress fit her perfectly.

"I love it!" Lisa exclaimed, twirling in front of the three-way mirror.

Debbie carefully pulled the veil out of its box, and Lindsay placed it on Lisa. It had a pearl-encrusted comb and fell to her waist with tiny seed pearls trimming the hem.

"It's gorgeous. I can't wait for the wedding," Debbie told her.

"Me, too." Lisa smiled.

They were getting married in May in the charming old church just kitty-corner to their house, and the reception was being held in their new home. Debbie was excited for their wedding. All the neighbors would be there. They always had a good time when they were together.

Lisa changed out of the dress, and Lindsay carefully hung and bagged it. "I'll bring Abby in to make sure her dress fits properly, too. She's grown so much these past two months that I hope it still fits," Lisa told Debbie.

"We can always alter it," Debbie assured her.

After Lisa left, Debbie thought about her neighbors and how many weddings there had been over the past couple of years. First, Kristen and Ryan, then James and Mallory. Now, Lisa and Avery. It seemed like the perfect neighborhood to fall in love in. She wondered when her turn would come. If ever.

She could dream.

* * *

Friday evening, Marc stood near the door, waiting for Debbie.

"Who are you waiting so eagerly for, boss?" Kyle asked, coming up alongside him. "Mandy is already here." He winked.

Marc bristled. He hated that Kyle was always trying to link him and Mandy. There was absolutely nothing between him and the yoga instructor. "I'm not *eagerly* waiting for anyone. Debbie, the woman from the other night, is coming in, and I want her to find me easily, that's all."

Kyle frowned. "The short blonde with the baggy sweats? She

hardly seems like your type."

"She's a client, Kyle," Marc said tightly. "Not all the women who walk into the fitness center are prospective girlfriends."

"Hey, you don't have to get so touchy. I've just never seen you wait like this for a client before. Well, except for your old flame, Alyssa. And she was a tall brunette. Can't blame a guy for thinking that you have a type." He elbowed Marc. "Tall, lean, and with legs that don't end."

Marc took a deep breath and let it out slowly. He couldn't blame Kyle for thinking the way he did. After all, when Marc had opened this particular center eight years ago—his first center that soon bloomed into twelve more throughout the following years—Marc did have a reputation for dating tall, lean model-type women. And he'd met Alyssa here too, when she'd walked in looking to lose a few pounds because she had an audition for a local television talk show. But now, Marc wasn't in the market for a woman who was just beautiful. He wanted someone who was sweet, smart, and could hold her own against him. Someone who cared about people and loved the simple things in life—like walking in the park on a crisp fall day or canoeing on the lake in the summer.

Yeah, good luck finding a woman like that, he thought.

Marc turned to Kyle, who was still standing next to him. The last thing he wanted was to scare Debbie off with Kyle saying something offensive to her. "Don't you have anything to do?" Marc asked.

"Oh. Yeah. Sure. I always do," Kyle said, giving Marc a salute and heading over to the workout floor.

Marc rolled his eyes just as Debbie walked through the automatic doors.

"What now?" she asked, looking suddenly self-conscious. "Is

this the wrong outfit too?" She wore the same sweatshirt as the last time but had on a pair of black yoga pants instead of sweat pants.

"What? No. I wasn't rolling my eyes at you," he blurted out. Then a small laugh bubbled up and out of him. "Sorry. That eye roll was for someone else. You look great. Are you ready to work?"

She grimaced. "I guess so."

"Don't sound so enthused," he teased.

He started her on the elliptical machine for ten minutes, then had her lift weights again. "Since we're in a crunch for time, I'm extending your workouts to thirty minutes plus ten for cool-downs," he told her.

"Hey. I thought this was Fit in 20," she complained, breathing hard from her elliptical workout.

"You're only working out three times a week. So I'm going to give you your money's worth," he said.

"You're going to kill me," she mumbled.

Before sitting down to stretch, Debbie pulled off her sweatshirt and tossed it over the weight machine bench. Marc stared at her with wide eyes.

"What?" she asked, looking around. She was wearing a baggy T-shirt underneath that didn't show anything.

"Is everything you own baggy?" he asked. "The most skin you show is your arms."

She glared at him. "I'm not here to put on a show. And believe me, if I wore the skimpy, tight tanks that the other women here wear, it would be an X-rated show."

His brows rose. "I saw you in that tiny dress, remember? There was nothing vulgar or X-rated about how you looked."

A blush crept up Debbie's neck and face. She dropped her

eyes to the floor. "I'm just not comfortable showing a lot of skin," she said softly. "It's not who I am."

He ducked his head and caught her eyes with his. "There's nothing wrong with that. I like you the way you are." He smiled, and she finally smiled back.

After their workout, Marc led her to the back room and handed her a bottle of water from a small fridge next to his desk. Bernie was lying in the room, nearly asleep, but his head rose when Debbie walked in.

She rubbed him behind the ears before taking a sip of water. "Thanks." Glancing around, her gaze stopped on several food containers on his desk. They were filled with cookies, brownies, and other treats. "You sure eat a lot of junk food for a fitness guru."

"What?"

She nodded toward the containers.

"Oh, those." He shook his head as if exasperated. "Some of my clients bring me homemade treats. I usually leave them in the lunchroom and the janitor eats them. Most of the employees here stay away from sugar."

Debbie's brows rose. "Treats? Why would your clients bring you baked goods?" Then it hit her. "Ah, I get it. These are from your female clients. Single female clients."

Marc had the good grace to look sheepish. "I don't encourage them. They just bring stuff. The brownies are from an older client who wants me to meet her daughter."

Debbie laughed. "So, you have women chasing after you, huh?"

He ran his hand through his hair. "Like I said, I don't encourage it."

She changed the subject. "Is this where the magic happens?"

"Magic?" he looked startled.

"Yeah. Is this the office where you decided that one gym wasn't enough, and you made plans for twelve more?"

He laughed. "Actually, it is. I mean, it doesn't look like much with this Walmart desk and metal filing cabinets, but it was my first office in my first fitness center, so I'm kind of partial to it. This is my home base for operations."

She glanced around the tiny room. "Looks pretty busy."

"Ha, ha," he said.

"Honestly, though, it's pretty amazing. Growing a chain of businesses on your own this way. And at your age. I mean, you're not *that* old, right?" she gave him a teasing look.

"Oh, you're just hilarious tonight, aren't you? Where have you been hiding this sense of humor?"

She laughed.

"I'm thirty-six," he said. "So yeah, it is kind of cool that I've been able to accomplish as much as I have at my age. But, once I set my mind to something, I'm like a dog with a bone. At least that's what my mother has always said."

"It's nice having something to be so passionate about," Debbie said. "I've yet to find that something."

"Really? What about your bridal shop?"

She shrugged. "That was my mother's dream. And she loved running that shop. I like it too, don't get me wrong, but it's not my dream job. But it does okay, and it pays the bills."

Marc sat on the edge of his desk and looked at her with interest. "What would you do if you didn't have the bridal shop?"

"Starve," she said, then chuckled.

"No, really. What would you rather be doing?"

"I don't know. I studied communications and marketing in college and took a few classes in graphic design. I really enjoyed creating things in the design class. But I've only ever used those skills for promoting the bridal shop. I'm not sure what kind of job I'd pursue if I didn't have the shop. And, I'm not an outgoing person, so a communications degree was kind of silly for me."

Marc frowned. "There you go again."

"What?"

"Putting yourself down. I'm sure you have to be friendly and outgoing at your shop or otherwise you'd lose clients. You have people skills. So don't put yourself down."

Debbie dropped her eyes. "It's just a bad habit, I guess. My mother always told me the same thing. But it's hard. I've never accomplished much on my own, and I've always been the invisible girl. It doesn't exactly give me high confidence."

"You're not invisible to me," Marc said gently. "Or to your friend, Lindsay. Or even to the friend who invited you to go all the way to the Bahamas to join in on her wedding. It seems to me that many people see and appreciate you."

"I get what you're saying," she told him. "I do have friends. But old habits die hard. And the Bahama bride is a whole other story. I won't bore you with that tonight."

Marc was about to ask her about it when there was a knock on his office door. Kyle cracked the door a little and peeked in. "Sorry to bother you, but someone was asking if you'd help them with a workout."

Marc sighed, disappointed. He'd wanted to stay here, talking with Debbie.

"Sure. I'll be out in a minute," Marc said. He turned to Debbie. "This conversation isn't over." He grinned.

They walked out to the gym together, and Marc retrieved her sweatshirt from the weight machine and handed it to her. "Don't forget this. It's cold outside."

"Thanks," she said. "I'll see you at ten on Sunday. The auction starts at eleven-thirty, and you'll want to look at the items beforehand."

"Great," he said. "I'll pick you up."

Debbie waved before walking toward the sliding door. At that moment, a woman with dark hair approached him, and he gave her a friendly smile. Before he went to help the woman set up a workout routine, he noticed Debbie had stopped a moment at the open door, then finally went through. He wondered if she'd forgotten something, or had meant to tell him something else. But she left, and he headed off to help his customer.

Chapter Seven

The next day at work, Debbie couldn't help but ponder the night before. She'd had a nice time with Marc, despite exercising. They'd teased each other and had a few laughs. But in his office, when she'd noticed all the goodies women left for him, it had reminded her that he was more than just a good guy. He was a handsome catch and he had the pick of just about any woman he wanted. She wouldn't even be considered for that list.

Debbie sighed. She'd been reminded of that again as she was leaving and saw the reflection in the sliding doors of Marc smiling sweetly at the tall, slender, dark-haired woman who'd approached him. It was the same smile he'd given Debbie just moments before. Her good spirits from the evening had deflated.

He was only being nice because he needs help decorating his house, she thought. She had to remember that. Because it would be too easy to get drawn into those warm, brown eyes of his. He spent his days around beautiful, thin women who were in better shape than she was. The most they'd ever be was friends.

Debbie was thankful that she closed the shop at three on Saturdays. After saying goodbye to Lindsay—who'd already told her she had plans for a fun night out with friends—Debbie went straight home. The sun was shining for a change and the temperature was in the upper forties, so she decided to go for a walk to the park and bring Chloe along.

"Don't worry," Debbie told the little dog as she put on her collar. "No more bicycle."

Chloe looked at her suspiciously but then seemed happy when they made their way outside and down the sidewalk. Of course, a block away Chloe whined about having to walk so far.

"Spoiled," Debbie said, lifting the dog and carrying her.

Marc had suggested she might want to walk on the days she didn't exercise at the gym. "It will burn calories and it feels good to get outside," he'd said. Debbie did like being outside when it was warm, but despite growing up in Minnesota, she had never enjoyed the cold weather. But today, as she walked along, she relaxed and enjoyed herself. She could feel the stress of the day melting away, and her thoughts turned to what she'd pack for her Bahama trip. She hoped that after two months of exercise, her shorts from last summer still fit her. She tended to put on a few pounds in the winter and that had been one reason she'd wanted to start exercising. She couldn't afford a brand new wardrobe of summer clothes. Plus, she wanted to look her best. And with Marc's help, she felt that she might actually make her goal.

Debbie arrived at Lake Harriet and turned onto the trail that bordered it. The lake was still frozen, and the slight breeze off the ice was crisp. But she'd worn her heavy coat and was already warm from walking the few blocks to the park. Chloe had snuggled in the crook of her arm and weighed so little Debbie barely even noticed the dog.

As she turned a curve, a big, dark dog came barreling toward her. Debbie let out a shriek and jumped from the path onto the snow-encrusted lawn. Coming out of the shadow was Bernie, panting heavily but excited to see her.

"Bernie! You scared the daylights out of me," Debbie said, letting out a long sigh.

The dog danced around her, jumping up to sniff at Chloe. The little white dog stared over Debbie's arm with interest.

"Bernie!" Marc yelled, coming around the corner. He stopped running when he saw Debbie. "Oh, no! Did he run into you? I'm so sorry."

Debbie laughed. "No. It was more like he ran to me instead. Although it did scare me until I recognized him."

Marc smiled, although he was breathing heavily like Bernie. "Sorry. But it's good seeing you out here, walking." He drew closer and looked at Chloe. "Looks like she's a spoiled one, though." He let Chloe sniff his hand before petting her behind the ears. The dog allowed him, seeming to enjoy the attention.

Debbie's heart warmed. She liked that he was good with pets. "Yeah. She gave up after only a block. But that's okay. It'll build up my muscles."

His eyes sparkled. She really liked his eyes.

"Marc! Where'd you go?" a female voice called, and then a tall, slender woman came running around the corner. She drew up close to Marc and stopped, barely out of breath. "There you are. I thought I'd lost you."

Debbie recognized her as the yoga/aerobics/spin class teacher, Mandy, from the gym. Her long, blond hair was pulled up into a ponytail and she wore a stretchy headband that covered her ears. Both she and Marc were wearing workout clothes from the gym and looked like life-sized advertisements. Who wouldn't want to join Fit in 20 after seeing these two together? Debbie suddenly felt short and dumpy standing there in her heavy coat and thick walking shoes.

"Bernie ran ahead of me when he saw Debbie," Marc told

Mandy. "So, I had to catch up."

"Oh. Hi," Mandy said, smiling with perfect white teeth at Debbie. "I recognize you now. I hear you're going to be joining my Wednesday night spin class."

Debbie tried not to groan. As part of her workout each week, Marc wanted her to join in on a spin class and one aerobics class. She was dreading both. "Yeah, I guess I will be," she said.

"Don't worry," Mandy said. "It's a fun class—and a lot of work. But you'll catch on quickly."

Debbie nodded. She highly doubted she'd catch on at all, let alone quickly. "I'd better let you get back to your run," she said, holding on tightly to Chloe and stepping off the grass onto the sidewalk. "See you later."

Marc waved, then motioned for Bernie to follow them as they ran off down the path.

Debbie's good mood disappeared as they did. "Come on, Chloe. Let's go home."

* * *

Marc ran alongside Mandy, wishing he hadn't agreed for her to join him. He would have preferred walking along with Debbie instead. He'd almost said it to her out loud, then stopped himself. He had no reason to be rude to Mandy. She was always pleasant and hadn't done anything for him to insult her.

They ran the rest of the way around the lake and then cooled down by walking to his house where Mandy's car was parked.

"This was fun," Mandy said as they stood beside her blue Ford Escape. "We should do this again."

Marc nodded but didn't commit himself. In truth, he enjoyed running alone with Bernie. He ran to clear his head and reduce stress. He wasn't enthused about having a regular running partner.

Except maybe Debbie.

That thought shocked him. *Why in the world would I think that?* Well, it wasn't actually a problem because he was sure running was the last thing Debbie would want to do. He grinned at the thought.

Mandy must have thought his smile was for her because she drew closer. "It's funny. I've known you for three years and I've never seen your house." She turned her eyes up toward the mansion.

Wow! Could she be more obvious? "Yeah, well, that's probably because I had a fiancé for most of that time," he said.

"But she's not in the picture anymore, is she?" Mandy asked, moving even closer.

Marc took a step back and stumbled over Bernie, who was waiting patiently behind him. He quickly righted himself. "No, she's not. Maybe you could see the house another time. I'm afraid I have to be somewhere soon and need to shower and change."

"Oh." Mandy looked disappointed. "Okay. Another time," she said, not completely deterred. She went around the car and got in, but rolled down the passenger window. "I'll see you at work on Monday." She waved and drove off.

Marc sighed. How did he get himself into these messes? He hadn't invited advances from Mandy in any way that he could think of, except being nice to her. But he was her boss, shouldn't he be polite? Years ago, he would have welcomed advances from a woman like Mandy. And he would have had fun and then that would have been that. Now, he was making up lies about having to be someplace else so he wouldn't have to show a pretty woman his house. But the truth was he didn't want to date random women anymore. Ever since he'd had a taste of being in a relationship, he preferred that to casual dating or one night stands. Even though it hadn't worked out between him and Alyssa, he hoped to one day find someone he'd click with. Someone sweet, smart, and kind. Someone who'd be interested in having a family.

"Someone like Debbie," he said aloud.

Bernie looked up at him with curious eyes.

"Did I just say that?" Marc asked, stunned by his own words. Yet, thinking about Debbie always made him feel warm inside.

"Come on, boy," he said to Bernie. "Let's go inside. It's a popcorn and movie night."

* * *

The next day, Marc showed up at Debbie's house at nine fifty-five. He was excited about going antiquing with her. This made him laugh to himself. If someone had told him he'd be excited about shopping for antiques ten years ago, he'd have said they were crazy. But he really couldn't wait.

Debbie walked outside, carrying two travel mugs of coffee, and got into his SUV.

"Hi," she said, handing him a mug. "I brought coffee."

"Hi. Thanks. You just became my favorite person." He smiled and noticed she was blushing. He loved that. She blushed at compliments like a schoolgirl. It was cute.

"Where's the bear today?" Debbie asked as she snapped on her seatbelt.

"Bear? Oh, Bernie. He's at home. I didn't think it would be a good idea to bring him to a place with expensive antiques. He's kind of a big galoot."

Debbie chuckled. "He's adorable, but yeah, he's a big dog."

"What about the puffball?" Marc asked, giving her a mischievous grin.

"The princess is worn out from her walk yesterday," Debbie said. "Or should I say, from being carried around."

They drove off toward St. Paul as Debbie directed him to the house where the auction was being held. It was located on one of the more prominent streets in the older section of town, where mansions were once owned by the very rich. Now, many had been transformed into apartments or townhouses, but the neighborhood was still very upper class.

"Sheesh. My house looks like a dump compared to these," Marc said, glancing around the neighborhood as he looked for a parking space.

"Great. What does that make my house? A shack?" Debbie asked.

Marc grimaced. "Sorry. Your house is cute. You'll have to give me a tour sometime so I can see your antiques."

"Right. Be prepared to be underwhelmed," she said.

They finally parked and walked down the street to the house. Marc noticed that Debbie had worn flats with her jeans today, probably anticipating they'd be standing and walking a lot. She looked cute with her hair up in a French braid and wearing a blue blouse and tan jacket. Her eyes turned an even deeper shade of blue because of the blouse.

Several people were milling around outside of the mansion and even more inside. Antique furniture filled the large rooms throughout the house, each with a number on it and a beginning bid price.

"These aren't exactly great bargains," Debbie whispered to Marc, pointing at the prices. "Do you see anything you like?"

"That dining room set is amazing," he said. "I love the dark wood and the curve of the chairs."

"It is beautiful," Debbie agreed. "It looks like Chippendale, and it's mahogany. Probably a later piece from the 1900-1920s."

Marc stared at her in amazement. "Wow. You really do know your antiques."

She shrugged. "Chippendale is easy to identify. The chair backs, curved legs, and feet give it away." She glanced at the list of furniture they'd been handed when they'd walked inside. "It is a Chippendale piece made of mahogany in the 1920s. That's the perfect period for your house. Are you thinking of sticking with mahogany throughout or choosing different shades of wood furniture?"

"I'm not sure," Marc said, looking confused. "Do I have to pick only one color?"

She laughed softly. "No. We can mix and match. But you don't want a messy hodgepodge of styles. Let's see what else you like."

Marc was overwhelmed by the many pieces for sale. He liked them all. There was a heavy desk he loved that also looked to be in the Chippendale style and some Barrister cases that would look great in his home office to store books. A cocktail table and end tables caught his eye, too, and upstairs in the master bedroom, he liked the sleigh bed and nightstands. When he handed his list to Debbie with all the pieces he wanted checked, she gasped.

"This will cost a small fortune! Maybe we should have talked about a budget for furniture first."

"Well, I figured I could bid on the items I like. I probably won't get them all if the prices go sky-high," Marc said.

"They already are sky-high to begin with. But I guess if you love all these items enough to spend that kind of money, that's up to you."

Marc paused. He liked each item, but he didn't know if he *loved* them. He could certainly live with them and not be unhappy. He looked again at the starting bids for each item. "Some of these are kind of high, I guess. I love the dining table. And the bedroom set. I can picture them in my house. Is that what you mean by loving them? That you can see yourself living with them?"

Debbie smiled. "It's been a while since you've had to worry about money, I guess. Personally, I'd have to be drooling over a piece before I'd pay that much. If you're comfortable paying these prices, then do what your heart tells you."

"Let's just bid on these items, and if they go too high, hit me to tell me to stop. Okay?"

"Okay," Debbie said, sounding skeptical.

In the end, Marc did win the dining table and chairs for a reasonable price. And he was having so much fun during the bidding war on the bedroom set that he didn't stop even when Debbie started hitting him hard enough to bruise his arm. He won the set, but when he realized how much he'd spent, he almost regretted it.

Almost.

"It's your money," Debbie said, looking perturbed.

Marc knew that was true, but he had asked for her opinion, and then he'd gone against it with his first purchase. He decided he'd better listen to her next time. After he'd paid and arranged for the items to be delivered to his home, they walked out to his car in silence.

"I did love that furniture," he said as they got into the car.

"I hope so," Debbie said. "Because you spent enough to

furnish ten houses."

For some reason, he felt like he should apologize. But it was his money. Why shouldn't he spend it however he wanted? "Where to next?" he asked, hoping they were going to shop some more. After buying those items, he was in the mood to buy more.

"There are a couple of shops we can go to. They're mostly good for small items, like occasional tables, light fixtures, and wall-hangings. But we can browse around."

They walked around the stores, which were jammed-packed with items from all eras. Debbie pointed out a coat tree with a bench that might look nice in the kitchen near the French doors, and Marc liked it too. There were Tiffany lamps that were right for the era, but he decided he didn't like them, and all sorts of decorative items, dishes, silverware, and glassware. A painting caught his attention. It had a wide, gilt frame and depicted an English countryside with men on horses on a fox hunt. The vivid green, red, and brown colors were what caught his eye.

"This would look good in my den," he told Debbie. "I mean, I know it's very masculine, but so is my den. It has dark wood bookshelves and wainscoting and that great tile fireplace."

Debbie studied the painting. "Yes. It would look nice over the fireplace."

"Should I buy it?" he asked.

She gave him a wry grin. "Do you love it?"

Marc laughed. "Yes. I think I do."

"Then you should buy it."

They left the shop with the painting, a tall lantern that would look nice next to one of the many fireplaces, and a beautiful rustic occasional table with wrought-iron accents for the foyer.

"The table will look good with that dead leopard you have on the floor," Debbie teased.

"That thing is going away along with all the other stuff. We'll need to find rugs, too," Marc said.

"I think we've done enough damage to your checking account for one day," she told him. "Besides, most of these small stores close by four on Sunday, and it's nearly that now."

They slid into his car, and Marc studied her a moment.

"What?" Debbie asked, frowning. "Is something wrong?" She smoothed her hair and pulled down the visor to look at her face.

"No, silly. I was wondering if you're hungry. We're near one of my favorite places. We could have a late lunch or an early dinner."

Debbie paused and looked as if she might say no. He hoped not. They'd been having such a good time that he wanted to spend more time with her.

"Sure. That sounds good. I'm hungry. What place is your favorite?"

"Gallagher's Irish Pub. Have you ever been there?"

Debbie grinned. "Oh, yeah. I've been there. A few times. Sounds good."

Marc wasn't sure if her smile was for the pub or for him, but he didn't care. He loved seeing Debbie smile. He started the car and drove toward the Nicolette Mall.

Chapter Eight

Debbie sat at a high-top table across from Marc. Gallagher's wasn't too busy this time of day, especially since it was Sunday. Football season was over, and baseball season was just starting, so there were no sport's fans filling up the place. When the waitress came to the table, it didn't surprise her who it was.

"Hi, Lindsay," Debbie said, smiling. "How has your day been?"

"Slow. And tips aren't that great today. I hope you two are big tippers." She grinned and handed them menus.

Marc stared at her, looking surprised. "Hi. I didn't know you worked here too."

"Only on weekends," Lindsay said. "The extra money helps."

"That's why I've never seen you here," Marc said. "I come in for lunch during the week. They have the best sandwiches and hamburgers."

"No argument there." A tall, dark-haired man joined their group as a chunky English bulldog followed behind him.

"Hi, James. How's it going?" Marc asked, greeting the newcomer. He got off the stool and stooped to pet Brewster, James's dog.

"I'm doing fine," James said. He turned to Debbie and

waggled his brows suggestively. "Debbie, you've been holding out on all of us. I didn't know you knew Marc."

"Right," Debbie said with a laugh. "I've been bringing all those *other* guys I've been dating to the neighborhood picnics."

Marc stood up from petting Brewster and cocked his head. "Neighborhood picnics? You both live in the same neighborhood?"

"Yep," James said. "Our house is only a few doors down from Deb's. Brewster has a crush on Chloe, but he tries to act casual about it."

Marc laughed. "Well, it is a small world."

"How do you two know each other?" Debbie asked James.

"I've been going to his gym for a couple of years now," James said. "At least, I try to stop in a couple of times a week. It's nice that it's not far from here."

Debbie tried not to grimace. The last thing she wanted was to run into someone she knew at the gym while she was looking foolish, exercising.

Lindsay took their drink order, and she and James headed to the bar with Brewster trailing behind them.

"That's really cool that you live near James. He's a great guy," Marc said.

"He is. And his wife is wonderful, too. In fact, Mallory runs a staging and design business, helping people decorate their homes. She's the person you should hire to help you decorate."

"But I like having you help me," Marc said. "We had fun today. And we get to do more of the same tomorrow, too." He winked at her.

Debbie chuckled and opened the menu. She was hungry, but she thought she should probably have a salad since she was trying to lose weight. Ugh! She hated dieting. A thought occurred to her as she looked at the food selection. "I'm surprised you haven't suggested a diet for me to follow along with my exercise."

Marc raised his eyes from the menu. "Generally, we do suggest a diet, depending on what the person is trying to accomplish. But in your case, you aren't overweight, so adding exercise should be all you need to tone up."

She gave him a sly look. "So, I can order the barbeque ribs with French fries and cheesecake for dessert?"

"Order whatever you like. As long as you keep exercising, it shouldn't matter."

"Right," she said, shaking her head. From the corner of her eye, she could see him grinning mischievously.

Lindsay brought their drinks and took their order. Debbie refrained from the high-fat foods and ordered a salad with grilled chicken instead. Marc went for the greasy cheeseburger and onion rings. Debbie didn't know how he ate like that and stayed in such good shape.

After Lindsay left, Marc leaned in closer to Debbie. "I did have fun today," he told her. "What's our next move for tomorrow?"

"Actually, I've been thinking that we didn't plan this very well. You should go through your entire house and make a list of the furniture you want to keep and a list of what you want to replace or add. Then you need to decide what you want to do with the furniture you're getting rid of. You might also want to consider going to furniture stores for some of your pieces. There are a lot of nice brands that make furniture that looks antique. For furniture you use a lot, you may not want an expensive item that you're afraid of ruining."

"Wow. You've given this some thought. Do you see why I need you to help me? I'd just start buying stuff and then realize I had no place to put it. So, what should I do with the other stuff?

Send it to Goodwill?"

Debbie nearly gasped. Even though she wasn't a fan of the furniture he had, she could tell it was high quality. It would be a shame just to give it away. "Let me talk to Mallory about that. She might know of a place where you can sell it. But first, let's use tomorrow to go through the furniture and make that list."

"Sounds like a plan," Marc said.

Their food came, and as they ate, Marc asked Debbie about the bridal shop. "How long have you owned it?"

"My mom opened it when I was just a baby. I think my grandparents helped her at first. She rented the entire house, and we lived upstairs where Lindsay lives now and she ran the shop below. It was actually a good idea to use the house for the business. People love those old Victorians, and for my mother, it was a dream come true. She loved antiques and old homes."

"You didn't mention a father. Wasn't he in the picture?"

Debbie shook her head. "No. They married very young and divorced before my mom even told him she was pregnant with me. I've never met my father. I don't even know what he looks like because my mom destroyed all the pictures she had of him."

Marc sat back, a serious expression on his face. "I'm sorry to hear that. Do you ever wonder about him?"

"No. My mom was a very sweet, vibrant woman. People adored her. So if she couldn't get along with him, I'm sure I wouldn't like him either." Debbie thought back to when she was a teenager and how she'd wished she'd known her father. But now, she didn't care. Her mother more than made up for her not having a second parent.

"So, after all these years, you still rent the house for the shop?" Marc asked.

"Oh, no. My mom bought the Victorian when I was little.

The owner didn't want it anymore and gave her a reasonable price. Then a few years after that, she bought the little bungalow where I live now. She rented out the upstairs of the Victorian to help make the payments. She wanted me to go to a better school district than the older house was zoned for, and that's why we moved. I've lived in that little house since I was around eleven."

"You own that Victorian house and the other one? That's amazing. Your mom left you some good real estate."

Debbie smiled. "She left me much more than that. She left me a way to earn a living and a bunch of wonderful memories. My mom was incredible. That's why I feel obligated to keep the shop running. It was her legacy."

Marc was eating the last of his fries, and Debbie had finished her salad. He smiled at her and his eyes sparkled. "Tell me, who are all these guys you bring to the neighborhood picnics?"

"What?" He'd completely thrown her.

"The long line of guys you were telling James about. I suppose I'm at the very back of that line." He grinned.

Heat rose to Debbie's face. She'd just been teasing James because he'd insinuated that she and Marc were together. "There is no line of guys. I was just being sarcastic."

Marc shook his head. "That's a shame. There should be. But that's everyone's loss but mine."

Debbie's breath caught in her throat. What did he mean by *that*? There was no way this extremely fit and handsome man would ever look at her twice.

"Now you're the one who's teasing," she said softly.

Lindsay appeared beside the table at that exact moment and dropped off their bill. "I'll see you on Tuesday, Debbie," she said with a wave.

Marc placed two twenties into the black folder, and they

headed out to the car. Their drive was quiet, mostly because the Sunday evening traffic was busy. As Marc pulled up in front of Debbie's house, he asked what time she wanted to meet the next day.

"I'll drop by around ten if that works," she told him.

"That's perfect."

She turned to him. "Thank you for dinner."

"You're welcome. It was fun." He glanced past her at the house. "Maybe the next time I'm here, you'll show me around inside?"

"Sure," she said. "Next time." Debbie stepped out and waved, then entered her house. She noticed that he waited until she was safely inside before driving away.

Yep. Marc was a gentleman. Too bad he was way out of her league.

With a sigh, Debbie picked Chloe up from the sofa. "Hey, baby. I'll bet you're hungry."

Chloe didn't disagree.

* * *

Monday morning, Marc woke up early and took Bernie out for a run in the crisp air. Then he showered and dressed so he'd be ready when Debbie came over. As he wandered around the house, looking at everything with a critical eye, he couldn't help but think of the day before. It had been so much fun going to the auction and then shopping with Debbie. She really knew her antiques and she kept him in line about his spending. He thought she had good ideas about mixing old furniture with new for the house and taking his time choosing things he loved. He'd never done that before, other than when he'd purchased this house. He'd fallen in love with it the moment he'd walked inside and no one was going to talk him out of it. Even Alyssa, who would have preferred a brand new house in a fancy development, couldn't stop him from buying this house.

"Maybe that's why she decorated it this way," he said aloud to Bernie, who'd been following him around the house. "As revenge for not getting the house she wanted."

Marc sighed. He'd never had much luck with women. He didn't need a psychiatrist to tell him why, either. In the past, he'd always gone for beauty over substance. Not that there weren't beautiful women out there who were also smart and successful. But he'd somehow found the ones who only cared about how they looked and how much money he could spend on them. He'd thought that Alyssa had been different, but in the end, they didn't have enough in common to keep the relationship together. Their break-up had been the final straw. He no longer wanted the fashion model type of woman on his arm. He wanted someone sweet, kind, and cute. Someone who cared about more than her hair or what the latest fashion was. Of course, saying that was easier than finding a woman like that, especially in his profession. A lot of pretty women came into the gym to keep in shape, which was good for his business, but not for his heart. He shied away from those women now, afraid they would be like everyone else he'd ever dated.

And then there was Debbie.

He'd never met anyone like her before. She was shy, smart, hardworking, and humble, yet she was also beautiful. He liked how down-to-earth she was. She intrigued him. And for the first time in years, he was unsure about himself. Debbie didn't fawn over him as the other women had. Which was another thing he liked about her—yet it confused him too.

"She probably thinks I'm a conceited snob," he told Bernie. Bernie didn't contradict him.

"You're supposed to disagree with me," Marc said. He reached down and ran his hand through Bernie's silky fur. "That's okay. I know you're just trying to stay neutral."

The doorbell rang, and Marc hurried to answer it. Debbie stood there in her wool coat and scarf, carrying Chloe in the crook of her arm.

"I hope you don't mind my bringing Chloe. She's been feeling left out the past few days."

Marc smiled. "Not at all. Come in."

She stepped inside and set Chloe on the floor. "Bernie won't eat her, will he?" she asked, looking concerned.

"I highly doubt it. Too much fur," Marc teased.

Bernie walked over and sniffed Chloe. She raised her tiny black nose to his big one, sniffed, then sauntered to the leopard rug and laid down, looking unconcerned. Bernie laid down too.

"Looks like they're going to get along," Debbie said. She took off her coat and scarf and Marc hung them in the closet. Digging through the big bag she'd brought along, Debbie pulled out a notebook and pen. "Shall we start in the living or dining room?"

"Wherever you'd like," Marc said. "Lead the way."

They started in the dining room since Marc had already purchased a table and chairs, and they could decide what else he'd want. Debbie wrote down everything in two columns—what to replace and what to keep. As they went through every single item, Marc realized that there were items he did want to keep.

"I've never cataloged everything so thoroughly," he said. "But there are a lot of items in the house that I do like. Or at least that will work with the new furniture."

Debbie smiled slyly. "I guess your ex-girlfriend's taste wasn't all that terrible."

"Well, she did pick me," he said.

Debbie rolled her eyes and continued assessing the furniture. "We should look for an antique hutch that will blend well with the table you bought. And a sideboard for the other side of the room. Do you have real silverware and china dishes?"

"No. I don't think so. Do you think I need them?" Marc asked.

"Do you ever entertain formally?"

"I've had the managers and their wives here for dinner during the holidays. Otherwise, no," Marc said.

"We could look at some dishes and see what you like. Probably something plain but elegant. I'm pretty sure you wouldn't want flowers on your plates."

Marc wrinkled his nose. "Probably not."

She laughed. "I'll add it to the list of things to look for. This room could use some new paintings unless you like these," she said. Marc shook his head vehemently, so she continued. "And possibly some glass sconces for the walls. I'd say six."

"Where would you put them?"

"One on either side of the fireplace and then two on that wall and two on this one across from it."

Marc watched where she pointed. "I've never thought of that before, but that would be nice. His brows waggled. "For all those candlelit dinners."

"Yes. Well," Debbie said, dropping her eyes to the list again. Marc's lips curled into a grin. He didn't know why, but he enjoyed teasing her. Probably because it got a reaction out of her. But instead of her telling him he was crazy, she always dropped her eyes shyly. He felt it was his job to tease the shyness out of her.

"And a large rug for under the table," she said, changing the subject. "Something with a beautiful pattern that'll break up all the wood in here. A soft red, maybe, or black with a paisley pattern."

"That sounds nice," Marc said.

He followed her to the living room next, but not before she wrote down to get rid of the leopard rug.

Debbie glanced around the room. "This is a beautiful room. I love the tray ceiling and the chandelier. And the large bay window with the seat at the front of the house. But it's the fireplace that really catches the eye. Is that marble tile around it?"

"Yep. Italian marble. And the mantel is walnut. That fireplace was one of many reasons that I bought this house."

"I can understand why," she said. "What about a framed mirror for over the fireplace? It would create a focal point."

"I love that idea," he said.

"And let me guess—you're a leather sofa kind of guy." She grinned.

"Guilty. Would that look okay in here?"

"I think it would look fine. Maybe a distressed leather, or a lighter brown. You could do a wooden coffee table and end tables with clear glass over the tops to protect them plus bring out the luster of the wood. And floor lamps instead of table lamps. I've seen some beautiful ones that would add character at a store downtown."

"You must frequent the antique stores a lot to remember those details," he said.

"I like to look. I can dream."

Marc was about to comment when the doorbell rang. He frowned. "Who could that be?"

"Oh, I'm sorry. I forgot to tell you I invited Mallory Gallagher to stop by and look at the furniture you don't want. She said she might be interested."

They went to the door together and greeted Mallory.

"Hi," she said, shaking Marc's hand after they were introduced. "I'm so excited to see the furniture you have. I've been staging some high-end homes lately, so I need quality furniture."

"Then you've come to the right place because it's all going," Marc said with a grin. He liked Mallory immediately. She had a warm smile that made him feel at ease. Dressed in jeans and a heavy sweater, she looked casual instead of stuffy or snobbish. "So, you're married to James. I eat at Gallagher's quite a bit."

"Yeah. James told me you both were in for a late lunch yesterday."

"There are no secrets in our neighborhood," Debbie said, looking embarrassed.

"I didn't know having lunch together was a secret," Marc said with a wink.

Marc ran to the kitchen to get bottles of water for all of them, and Debbie showed Mallory the living room and dining room furniture he wanted to sell. After Marc returned, they walked around the house, and Mallory took notes of the pieces she'd like to buy.

"I can't buy too many, but I do want this list of items for sure," she said, handing Marc the sheet after they'd scoured every room. "Write down a price when you have time, and we'll see if we can work out a deal."

"Okay. Great." Marc was pleased the old furniture would have a new home.

As they walked Mallory to the door, she glanced down at the leopard rug where the dogs were sound asleep. "It looks like they've found the item they want to keep," she said, laughing.

Debbie winced. "Well, maybe Marc can keep it in the family room in the kitchen if Bernie likes it so much."

"Bernie never sleeps on it. He's just flirting with Chloe."

"Oh, oh," Mallory said. "Brewster has competition for Chloe's affections. I'm not sure I have the heart to tell him."

They all said goodbye, and Marc and Debbie went back to working on their list.

"I like Mallory. She seems nice," Marc said as they headed for the den.

"Yeah. Everyone in my neighborhood is great. You'd like all of them, I'm sure," Debbie said.

"Maybe you'll invite me to one of those neighborhood picnics so I can meet them."

Once again, Debbie looked flustered. "Let's get back to work," she said hurriedly.

They made a list of items for the den, and Marc offered to order in lunch. "Do you like Chinese takeout?" he asked.

She glanced at the garish clock in the den. "It's getting kind of late. Remember, I still have to meet my trainer at the gym later for a torture session. Chinese might be too heavy."

He saw a glimmer of a tease coming from her eyes. Ah, ha! He was rubbing off on her. Just as he was about to offer to make a salad, the doorbell rang again. "Were you expecting anyone else?" Marc asked.

Debbie shook her head.

Marc hurried to the front door, and Debbie trailed behind. The dogs had left the leopard rug and were snuggled up on the fluffy white rug in the living room. Marc opened the door, and there stood Mandy.

"Hi. I hope I'm not bothering you. I was thinking about you and thought I'd stop in for that house tour," she said, smiling wide. She raised a paper bag. "I picked up chicken wraps from Arnie's that I know you like. Have you had lunch yet?"

Marc stood there, speechless. "Well, uh." He glanced back to where Debbie was standing in the hallway beside the staircase. "I was kind of busy."

"We can be finished for the day," Debbie said hurriedly. "Hi, Mandy. I was just leaving anyway." Debbie grabbed her coat from the closet and slipped it on.

"Oh, I didn't know you had a guest," Mandy said, looking genuinely sorry. "I don't want to intrude."

"You're not intruding," Debbie said. She turned to Marc. "We have a good start for now. Go ahead and have lunch with Mandy. I'll see you at the gym." She hurried out the door.

Marc stood frozen. Debbie was scurrying out the door and he hadn't had a chance to say anything. He didn't want to have lunch with Mandy. He wanted to spend the rest of the afternoon with Debbie. Unfortunately, she had already reached the steps that went down to the street. He rushed past Mandy. "Debbie! Wait!"

She stopped and stared at him.

"You forgot the puffball," he said, remembering Chloe was still in the house.

Debbie's mouth dropped open. "Oh. How could I forget her?" She came toward the house again, and Marc went inside and picked up Chloe. Mandy was already inside the house and standing by the staircase. He brought Chloe outside to Debbie, who'd made it to the front steps.

"Thanks," she said, tucking Chloe under her arm and turning to rush off.

Marc reached for her arm and stopped her. "I didn't ask Mandy over," he said softly so the Mandy wouldn't hear. "I had planned on spending the entire day with you."

Debbie turned. "It's fine. We've done enough for one day. Go, have some fun." She spun and headed away.

Marc wanted to run after her, but he stopped himself. Debbie said it was fine, but he knew it wasn't. She'd looked upset. Still, he didn't want to be rude to Mandy either. With a sigh, he walked back inside the house and closed the door.

Chapter Nine

Debbie drove the short distance home with tears in her eyes. She didn't even understand why she was crying. She and Marc had a business arrangement—her antique knowledge in exchange for his training abilities. They were only working together. Why on earth was she so upset?

She wiped her tears with the sleeve of her coat and pulled into her garage. She knew why she was upset. She'd had fun going through the furniture with Marc, and she hadn't wanted it to end. It was work, but with him, it didn't feel like it. He had such a light-hearted way about him that it brought out her light-hearted side. She enjoyed his teasing and giving it right back. Debbie hadn't spent time with a man that made her feel comfortable in a long time. And with Marc, she felt very comfortable.

But then again, he acted friendly with everyone. She had to remember that. She wasn't special to him in any way, just another woman that he was friendly with. From the little she'd seen, he'd had a lot of practice with women.

Her good mood from earlier now crushed, Debbie lifted Chloe from the seat and went inside the house. She was hungry, so she made a light lunch in her small kitchen and sat at the little antique breakfast table by the window. The day had warmed a little, and she watched as Lisa and Avery walked down the sidewalk, pulling little Abby in her wagon. The sweet little girl was bundled up in her jacket, scarf, and stocking cap, a few of her red curls peeking out.

Debbie sighed. Everyone in her neighborhood was pairing off and having children—everyone except her. Kristen and Ryan had just had their second child, a little boy they'd named Joshua. James and Mallory had little Shannon. Debbie adored all the happy families around her, but she felt left out. When would her turn come?

Debbie thought back to her only serious relationship when she was in college. She'd met Colin Williams in her senior year in an advanced graphic arts class. He was a little nerdy, which she'd found adorable, and they'd bonded while working on a group project for class. He'd been an everyday kind of guy, and Debbie had liked that about him. They'd dated for two years, and in that time, became engaged. Both had graduated with a communications degree, and Colin had found a job in downtown Minneapolis in the human resource department of a large company. Debbie had continued working at the bridal shop with her mom but had dreamed of finding a graphic design position downtown once she and Colin were married. But as she planned their small wedding, everything changed.

Debbie's mother hadn't warmed to Colin the way Debbie had hoped, but that hadn't stopped her from being excited about her future. Then little things started to happen. A broken dinner date, Colin claiming to be putting in a lot of overtime at work, and then weekends when he was too busy to meet up with her. All signs pointed to his losing interest, but Debbie refused to see it. He changed too. Colin was going to the gym and buying tailored suits. He moved out of his small apartment and into a larger townhouse. Debbie had thought Colin was making those changes for her but found out that wasn't the case. When she dropped by the townhouse one evening, he'd been there with a beautiful, tall, slender woman. He finally admitted to Debbie that he'd found someone else he cared about and he was sorry to hurt her. But he didn't look sorry. He looked like he was happily moving on.

Debbie sighed. It didn't hurt anymore, not like it had at first, but it still stung. She'd felt so stupid. How could she have not seen the signs? He'd changed and left her behind, and she was still stuck in her old life after all these years.

"It was for the better," she said aloud, as she'd told herself so many times before. But it had turned her into a more guarded person. She'd never been a social butterfly, but after that experience, she'd gone deeper into her shell. Opening herself up to loving someone again wasn't going to be easy. Protecting her heart was better than giving it away to be broken again.

"And that's why I need to be extra careful around Marc," she told Chloe as she lifted the dog into her lap. "Because he'd break my heart for sure."

* * *

Debbie arrived at the gym five minutes before her workout. To her surprise, Marc was once again standing at the door, waiting for her. She wasn't sure if she was flattered or annoyed.

"You know, I can find my way inside without you waiting for me," she said, sharper than she'd intended.

"I know that," he said, looking a bit stunned.

They walked to the workout room, and Marc turned on a treadmill for her. She slipped off her sweatshirt and stepped on, already knowing that she'd be on the torture device for at least ten minutes, if not twenty. The machine began at a slow pace.

"You don't have to stand there a watch me the entire time," Debbie said. "I can speed it up on my own. I'm sure you have other people to help."

Marc stood there, looking unsure. Finally, he said, "You're angry about Mandy showing up, aren't you? I promise I didn't invite her over. She's just been a bit overly friendly lately. I'm trying to be nice about it because she works here, but I'll have to tell her I don't date employees. It gets messy."

Debbie touched a button that sped up the treadmill. She didn't really want to go faster, but she knew she should. Also, the noise would drown out Marc's attempt at making excuses.

"Aren't you going to say anything?" Marc asked.

"About what? I don't have a problem with you and Mandy. She seems like a nice woman. If you have a problem, you should take care of it instead of leading her on."

"I'm not leading her on," Marc protested, but he was drowned out by Debbie increasing the speed of the machine again. Finally, he gave up and walked to the other side of the room to help someone else.

Debbie's heart pounded in her chest—not from the workout, but from her growing anger. Anger at Marc, but mostly, anger at herself. She had no reason to be snide to Marc, but she couldn't help herself. What was wrong with her? Why did this guy bring out the best and worst in her? She hit the machine's button again and walked even faster, trying to burn off her angry energy.

By the time Marc returned to slow her down, she was sweating and her muscles ached. She'd gone too fast for too long and wasn't used to it. All because she was acting stupid about this guy.

"Let's go lift some weights," Marc said, sounding very professional.

Fine, Debbie thought. *Let's keep this professional.*

She sat on one of the weight benches and started pulling the weights. She tugged hard at first, but soon her back and arm muscles hurt, and she slowed down. Finally, she called it quits. "I'm done," she said.

Marc nodded. "Let's stretch before you leave."

Debbie sat on the floor opposite him and started stretching as he'd shown her before. Marc stretched too, staying silent. But when she dared to look at him, she saw he was watching her with those warm, brown eyes, and it was her undoing. She let out a big sigh, and her shoulders slumped.

Marc instantly looked concerned. "Are you okay? Did I work you out too hard?"

Debbie shook her head, all her anger spent. She'd had no reason to be angry to begin with and now she just felt foolish. "I didn't mean to sound so snippy earlier. I'm sorry," she said softly.

"That's okay." He gave her one of his sweet grins. "Actually, I think I deserved it."

That made her smile. "No. You didn't. But can I give you a little advice?"

"Sure."

"If you aren't interested in Mandy, then you should let her know right away. Leading someone on, even if you're trying to be nice, is more hurtful than the truth. Every woman deserves the truth," Debbie said.

Marc nodded. "You're right."

Debbie stood, grabbed her sweatshirt, and slipped it on. She was hot and sweaty and worn out both physically and emotionally. "I'll see you on Wednesday."

"Spin class that night," he added.

Debbie rolled her eyes, waved, and headed out the door.

* * *

Marc watched Debbie leave, relieved she was no longer angry at him. He hadn't understood why she'd been so upset because he'd explained he hadn't invited Mandy over. But now he felt he had a little insight into why Debbie had been mad. Her advice to not lead Mandy on came from the heart. Possibly from a heart that had been broken once before, by someone who'd led her on. The thought of a man doing that to Debbie irritated him. She was so sweet, how could anyone do that to her? Then again, he'd been guilty of the very same thing—not telling a woman the truth right away to spare her feelings. And Debbie was right. Doing that didn't help anyone in the end.

"Is your little sweetie gone for the night?" Kyle asked, coming up behind Marc.

His words gnawed at Marc's nerves. He turned abruptly and glared at Kyle. "Do you mean is my client gone? Yes, she is."

Kyle look startled. "Hey, I didn't mean anything by it. It's just that you seem to spend a lot of time with that woman, so I can't help but think you have a thing for her."

Marc frowned. Why did Kyle always sound like a jerk to him these days? "That woman's name is Debbie, and I'm working with her, so I don't see why it's any different than my working with anyone else who comes in here."

Kyle raised his hands. "Okay. Okay. Sheesh. You sure have been touchy lately. I was a little confused by it anyway. She's definitely not your type." He walked away into the workout area.

Not my type? Marc pondered that. What would Kyle know

about his type? Marc felt he'd be lucky if a woman like Debbie were in his life. He smiled. Of course, she'd probably not feel as lucky as he would. She was too smart to be involved with a man like him. He'd probably drive her crazy.

Throughout the evening, Marc helped several members with training or operating the machines. Most of the clients who sought him out were women. All ages, all sizes. Some were regulars who flirted brazenly with him while others were the motherly type who brought him cookies and brownies and all the treats he didn't need. He found that endearing, but he wondered if he'd been casually flirting with these women all along, and that was why they were so sweet to him.

Cripes! Debbie's advice was really getting to him!

He was conscious of being as professional as possible with everyone, and he was going to speak with Mandy after her classes about their relationship staying platonic. Unfortunately, she left immediately after her last class and he didn't have a chance to talk to her. He decided he would first thing tomorrow evening.

"Hey, boss," Kyle called from across the room. "Phone call for you."

Marc excused himself from the woman he'd been showing how to use the rowing machine and headed toward the back room. "I'll take it in my office," he told Kyle.

Marc sat at his cluttered desk and lifted the phone from its cradle. "Hello. This is Marc."

"Hello," a woman's voice said on the other end. "I'm sorry for calling so late but I was told you only work evenings."

"Yes. That's one of the perks of being the owner," he said lightly. "What can I do for you?"

"My name is Melinda Jones, and I'm the manager of human resources for McGregory Medical Supply. We're thinking of adding a gym to each of our office buildings in the metro area and possibly across the country. But we thought instead of just setting up some equipment and hoping our employees used it, we could partner with a chain of gyms to set something up. Would you be interested in meeting and discussing such a proposal?"

Marc was stunned. What a fantastic opportunity, just falling in his lap. "Why, yes, I would be interested in talking to you about it."

"Wonderful. I'd like to get together as soon as possible, but my next two weeks are packed solid during office hours. Would you be open to having dinner on Wednesday night instead, and we can talk then?"

"Wednesday night sounds perfect," Marc said. They set a time and place and soon hung up. Marc fell back into his chair, still shocked by what they were proposing. But it made perfect sense. He could set up fitness centers inside their office buildings and even have trainers come in to work with employees. It would be a whole new market even he hadn't thought of.

Excitedly, Marc opened his laptop and began researching McGregory Medical Supply. He'd get a little background on their company and then set up a proposal for gym equipment. He was so excited that ideas were running through his mind like wildfire. And that was when it hit him—Wednesday he was supposed to be here for Debbie.

He contemplated that a moment. Well, he had told Debbie that was spin class night, so he really wasn't going to be helping her anyway. But he had thought he'd join in on the class to see how things went for her. He didn't want her to think he'd abandoned her.

"She'll understand," he finally told himself. "She's in business too, and this is important." He would text her that he couldn't be there Wednesday, but she should go to spin class, and he'd catch her on Friday.

Excited again, he began typing up a proposal on how to implement an office gym for McGregory Medical Supply.

Chapter Ten

Tuesday was predicted to be in the high forties, so Debbie wore a pair of dress pants to work and brought along sneakers to change into.

"We're going to walk at lunchtime," she told Chloe, who didn't look very excited about it. "No more being lazy. I have to make myself exercise if I want to lose this weight."

Once at the store, Debbie was busy with customers and unpacking stock and orders that had arrived. Every January and August she ordered the new lines of bridal gowns and brides-maid dresses. She also ordered in dresses with a younger flair for teens to wear to prom in the spring. When the orders started coming in, it felt like Christmas. So many packages and new items to admire.

Lindsay came downstairs around noon and took over so Debbie could go on lunch break. Debbie had already opened up several cartons of dresses and had hung them on the rolling rack to steam.

"Look at all these gorgeous dresses!" Lindsay exclaimed, looking through them. "I love when the spring line comes in."

Debbie nodded. "The colors are always so beautiful."

"Yes, and it also means that summer is on the way," Lindsay

said, grinning. "I can't wait for warmer weather."

"The sun is out today, and it's supposed to be tolerable," Debbie said. "Chloe and I are going walking after I eat my lunch."

Lindsay glanced over at the little white dog curled up on the tufted chair. "I see that Chloe is pumped up for this walk."

"She doesn't have a choice. And neither do I," Debbie said. "I'm serious this time about losing weight."

Lindsay smiled indulgently. "You look fine, but good for you for working at staying healthy. Go ahead and take your break and I'll pull these out to the front and work on steaming them."

Debbie picked up Chloe and brought her to the office in the back room to feed the little dog her lunch and eat her own. After eating baby carrots, half an apple, and half a turkey sandwich, Debbie slipped on her running shoes and coat, clipped on Chloe's leash, and said, "Here we go little girl."

Chloe sat down and glared at her.

"I'm not carrying you the entire time," Debbie told the little dog. "You could use some exercise too."

Debbie imagined Chloe rolling her eyes at her, but the dog finally stood, and they walked out the back door of the shop.

The day had warmed to forty-nine degrees, and the sun was shining. It felt absolutely wonderful. They walked down two blocks and then turned. This part of town had once held many upper-class Victorians, but now those older homes had been repurposed as cute gift shops, second-hand clothing stores, and antique shops. They were quite charming and the big bay windows in the houses made perfect display areas for the shops. Debbie peered into the windows as she passed by, waving at the other proprietors who saw her. Most of the owners were middle-aged and older, just as her mother had been. The uniqueness of the area did bring in many curious tourists in the summer and locals shopped for gifts at Christmastime and all winter.

After a time, Chloe refused to budge another step, so Debbie picked her up and stopped in front of an antique store. Inside the window, she saw the most beautiful grandfather clock. It was tall and made of mahogany with a glass door where the pendulum swung. She could picture it standing in Marc's entryway, or maybe even in the living room. She went inside and took a picture of it so she could show it to him. That's when she saw the message from Marc on her phone.

"Hi, Deb. I'm afraid I won't be at the gym on Wednesday because I have a meeting. But you have spin class that night anyway, and Mandy will take good care of you. I'll see you Friday for sure. Marc."

"Great," Debbie muttered. "I'm being delegated to Miss Tall, Leggy, and Blond." The minute she said it out loud, she realized how horrible it sounded. Mandy was a pretty woman, and Debbie shouldn't judge her for it, just as she didn't like being judged by her appearance. Her shoulders sagged. Maybe the problem with her attitude had more to do with her feelings of inadequacy than with how she thought everyone else around her perceived her.

Debbie pulled Chloe up closer and looked the dog in the eye. "Do you think *I'm* the problem?"

Chloe looked like she might want to shrug.

"Hi, Debbie. What can I help you with today?" An elderly man came up behind her, making Debbie jump.

"Oh, Mr. Truman. I didn't know you were standing there. How are you?" Debbie asked. *Sheesh! I hope he didn't hear me talking to my dog.*

"I'm fine, dear," he said, his inquisitive eyes peering over his half-moon glasses. Debbie had known Mr. Truman since she was ten years old. He was a kind man with an eye for antiques and also fixed old clocks and watches. "And how is beautiful little Chloe today?" he asked, reaching out to pet the dog.

Chloe lapped up the attention.

"She's fine. We were enjoying a walk in the sunshine when I saw this beautiful grandfather clock in your window. I took a picture for a friend. He's looking for antiques to fill his 1920's house with."

"Ah. That's wonderful. Yes, that's a beautiful clock. Bring him in anytime to see it. I'll give you a good price." Mr. Truman smiled.

"Thank you. I will. I'll see you soon," Debbie said, waving and hurrying out.

"Bye, dear," he called after her. "And don't worry. I talk to my cat all the time."

Debbie turned, surprised, and his eyes sparkled mischievously. Then he walked back toward the counter.

"Great," Debbie said to Chloe. "He had heard me." Oh, well. What's one more person thinking she was strange?

On the way back to her shop, Debbie kept thinking about her realization that she might be the one who needed the attitude adjustment. She was always the first one to put herself down before anyone else could. And she was very critical of herself. She'd always looked at herself in the way she thought others did. But maybe that was all in her mind. Did anyone else besides her care if she was chubby?

Curvy, Marc had called her. And he'd even asked why she was so hard on herself. She hadn't believed him when Marc had said she'd looked beautiful in the poufy strawberry dress. She'd thought he was simply being nice. But maybe he had meant it.

Debbie walked into the shop, and the little bell on the door jingled. She set Chloe on the tufted chair as Lindsay came out from the back room. Lindsay was making a funny face and pointing to the dressing rooms and Debbie couldn't figure out what she was trying to tell her.

"What?" Debbie asked aloud. A head poked out from behind a dressing room curtain, and Debbie realized it was Felicia.

"Debbie! How wonderful! I was so disappointed when your assistant told me you were out for lunch. Come over here. I have the dress on. You *must* see it!"

"I'll be there in a moment," she told Felicia, pulling off her coat and heading for the back room. The last thing she wanted was to stand next to tall, skinny Felicia with her sneakers on. Debbie needed her heals.

"Don't make me wait, dear," Felicia begged. "Please come now."

Debbie gritted her teeth and threw her coat over the counter. Lindsay picked up the coat and whispered, "I tried to warn you."

"I need my heals," Debbie mouthed to Lindsay, and the other woman nodded and ran to the back room.

"Debbie? Where are you?"

Sighing, Debbie walked to the dressing rooms. Felicia was standing on the small platform in front of the three-way mirror, looking absolutely dazzling in her wedding gown.

"Isn't it perfect?" Felicia asked, twirling.

"It is. You look gorgeous," Debbie said, smiling warmly. It was the truth. Felicia had chosen a strapless dress made of satin and chiffon. Fabric gathered and crisscrossed on the bodice, coming down to a tiny waist then slowly flowing out to the floor. Tiny crystals glittered around the waist, and crystal buttons trailed up the back. It was simple yet stunning, giving off a frothy appearance perfect for a beach wedding.

"Thank you, sweetie," Felicia said, bubbling all over. "It's perfect. I don't think I need any alterations." She stepped off the platform and stood next to Debbie. "What do you think?" Felicia spun so Debbie could inspect the fit.

Debbie studied it with a trained eye. Felicia was right. Her size two dress fit to perfection. Even the length was fine with the heels she wore. "I think you're right. The fit is perfect."

Felicia stopped and smiled down at Debbie. She had the cutest brunette bob, and her brown eyes twinkled, although Debbie thought it might have more to do with the glittery eye shadow she was wearing.

Felicia suddenly frowned. "My goodness. Have you gotten shorter?" She gave Debbie the once-over with her eyes.

Debbie's heart dropped. She'd almost forgotten she wasn't wearing heels. "No, no. I'm wearing my sneakers right now. I just came back from a walk."

"Oh." Felicia's pretty heart-shaped face creased. "You really shouldn't wear flats, dear. They don't do a thing for you."

Any positive energy Debbie had felt earlier disappeared. She felt like the same short, chubby girl she'd been in high school. Lindsay came in at that exact moment, bringing her heels. "

"Sorry," she said softly. "The phone rang while I was getting these."

Debbie quickly shucked her sneakers and slipped into her three-inch heels. "There," she said, facing Felicia and putting on a fake smile. "Better?"

Felicia brightened. "Yes. A little better. A girl like you needs the extra height."

Debbie saw Lindsay's expression turn red with anger so she practically pushed her out of the dressing rooms. "Thanks,

Lindsay," she said hurriedly. Lindsay left but not before tossing Felicia a nasty look.

Felicia was oblivious to the drama she'd caused. "Your assistant said the rest of the bridesmaid dresses were here. I'll take those with me, too, and if the girls need any alterations on them, they can bring them back. What's the latest date they can have them altered?"

Debbie thought a moment. The wedding was the first weekend in June, so there were about nine weeks left. Since her mother's passing, Debbie had hired a woman to do alterations, and she was always busy, especially during wedding and prom season. "I'd suggest they get them back here in the next two weeks; otherwise I can't guarantee the alterations will be finished on time. We're cutting it a little short."

Felicia nodded, hardly paying attention as she admired herself in the mirror. Her eyes caught Debbie's staring at her in the mirror, and she smiled prettily. "I'm so happy you're coming to the wedding. It's going to be such fun. You've made your plane reservations, haven't you?"

Debbie tried not to wince. She hadn't yet. And she knew that window was closing soon. "I was going to do that tonight," she said.

"Oh, darling. You must do it soon. Those planes fill up fast."

"I know," Debbie said, nodding. "I promise I will tonight. I also meant to ask if there are any more rooms left in the block for the wedding guests. I might be bringing a plus one."

"Oh." Felicia turned, and her lips formed a perfect o. "I had no idea you were bringing a date. I don't think there are any more rooms at the group price, but I'm sure the resort will have open rooms."

"Okay. I'll confirm if he's coming first, then we'll book his room." Debbie could tell Felicia was shocked to hear she was bringing a date. It made her feel a little better after being put down about the flat shoes.

"Is it anyone I know?" Felicia asked.

"No. He's someone I've met recently, and he's thrilled to go on a Bahama vacation. I'll let you know for certain whether or not he's coming."

"Well, I'm so happy for you," Felicia said, her smile slowly returning. "I can't wait to meet him." She turned and walked into the dressing room, and Debbie helped her out of the gown. She and Lindsay carefully hung and tagged all the dresses and helped Felicia place them in her car.

"I'll see you soon," Felicia said, giving Debbie a side hug then waving as she got into her car.

Debbie and Lindsay stood on the sidewalk and watched her drive away.

"I can't stand her." Lindsay crossed her arms. "She's intolerable."

They went inside the shop. "She's not really that bad. Just a little self-centered," Debbie said.

"A little?" Lindsay grimaced. "She treats you terribly. And she flounces all around like she's the queen and calls me your "assistant" even though I've told her my name a hundred times. She's a horror! Are you sure you want to spend six days on an island with her?"

"It won't be so bad," Debbie said. "The wedding is the second day we're there, and then I'm sure I won't see any of the wedding party the rest of the time. I'm looking forward to sitting on the beach and watching the waves while reading a good book."

Lindsay grinned. "That does sound fun. Maybe it won't be so bad after all."

Debbie nodded as she thought about the possibility of Marc being on the island too. He'd said he'd go with her as part of their deal, but had he meant it? And would she actually hold him to it? Even though they'd be going as just friends, she couldn't help but feel a tingle of joy at the thought of it. He was fun to be around, and they could have a great time.

But then again—he'd see her in a swimsuit. Ugh!

Well. She'd cross that bridge when she came to it. Debbie would book a flight for both of them and another room for Marc tonight and then confirm with him on Friday if he was positive he was going. Of course, that would be only if she survived spin class tonight.

* * *

Debbie arrived at the fitness center right on time and missed seeing Marc's smiling face waiting for her. She'd known he wasn't going to be there, but it was still disheartening. As she walked past the desk to check the time of the spin class, the manager, Kyle, stopped her.

"Hi. You're Debbie, aren't you?" he asked.

She nodded.

"Marc isn't here tonight, so he told me to look out for you. He's gone off to a 'meeting,'" Kyle made air quotes with his fingers, "if you can believe that." He laughed at his joke. "All I know is I saw the beautiful woman he was having the meeting with and I certainly wouldn't say no to her."

Debbie stared at him, appalled, wondering why he felt the need to say this to her. She didn't even know this guy. "I know Marc isn't here. I'm going to the spin class tonight anyway."

"Oh. Okay. Well, have a good class. And if you need help

with stretches afterward, let me know." He winked at her and turned away. Winked! It made her skin crawl.

"Hi, Debbie," a female voice said from behind her. She turned, and there stood Mandy looking as cute as ever in her stretchy outfit with her long ponytail bobbing.

"Hi, Mandy. How are you tonight?"

"Great! I hear you're coming to spin class. Follow me, and I'll find you a good spot and show you how the bike works. Marc said it was your first time."

Debbie followed her into the room.

"Grab a towel," Mandy said as they passed a pile of white towels beside the door. "Believe me; you sweat so much in this class that you'll need one."

Debbie did as she was told and followed Mandy to a bike in the second row. There were five rows in all with five bikes across. The room was quite plain, actually, but there was a big-screen TV in front with a bike on a pedestal that she assumed was Mandy's.

Mandy showed her how to operate the bike and told her not to worry about keeping up for the entire class if she became too tired. "Spin class is a lot harder than most people think. It's nothing like going on a bike ride. So if you get tired, slow down. We're not about overdoing it here at Fit in 20. We want you to be able to keep coming back." She smiled, and Debbie couldn't help but like her. Mandy seemed like a nice person and was only trying to help her.

Soon, women and men of all ages and sizes came into the room and found a bike. Mandy went off to help two other newbies get settled. Debbie placed her water bottle in the slot on the bike and slipped off her sweatshirt. She knew she'd be too hot wearing it. Today after work, she'd gone to a sports shop and bought a modest tank top that didn't look too obscene on her. She'd also bought another pair of exercise pants that went down to her calves. She hoped she didn't look too ridiculous, although she was wearing exactly what everyone else was wearing.

Mandy passed her on the way to the front of the class and touched her on the arm. "Cute outfit." She continued walking to the bike in front.

Debbie knew Mandy was being sincere—she had no reason not to be—and it boosted her confidence. She waited as Mandy addressed the class and then turned on some soothing music they could spin too. The television screen came on behind her with a calming scene of a trail through the woods.

"Let's start slow and enjoy the nice ride through the woods," Mandy said over the music. Everyone started pedaling their bikes in slow rhythm to the music.

This isn't so bad, Debbie thought. *In fact, it's kind of nice.* She rode along, feeling her muscles warm up and pretended she was out for a nice ride in the park. Then the music grew louder in a pounding beat, and everyone sped up. Debbie sped up too, and then Mandy had them standing up and pedaling, and soon her legs felt like rubber. Debbie glanced at the clock on the wall and was horrified to see they still had fifteen minutes to go.

This class *was* going to kill her after all!

Halfway through, Debbie had to slow her speed. She was breathing heavily, sweating profusely, and wasn't sure she'd be able to walk after the class. Mandy smiled over at her and nodded that she was doing the right thing, slowing down. Debbie used the towel to wipe her face and hung it around her neck. She glanced to one side and saw the man beside her racing along as if it was the easiest thing in the world. She glanced to the other side and saw a woman around her age going as slowly as she was.

That made her feel better.

At the end of the class, after they'd slowed down the pace for a couple of minutes, Mandy thanked everyone for coming. She did stretches on the platform, and many of the bikers followed suit next to their bikes. Debbie stretched along with them, hoping she'd be able to walk tomorrow.

"How did you like the class?" Mandy asked after they'd all cooled down, and everyone was leaving.

"It was great until we actually started pedaling," Debbie said.

Mandy laughed. "I know. It's a tough class, but you did fine. Once you get used to it, you'll be sailing along like some of the others."

"God help me," Debbie groaned.

"What does Marc have planned for you next?" Mandy asked.

Debbie picked up her sweatshirt from the handlebars and slipped it on. "He said aerobics on Friday with some weights afterward."

"Great. I teach aerobics too." Mandy stood there a moment as if she meant to say more. Debbie wasn't sure if she should say goodbye or ask her what was on her mind. They both started moving toward the door. Finally, Mandy spoke up.

"Can I ask you a personal question?"

"Okay," Debbie answered, a little unsure.

Mandy looked uncomfortable, too, but continued. "Are you and Marc seeing each other? Because, if you are, that's great. I just need to know, so I don't butt in anymore."

"Oh." Debbie was stunned. She hadn't expected that question. "No. We're not seeing each other in that way. I'm helping him find antique furniture for his house in exchange for him helping me lose weight and tone up. Nothing is going on between us."

Mandy let out a sigh and looked relieved. "Okay. I wasn't sure. He seemed a little upset when I showed up at his house the other day, and honestly, I was a bit confused. I mean, he's always so nice to me here and I thought I'd felt a connection between us. But now, I'm not so sure."

Debbie's heart went out to Mandy. She sounded confused about how Marc felt about her. That was precisely why Debbie had told him to be upfront and honest with Mandy if he wasn't interested. It irritated her when men led women on.

Debbie placed a hand on Mandy's arm. "You're not stepping on me or anyone. As far as I know, he's not seeing anyone else. He and I are just friends, nothing more." She smiled, and Mandy smiled back, looking reassured.

"Great. I guess I'll see what happens, then," Mandy said. "Thanks."

Debbie nodded, and both women went their own way. As she drove home, Debbie was surprised at how unsure of herself Mandy had seemed. Mandy was a beautiful, self-reliant woman, but she seemed as uncertain about relationships as Debbie was. She'd always thought the beautiful girls were more confident about themselves. Maybe that wasn't true after all.

What Debbie did know for certain was she was going to give Marc an earful about not having talked with Mandy yet about his wanting a platonic relationship with her. It wasn't fair leaving her dangling like that. Debbie knew how it felt and she wasn't going to let him do that to Mandy.

Chapter Eleven

Marc sat in his office at Fit in 20 on Friday evening, going over paperwork for his potential partnership with McGregory Medical Supply. Bernie was sound asleep on the rug in front of his desk, worn out from his run earlier. Marc had had a successful meeting with Melinda Jones over dinner on Wednesday night, and he was excited about the prospect of moving forward and working with them. She'd asked him to detail the costs of such a venture before they set up anything concrete. She'd also asked him to keep their prospective partnership confidential until they were able to sign a contract. That was the toughest part. Marc wanted to tell everyone about this fantastic opportunity to expand Fit in 20 in the workplace, but he respected her wishes.

There was a knock on his door, and he called for the person to come in. When he looked up, Debbie was walking to his desk with a determined look on her face. She glanced down to avoid stepping on Bernie.

"What's wrong with you?" she demanded.

Marc stared at her, shocked. "What?"

She crossed her arms and glared at him. "You haven't told Mandy yet that your relationship with her is strictly business. You've been leading her on. The poor woman doesn't know how you feel about her. And to make matters worse, she likes you. You have to let her down easy now, or else it will get messy, and she'll end up quitting."

Marc tried to grasp what Debbie was saying. "I'm not leading her on."

Debbie gave him a withering look. "Of course you are. You lead on all the women in the gym. You flirt endlessly, and some of these women take it differently than you intended. You can't do that to people. It's not right."

Marc frowned. Was he doing that? He was just being nice. Wasn't he? "Wait. How do you know how Mandy feels?"

"Because she told me. We had a chat after spin class, which killed my legs, by the way. She's so confused about the signals you're sending. Just stop doing it! It hurts people more than you realize."

He stood and walked around to the other side of the desk where Debbie was. Bernie was wide awake now, sitting between them, his head going back and forth as he watched each one talk. When Marc looked down into Debbie's eyes, he saw pain. He could tell she knew what she was talking about.

"I'm sorry. I had meant to talk to her, but then something came up, and I've been immersed in it. I'll talk to her tonight, after her last class. I really never meant to lead her on."

Debbie's stance relaxed, and she dropped her arms to her side. "Good. Sorry I got so mad, but I hate when people get their signals crossed and someone gets hurt."

He nodded. "I never meant to hurt anyone."

She gazed up at him. "I'm sure you don't mean to. But women fall easily for you. You need to be careful."

He cocked his head. "What women?"

Debbie rolled her eyes. "Certainly not *this* woman."

Marc laughed, and then Debbie joined in.

"Okay. I have my aerobics class in a few minutes, thanks to you." She tossed him a dirty look. "But can we talk a little afterward? I have a couple of questions."

He nodded. "Yep. We're hitting the weight machine after. Remember?" His eyes sparkled mischievously.

Debbie shook her head and pointed at him. "That's the look. That's what gets you into trouble with women. See you after class." She turned and left the room.

Confused, Marc walked into his small bathroom and stared in the mirror over the sink. *What look is she talking about?* He studied his face a moment, then gave up. Maybe she was teasing him. He didn't have a *look*.

Later, after the aerobics class was over, Marc met up with Debbie, and they walked to the weight machine.

"How was class?" he asked, giving her a knowing grin. She was damp with perspiration, and her face had turned pink. He thought she looked adorable.

She glared at him. "You're trying to kill me. I know you are."

"Yep. That's our motto here at Fit in 20. We aim to kill."

"Ha, ha. Now you're a clown."

They worked on the weight machine for ten minutes, then cooled off with some stretches.

"How was your meeting on Wednesday?" Debbie asked him now that she had her breath back.

His brows rose, then he remembered he'd texted her that he'd be in a meeting. "Good. Great, actually. I can't say anything yet, but this may be an amazing opportunity for my company."

"That's wonderful." Debbie looked sincerely happy for him as she stretched her leg muscles. "I hear the woman you had the meeting with was a real hot number." Her eyes twinkled.

"Who told you that?"

Debbie chuckled. "Never mind. I just found it funny. I think some people around here have the impression we're an item, and they wanted to make sure I knew you were out with another woman."

"Hm," Marc mused. He had a good idea who that person was who'd said that to Debbie. "I suppose she is a pretty woman, but it wasn't like that. I was at a real meeting."

"Good to know," she said.

Marc watched her a moment as she stretched over one leg, then another. He noticed she was wearing a tank top with her leggings. It fit her well—very well—and she looked incredible. He knew better than to mention that, though, because she'd become self-conscious and put on her sweatshirt. "Some people think we're an item, huh? Would that be such a bad thing?"

Her head rose from her stretch, and she stared at him. "A bad thing that they think it?"

"No. A bad thing if we were an item."

Debbie studied him as if gauging whether or not he was teasing. "It's that kind of flirting that gets you in trouble," she said sharply. She stood and reached for her sweatshirt.

"Don't be mad at me again," Marc pleaded, also standing. "I can't take you always being mad at me. No more teasing, okay? I promise."

Debbie nodded. "Fine."

He knew better than to believe that *fine* meant fine. "You said you had something to talk to me about."

"Right. Well," Debbie looked around to make sure no one close by could hear. "About that Bahama wedding I'm going to. You mentioned you'd come as my plus one, but you don't have to if you've changed your mind. I had to book the flight and your room before it filled up, but I can cancel both if you were only kidding about going along."

"I never kid about a Bahama vacation. I do want to go with you—it's part of the deal. I'll reimburse you for the flight and room. Thanks for booking it for me."

"Oh. Okay. It should be fun once the wedding is over."

"I'm looking forward to it."

Debbie stood there looking awkward, then pulled out her phone. "I almost forgot. I saw a beautiful grandfather clock in an antique store near the bridal shop. Here's a picture."

Marc looked at the photo. "It is beautiful. I love it. Where were you thinking of placing it?"

"Maybe the entryway. Or the living room. It would look good in numerous places in your house. I'll take you to see it on Sunday, and you can decide if you want it."

"I want it," Marc said. "I'm looking forward to going shopping again. Also, they delivered my bedroom set and dining room table yesterday, so I called Mallory to pick up the old items. We settled on a price, which I was happy with."

"That's good. I'm glad it's taken care of."

"Me, too. Mallory also said she'd like the first look at other items as we dispose of them in case she'd like to buy them."

"Great. We'll keep track as we replace things," Debbie said.

Marc was just about to ask Debbie if she'd like to meet for dinner on Saturday, but Kyle interrupted them. "Phone call, Marc."

"I was just leaving anyway," Debbie said. "See you Sunday." She hurried out of the gym before he could stop her.

Disappointed, Marc watched her leave, then went to grab the phone.

As he worked that night, Marc thought about what Debbie

had said. This wasn't the first time she'd accused him of flirting with women. It was such an ingrained habit, he didn't even know he was doing it. But as he worked with women that evening, Marc was conscious of how he spoke and when he smiled. He didn't want to give women the wrong impression. But it was hard. Teasing and being friendly was his normal behavior. That's why people responded well to him. But he also knew he had to be more careful.

Except with Debbie. He liked flirting with her.

That thought surprised him, but he knew it was true. That was why he'd wanted to invite Debbie out to dinner. She was different from anyone else he'd ever known. And she didn't let him get away with anything, even if he smiled sweetly. She told him the truth. Marc liked that the most. She was completely honest, and it was refreshing.

Just before closing, Marc took Mandy aside and explained that he appreciated her work at the center and thought of her as a friend but needed to keep their relationship platonic. He did his best not to sound like an arrogant jerk who thought she was in love with him. Mandy took it well, though, and he was relieved she had. It could have ended up messy.

"Well, Bernie," he said when he entered his office to get his things and go home. "I guess you and I have to change our ways. No more flirting with the ladies."

Bernie looked at him as if he were crazy. Maybe he was. They headed out and locked up.

* * *

Sunday morning at eleven, Marc was at Debbie's front door as they'd planned. She opened it, already wearing her coat.

"Any chance I could get a tour of your house?" he asked before she shut the door.

Debbie looked hesitant. "There's not much to see."

"Hey. I showed you mine. Isn't it only fair you show me yours?" He grinned mischievously.

"You're terrible," she said but opened the door wide. "Come in and be prepared to be underwhelmed."

He walked into the entryway and glanced around. The house was an open concept style, which surprised him for a small bungalow. On the right was the kitchen with an island and a spot by the front window for a little table. On the left was a cozy living room with a fireplace and a large picture window in front.

"You have a fireplace," he said. "Is it wood or gas?"

"Gas. My mom had it converted when we bought the place. It heats the room quite well. I love having a fireplace."

"Me too," he said.

She laughed. "You have a fireplace in every room. You'd better like them."

She walked with him to the back of the house, where there were two bedrooms, a bathroom, and a laundry room. They came back toward the kitchen, where the dining room table sat.

"That's definitely an antique, isn't it?" he asked, walking over to it. The table was made of oak and had a rustic distressed look. Four matching chairs sat around it with a long bench on one side. Marc ran his hand along the top of the table. "It's beautiful."

"Thanks. It's one of my mother's greatest finds. The little table by the window in the kitchen is an older one too."

"Cute. I can see you sitting there in the morning with Chloe in your lap, drinking coffee," Marc said.

Debbie chuckled. "That's exactly what we do."

He grinned.

She showed him the grandfather clock in the living room and the antique curio cabinet. "We didn't collect knick-knacks, so it's filled with some of our favorite china. My mother loved buying old china."

"She had wonderful taste." He looked at Debbie thoughtfully. "I wish I'd met her. She sounded like a special person."

Debbie nodded. "She was. I'll never be half the woman she was."

"I highly doubt that. You're an incredible person from my point of view."

Her face reddened at his compliment, which Marc found charming. "Thanks for showing me your house. I love it. I'm so glad you're helping me with mine. It needs this type of charm to make it feel like a home."

They headed out to his SUV. Debbie directed him to go to her bridal shop so they could visit Mr. Truman's store. "He's a sweet, elderly man who's had the antique shop since I was a girl. His wife died a few years ago, and I think he continues to run it so that he isn't lonely."

"That's sad," Marc said. "Yet, kind of neat. It's hard to believe that anyone stays married forever anymore. That's what I want. A happily-ever-after that lasts until the day I die."

Debbie's brows rose. "Wow. You're in a very romantic, nostalgic mindset today."

He grinned. "You didn't think I had it in me, did you? I thought I'd lost that feeling, too, until we started shopping for antiques. I think these beautiful pieces from the past are reminding me that some things do last. I like believing in love lasting forever."

She nodded. "Me, too."

Marc smiled. He liked that they were in the same mindset.

They parked in front of the antique store and went inside. As soon as the bell chimed over the door, Mr. Truman was making his way toward them.

"You're back just as promised," he said to Debbie, a twinkle in his eye.

"Hi, Mr. Truman. This is the person I was telling you about. Marc Bennett. He's filling his house with antiques, so show him everything you have."

Mr. Truman laughed. "Buy it all. Then I'll retire and move to Florida."

"You wouldn't leave us, would you, Mr. Truman?" Debbie asked.

"I don't see me leaving anytime in the future," he said. "But one never knows."

Debbie pointed out the grandfather clock to Marc, and Mr. Truman took over explaining about its age and where it had come from. "I picked it up from an auction over on Summit Avenue in St. Paul," he explained. "From one of those large mansions from the 1900s that had sold with all the old furniture. The new owner didn't want the furniture. They were going to turn the place into an apartment building." The older man shook his head. "Such a shame to see those grand houses go like that. But good for us, I guess. We get to keep these wonderful treasures from the past."

"It's beautiful," Marc said, running his hand over the smooth wood. He liked the beveled glass over the pendulum and the gold accents on the face. "And it still works."

Mr. Truman nodded. "All my clocks are in working order," he said proudly. "I fix clocks and watches. You just have to make sure to wind the clock with the key once a week to keep it running."

"I want this," Marc said. "Knowing it came from one of the stately mansions on Summit makes it even more special."

Debbie smiled at him, and his heart warmed. He knew her smile was an appreciation for his understanding of how special this piece was. But her smile meant even more than that to him. It made him feel as if they were connecting or bonding somehow over these shopping trips. He liked that.

They wandered around the shop, and Debbie pointed out small items that might interest him. An antique bellows to hang by a fireplace, possibly in the den, and a decorative glass fire screen that would look perfect in the living room. They found a large, framed mirror that would fit in well over the fireplace in the living room, too. As they came to the section with hanging clocks, she pointed out one framed in wood with a little glass door over the hands. "That would look much better in your den than that garish one you have."

"Sold!" Marc said. "I love it."

Marc purchased all the items, and Mr. Truman told them he'd have them delivered on Tuesday. They waved goodbye to him on their way out, and Marc turned to Debbie. "Where now?"

"Oh, I have a full day set up for you," she said, laughing.

"Great. I can't wait." He drove in the direction she told him. Marc was surprised how much he enjoyed scouring the antique shops. But then, he knew it had more to do with shopping with Debbie. She was the one who made it fun. That thought made him smile.

Chapter Twelve

Debbie enjoyed her afternoon of antiquing with Marc so much, that when he asked her if she'd like to have dinner, she accepted immediately. She hadn't wanted the day to end. He suggested a corner pub not far from her house, and they went inside. It reminded her a little of Gallagher's, only smaller in size.

Once seated in a corner booth, Marc ordered a beer, and Debbie asked for half a glass of white wine.

"I'm not much of a drinker," she told him. "But we have to celebrate all your great purchases today. I love the leather chairs we found for your den, and the Barrister cases were beautiful. But the grandfather clock was the best one of all. So much history in that one."

"I agree. I love that one." He raised his glass. "To us. For our impeccable taste."

Debbie giggled. "To us." They clinked glasses, and each took a sip.

The waitress returned and took their order, then departed again.

"What's on the agenda for tomorrow?" Marc asked, his eyes twinkling.

"I thought we should go to furniture stores and look for sofas for your living room. We should probably try to work on one or two rooms at a time so you don't have a mess of mismatched furniture all over the house. There's an estate sale later in the afternoon we should hit, too. They had hutches and occasional tables listed. You might find something for the dining room or the living room."

"Sounds good to me. You're the boss."

Debbie shook her head at him. "It's easy to go shopping when the person buying doesn't even look at the price tags. I hope you're as rich as you think you are because this is costing you a fortune." She was teasing him, but also a little concerned. The grandfather clock alone would cost her a month's profit at the shop. She couldn't imagine having that much money to spend all at once.

"I'll be fine," he said. "And I do look at the prices when you aren't watching. I'm not that crazy. I just want to impress you by letting you think it doesn't matter."

She studied him, wondering if he was still teasing. She wasn't sure. "It'll take more than spending a lot of money to impress me," she said softly.

Marc leaned on the table, closer to her. "So, what is it that impresses you?"

"Honesty. Integrity. Loyalty. And being kind to animals. That's one of the most important things."

"I'd like to think I'm all of that," he said solemnly. "At least you know I love dogs."

Their food came then, breaking up their serious conversation. Debbie had ordered a grilled chicken salad, and Marc had gone for the juicy cheeseburger and fries.

"How on earth do you eat like that and not get fat?" Debbie asked him. "I'd gain five pounds just looking at it."

He laughed. "Remember, my life is exercise. I run almost

every day and then I'm in the gym most nights. I can afford a few fatty calories once in a while."

She rolled her eyes. Men had it so easy.

As they ate, Marc turned serious again. "I talked to Mandy Friday night. I tried my best not to make it sound like I was an arrogant jerk thinking she was in love with me. I think she understood, and hopefully, won't hate me. I have this ridiculous need for everyone to like me. I've been thinking about what you said about my flirting with everyone, and I think that's why I do it. It's my way of being nice. I guess it doesn't always come off that way, though."

Debbie was surprised by his admission. But she understood. "I'm glad you talked to Mandy. She thought there were vibes between you and her, and it confused her. I get what you're saying, though. Sometimes just being nice to someone can appear as flirting. It's not always easy to tell the difference."

Marc nodded. "I would never intentionally try to hurt some-one's feelings. Believe me, I know how it feels, and I'm not that guy."

"I believe you," she said quietly.

"Can I ask you a personal question?"

Debbie's eyes darted up, and her heart gave a jolt. "Maybe."

"I have a feeling someone led you on once and hurt you deeply. Am I right?"

She dropped her eyes. Debbie wasn't sure she wanted to share that story with Marc. It made her feel like such a loser.

"I'm sorry. I shouldn't have said anything. I didn't mean to embarrass you," Marc said quickly.

She took a deep breath. He'd been honest with her, and she should be the same with him. "You don't have to be sorry. You just surprised me with how intuitive you were. Yes, someone did hurt me and led me on for months before finally telling me the truth. After college, I was engaged to a man who I thought I could trust. But he started seeing someone else and didn't tell me we were over even though I was planning our wedding. Can you imagine?" Debbie dared to look into Marc's eyes but she didn't see any judgment there. Only warmth.

"No, I can't. That's a terrible thing to do."

She nodded. "When he finally told me, I felt like an idiot. How could I have not known he was cheating on me? And there I was, buying a dress and setting up a venue. Planning my life, except it was a life he didn't want. And to make it worse, the woman he chose was the complete opposite of me. Tall, thin, beautiful." She shook her head. "That experience has made it hard for me to trust again."

"I'm sorry," Marc said, sincerely. "But I hope you realize that he was the idiot, not you. Anyone who can't see how special you are is an idiot."

His words surprised her. Special? Her? Surely he was just being nice. But as she gazed into his eyes, she only saw sincerity. The sweet look on his face tugged at her heart.

The waitress came with their bill and broke whatever spell they'd been under. Marc paid, then walked her back to the car. Once they reached her house, he got out and walked with her to the door.

"I'm glad you felt comfortable enough to confide in me," he said, standing close to her on the front stoop. "I don't usually have serious conversations with people anymore. It always seems like I'm just skimming the surface with the people I know. It feels good to have someone to talk to."

"I know what you mean. I have a few close friends, but we don't generally talk about personal things. Anyway, at least now you can understand why I'm so critical of myself. I've been passed over a few times for the beauty-queen type. It's hard on the ego."

Marc caught her eyes with his. "You're beautiful and don't ever tell yourself that you aren't."

Debbie felt heat rise to her face. "Thanks," she whispered. She turned quickly, opened the door, and stepped inside. "I'll see you tomorrow at ten."

He smiled. "See you then. Goodnight." Marc headed back to his car.

"Goodnight," she called softly after him, then closed the door.

Chloe was sitting on the floor, staring up at her as Debbie turned around. She scooped up the little dog and twirled around. "He thinks I'm beautiful," she said happily. "Beautiful! No one has called me that in a long time. Well, Lindsay says it, but I always think she's just being nice."

Debbie put away her coat and went into her bedroom to change into comfy sweats. Of course, Marc had told her she was beautiful before, and not to put herself down. But she hadn't believed him then. This time, it was the way he said it. He'd sounded like he meant every word.

Or was he just being kind?

Chloe sat on the bed where Debbie had placed her and stared hard at her.

"Okay, okay. I won't go negative on myself," she told the dog. "But I also won't get all giddy, either. Marc and I are just working together. That's all." But then she smiled again. *And we're going to the Bahamas for six days together, too.*

For the first time since being invited to Felicia's wedding, Debbie was excited she was going.

* * *

The next day as Debbie dressed, she noticed something exciting. The jeans she put on were a little loose. She tugged at the waistband and stared in the mirror. It wasn't her imagination—there was space between her waist and the jeans.

A huge smile spread over her face. Two weeks of exercise at the gym plus walking daily and eating healthy had helped her slim down. She didn't care if it was less than an inch. It was something, and it made her feel good about herself.

"I'm losing weight!" she said excitedly to Chloe as the little dog lay on the bed. "And I still have a couple of months to go." Maybe she'd become so slender she'd have to alter that puffball strawberry dress. That would be amazing.

There was a knock on the door, and Debbie went to answer it. Marc stood there in one of his lightweight workout jackets, grinning at her.

"It's going to be in the sixties today," he said. "Spring is finally here."

Debbie beamed. "More good news! Let me grab my jacket, and we can go."

Once they were in the car, Marc turned to her. "I'm glad to see you smiling. What was the other good news?"

She suddenly felt shy. It would sound silly to someone like Marc that she was excited her jeans were a little loose. He was so fit and looked great in everything he wore, while she still looked chubby despite the loss.

"Aren't you going to tell me?" he asked.

"It really isn't *that* great. I noticed my jeans weren't as tight today as they have been in the past. I think all this exercise is working."

His eyes lit up. "That's wonderful! Congratulations! That's where you first notice you're toning up—when your clothes get looser. I'm so happy for you."

Debbie couldn't help but smile. "It isn't all that much, but it's a start."

"But it is a big deal," he said. "You've been working hard, and now your progress is showing. It makes you want to work out even harder, doesn't it?"

Debbie rolled her eyes. "You're trying to kill me," she said. But they both grinned. She liked that he was happy for her.

She directed him to a furniture store where she knew they sold high-end leather sofas and other good pieces. "You don't have to buy here," she said. "Plenty of places sell leather. But this place sells high-grade leather, so I wanted you to see their items first."

"Don't I want high-grade leather?" he asked, looking confused.

"Everyone wants high-grade leather, but we all can't afford it. Let's look and see if you like anything."

They wandered around the store, and when they came to the sofas, Debbie ran her hand over the back of a light brown sofa with thick cushions and rolled arms. The leather was so soft, it felt like satin under her fingertips.

"Feel this," Debbie said. "You won't believe how soft it is."

Marc's hand pressed down on the sofa's cushion, and his eyes grew wide. "Goodness! This is amazing." He sat down and sank into the cushion. "Okay. I get it now. We all want high-grade leather."

Debbie chuckled and sat down beside him. It was like floating on a cloud. "Isn't it wonderful? I could fall asleep on this right now."

They looked at several styles, and Marc decided he liked the first one they'd sat on. "I like the color and design of it. And there's a loveseat and chair to match. I want them all."

"Aren't you going to look at the price tag first?" she asked.

"No. I don't want to ruin the moment. I *want* this sofa even if it costs a fortune. In fact, let's pick out another set for the family room in the kitchen, too. The leather in there now doesn't even compare to this. Maybe Mallory would like to buy those for her business."

Debbie had trouble believing that a person could spend that much money in one day, but she had no idea what Marc earned from his businesses. *It's his money,* she told herself. *Let him enjoy it.*

They chose a light tan colored sofa and loveseat for the family room, and the sales clerk was all too happy to order the items for them.

"I think you made his day," Debbie said with a laugh.

"Good." Marc smiled over to her. "I like making someone's day happy."

Once in the car, Debbie gave Marc directions to the location of the estate sale. It was out in Chanhassen, and when they pulled up to the mini-mansion, both stared at it in surprise.

"I didn't know there was such a grand house out here," Debbie said as Marc parked the car behind a long line of vehicles. "Do you think someone famous owned this?"

"Do we have anyone famous who lives around here?" Marc asked.

Debbie shrugged. When they walked inside and took a pamphlet listing the items for sale, it told them who'd owned the house.

"I've never heard of him before," Marc said. "It says he made his money in real estate. I can believe that seeing the acreage this place is on."

They walked around the house, pointing out furniture that caught their eye. Marc fell in love with an antique mahogany desk that had leather imbedded in the center of it for the writing area. "This looks like something I'd want," he said, glancing at Debbie.

"It's beautiful, but did you see the starting bid?"

Marc shrugged. "I probably won't win it anyway."

But during the auction, much to Debbie's surprise, Marc won not only the desk but also an antique hutch for the dining room and oak end tables for the living room.

"Looks like I got lucky today," he said, winking at her. She thought he was crazy. He'd spent so much money. She couldn't even imagine having that much to spend freely.

By the time Marc paid for his purchases, it was getting late.

"I think we're done for the day," Debbie said. "Your credit card needs a rest, and I have a date with an evil workout trainer later."

"I hear he's one of the best," Marc said, a teasing glint in his eyes.

"Don't believe everything you hear," Debbie responded, hiding a smile.

As Marc maneuvered the car onto the highway toward Debbie's home, she asked, "Can you tell me yet about that great deal you're putting together?"

Marc glanced over at her. "I wish I could, but I promised not to say a word until the final contract is signed. But it's big. And it just fell into my lap, or so it seems."

"I'm sure the excellent reputation of your gyms and how you run them is what made it fall into your lap. A lot of hard work has led up to this deal," Debbie said.

Marc looked thoughtful. "I hadn't thought of it that way. However it happened though, it will more than pay for my furniture shopping." He grinned at her. "And I should be paying you for your help. This is a big job. What you're doing for me is worth much more than three days a week of working out."

"I don't mind," Debbie said, and she meant it. She knew that if she weren't spending time with Marc looking for antiques, she'd just be at home on her days off, wishing she had something to fill her time. "It's been fun."

He beamed. "It has been fun."

Marc pulled up in front of her house just as Mallory walked by with little Shannon in her wagon. Mallory waved and came closer to the car as Debbie stepped out.

"Hey there," Mallory said. "Were you out shopping again?"

Marc waved from inside the car. "Yes, we were. And I have a lot more furniture for you if you want it."

"Really? I'd like to look again if you don't mind," Mallory said.

"Anytime you want. Just let me know," Marc said. "You'll have to consult my decorator first, though." He pointed to Debbie.

Debbie moved away from the car with Mallory and waved as Marc drove off.

"His decorator, huh? Are you my competition now?" Mallory asked good-naturedly.

Debbie laughed. "No. I could never compete with you. Marc decided to buy new leather sofas for the living and family rooms, so his other leather sofas are up for grabs if you want them. And a few end tables, and a desk. We can meet at the house sometime this week if you'd like to look them over again."

"Sure. That sounds great." Mallory studied Debbie a moment. "You look different. More relaxed. Happier." Her blue eyes twinkled. "You must be enjoying spending time with Marc."

Debbie couldn't help but smile. "I do enjoy spending time with him. We have fun going to estate sales and antique shops. It's crazy how much money he spends, but it's fun. And I love going furniture shopping and helping him pick out items for his house. I used to love doing that with my mother, but I hadn't realized how much I'd missed it all these years."

"And you're good at it. Really good," Mallory said. "You have an eye for design and style. I knew you were talented at selecting beautiful dresses but I had no idea how talented you were with furniture."

Debbie's face heated up with embarrassment. She wasn't used to being complimented, even by her neighborhood friends. She adored all of them, but they usually kept their conversations away from personal issues. "I just enjoy it."

"I think it's more than that," Mallory said as if she saw something in Debbie that even she hadn't noticed in herself. "And if you ever want to change careers, let me know. My business is growing so quickly, it's become too much for my sister and me. At some point, I'll need to hire an employee or bring in another partner. It's great that it's doing so well, but I never expected it to take off so quickly."

Debbie was surprised by her offer. Had she been serious? "Working with you would be amazing, but I doubt I'll ever be able to leave the bridal shop. It was my mom's dream for me to run it."

Mallory patted her on the arm in a friendly gesture. "But what is your dream? You're good at so many things. It's nice to have a choice."

Debbie wasn't sure how to respond. A choice? Did she really have one? She'd been working in the bridal shop for so long that she'd thought that was all she'd ever do. Yet, hadn't she longed to do something else? Did she dare?

"Well, let me know when I can drop by Marc's house again. I'm off to Lisa and Avery's house. I'm going to help Lisa with decorations for the wedding and Abby and Shannon are having a playdate." She waved and said goodbye.

Debbie walked toward the front door of her bungalow as ideas swirled around in her head. She didn't know if she ever dared to make a big change in her career. But it was nice knowing that someone thought she could.

Chapter Thirteen

Marc smiled as he watched Debbie ramp up the treadmill to go faster. He hadn't asked her to; she'd done it on her own. He knew that she was encouraged by losing that little bit of weight and it made her happy. It made him happy too. He'd enjoyed seeing her face light up this morning when she'd told him her jeans were loose. She'd looked so pretty with those big blue eyes fringed in thick lashes and her cheeks pink with excitement. She'd left her hair down earlier today, too, and it was so thick and wavy, she'd looked beautiful.

He just wished she could see how beautiful she was both inside and out.

Except he'd better not tell her to look in a mirror right now or she'd think he was crazy. Her hair was pulled back in a French braid, and her face was red with exertion, perspiration damp on her skin. Actually, Debbie looked pretty good this way, too.

"What are you staring at?" Debbie said, glowering at him as she slowed down the machine. "If you were any kind of gentleman, you'd be on the machine next to me, sweating too."

Marc laughed. "This is your time to sweat, not mine," he teased. "I get my run outside every day."

As Debbie used the weight machine, Marc commented,

"You realize you aren't huffing and puffing as much as you did that first few times. That means you're getting into shape."

"I'll still be sore tomorrow," she said. "But you're right. It's not as bad as it was. And walking on the days I don't come here has helped too. I feel so much better."

They sat on the mat and stretched. "So, what will I need to pack for this wedding in the Bahamas?" Marc asked.

Debbie looked thoughtful. "A suit for the wedding, or at least a shirt, tie, and nice pants. And something dressy for the groom's dinner the night before. Other than that, just shorts, shirts, and swim trunks."

"Ah. I can't wait." His eyes sparkled. "And you'll be packing a bikini or two, right?"

Debbie grimaced. "I don't want to think about that yet. It's your job to make sure I can wear a swimsuit without humiliating myself. Otherwise, I'm buying a mou mou."

"God, no!" Marc said, making a face. "I'm going to work you extra hard to make sure that doesn't happen."

After the workout, he grabbed a couple of bottles of water and they sat back against the wall away from the workout area.

"Mallory said she'd like to come over and look at your furniture again. Maybe sometime this week, if that works for you," Debbie said.

"Anytime. I'm usually home until four every day. Or, I can give you a key, and you can show her in."

Debbie's brows rose. "You'd trust me with a key to your house?"

"Why not? I trust you. Besides, I know where you live. I can find you if you abscond with the family silverware." He laughed, and she did too.

"You're crazy, you know that?" she said.

Marc looked down at her, enjoying how easy it was for them to be together. There was no pretense between them—they were simply themselves, flaws and all. He couldn't remember when he'd felt this comfortable with a woman. Alyssa, his last girlfriend, had always wanted to put on airs and show off his money. He'd never understood that. Yes, he lived in a big house and he could afford expensive things, but he was still the same guy he'd been before he had money. Debbie was different. She wasn't impressed by his wealth, or affected by it. It was so refreshing.

"I'd rather be crazy than sane," he said, leaning closer to her. "Sane isn't any fun." He gazed into her eyes and felt a twinge in his stomach. Butterflies? He wasn't sure, but he did know that at that moment, he wanted to kiss her.

"Boss. Telephone. Sounds like another pretty lady," Kyle called over to him.

Debbie pulled back as if she'd been slapped. "I have to go. You're busy. I'll see you on Wednesday, if not before." She stood to leave, and Marc jumped up to stop her.

"Wait. I'll walk you to your car," he offered, following close behind her.

"Don't bother. You have a phone call." Debbie waved and headed out the door.

Marc stood there, his anger at Kyle welling up inside him. He strode past the desk on the way to his office, but not before stopping next to Kyle. "You'd better watch how you talk around here, Kyle. Saying crap like 'it sounds like another pretty lady' isn't acceptable. Got it?" Marc didn't wait for Kyle to answer. He strode off to his office to answer the phone.

* * *

Debbie rushed to her car, the cold night air feeling good on her flushed face. She'd been having such a fun time all day with Marc that even exercising tonight hadn't ruined it. And then, as they'd sat there, drinking water and teasing each other, she'd thought Marc was going to kiss her. He'd been looking into her eyes so deeply, and she'd been drawn into his, too. And she'd wanted to kiss him. More than she'd ever thought possible. Then that manager of his had broken the spell.

Sounds like another pretty lady. Those words had jolted Debbie back to reality. Another pretty lady. As if he had a line of beautiful women strung out around the block. Well, maybe he did. It wouldn't surprise her. A guy who looks as great as Marc would have a flock of gorgeous women after him. Hadn't she already seen proof of that? Why on earth would he want to bother with her?

Once Debbie arrived home, she lifted Chloe into her arms and held her tight. "It's just you and me, girl," she said, a tinge of sadness in her voice. It would always be just her and Chloe. Unlike Marc, Debbie didn't have a flock of men waiting to date her.

* * *

Over the next two days, Debbie didn't have time to think about Marc or the women in his life. Prom and wedding season was upon them. Even though Debbie planned months in advance for this busy time, it always surprised her how it suddenly crept up on them. Boxes and boxes of orders came in all at once and she and Lindsay were busy unpacking dresses, steaming them, setting up displays, and tagging special orders. Teen girls came in with their mothers to try on dresses they had either ordered or to find ones they loved. Alterations skyrocketed in April. Debbie kept a special calendar in the backroom to keep track of who needed dresses and when, and it started filling up quickly.

They were so busy making room for the sample dresses and processing the orders that Debbie hadn't been able to walk at lunchtime on Tuesday or Wednesday. But she was getting so many steps in between the back room and the storefront that she felt like she'd walked ten miles a day—in heels.

"Don't you just love this time of year?" Lindsay asked Wednesday afternoon while helping a group of teenaged girls try on a multitude of dresses.

Debbie thought she was being sarcastic, but when she saw the excited glint in her eyes, Debbie realized she'd meant it. "I guess," she said. "I mean, it's our bread and butter but it's a lot of chaos most of the time."

"But it's exciting," Lindsay said. "All the beautiful new gowns and the excited customers looking to find that perfect dress. And when they do, they're so happy. I love it."

Debbie watched Lindsay as she cheerfully helped customers, seeing her as if for the first time. Lindsay had been working for them for years, but Debbie had never noticed that she actually enjoyed her work. When Debbie was younger, it had been fun helping her mother in the shop, and as a teenager, it had been exciting to open the boxes of dresses each season. But now, it was just work. The excitement had faded for her. But Lindsay seemed to thrive on it.

After they closed the shop Wednesday evening and were picking up the many dresses to hang up, Debbie asked Lindsay, "So you really enjoy all of this?"

Lindsay laughed. "Sure. Why do you think I've worked here all these years? I love working with you, and I adored your mom.

And I like helping women find the dress of their dreams or the girls find that special prom dress. It's fun."

"That's great. I'm glad you're so happy here."

Lindsay placed a plastic cover over a dress and carefully hung it on the display rack, then turned to Debbie. "Why did you think I've stayed all these years?"

She shrugged. "I never really thought about it, I guess. I've always done this because my mom had the shop and it just fell to me after she passed. I guess I thought it was just a convenient job for you, and that's why you stayed. Not that I'm not appreciative, because I love working with you, but I thought someday you would come and tell me you'd found something better and then move on."

"Move on? Where would I go?" Lindsay asked, her expression amused.

Debbie lifted yet another dress off the dressing room floor and zipped up the back. For the life of her, she couldn't understand why people threw a $300 dress on the floor. "Have you ever thought of owning your own shop?" she asked Lindsay.

Lindsay stopped and looked at her. "To be honest? Yes. But I'd never be able to afford to do that—at least not until years down the road." She cocked her head. "Are you trying to get rid of me?"

"No, no," Debbie said, shaking her head. "Never. I was just curious if you've ever thought of what else you might do someday."

Lindsay shrugged. "As of right now, you're stuck with me. I have no other plans. I like what I do."

Debbie nodded as they continued hanging up dresses and straightening the store. She thought again about Mallory's offer to change her career. It would be interesting to do something different. But would it be any different than this? Here, she found beautiful dresses for women to wear on special occasions. Working with clients finding furniture that suited their style would be similar, wouldn't it? Yet, the thought of doing that instead of running the bridal shop excited Debbie.

Later, at home, after patting Chloe goodbye and heading out the door, Debbie had a text from Marc.

"I'm afraid I have another meeting tonight and won't be at the gym. Have fun at spin class and I'll see you on Friday."

"Have *fun* at spin class? Obviously, this guy has never taken the class before," Debbie muttered to herself. She was disappointed Marc wouldn't be there, but she knew how important this secret deal of his was. She hoped it went well for him.

Mandy led a heavy workout in spin class and by the end, Debbie's legs felt like spaghetti noodles. But she forced herself afterward to use one of the weight machines for ten minutes and then sat down and stretched. As she was stretching, her neighbor, James, stopped by a minute to say hello.

"Hey, Debbie. This is the first time I've seen you here. How's it going?" James asked.

She complained good-naturedly about the spin class and he laughed. "No way I could get through that one. Good for you. I'm just going to hit the treadmill for thirty minutes, then go back to the pub. My sister wanted tonight off, so I'm filling in for her. You should stop by on your way home for dinner and say hi."

"Where are we stopping by?" Mandy asked, coming up to them. "I'm starved."

"Gallagher's," Debbie said. She introduced James and Mandy.

"I love Gallagher's." Mandy turned to Debbie. "Do you want to go for a quick bite? The new woman I hired is taking over my last two classes tonight, so I'm free."

Debbie hesitated a moment. Then she told herself to stop being so silly. Mandy was nice, and it might be fun to get to know her better. "Sure. But I didn't bring a change of clothes."

Mandy waved her hand through the air to dismiss the problem. "Don't you know that yoga pants are the new jeans? You look fine."

James said he'd see them later and headed for one of the treadmills. Debbie followed Mandy inside the women's locker room and tried to make herself presentable. All she had was her old sweatshirt to wear over her tank and workout pants.

"Here," Mandy said, opening her locker. "Wear this. Marc gives us gym clothes all the time. I have a bunch of jackets." She handed Debbie a sleek black workout jacket that zipped up the front and had the company name and logo on it.

"Uh, I doubt if this will fit me," Debbie said, looking at how lean Mandy was compared to her.

"It'll be fine. Try it on."

Reluctantly, Debbie slipped it on. She was shocked when the zipper actually went up easily and the jacket fit her well, except for the long arms but she could fold the cuffs. She stepped up to the mirror and stared at herself in astonishment. She looked good. Her waist had slimmed down a little, and the jacket made her look slender.

"See. I told you it would fit," Mandy said, smiling. "I think you have the wrong image of yourself in your head."

Debbie nodded. Mandy was right. Marc had basically said the same thing to her. She always thought of herself as short and chubby. Well, she was short, but looking in the mirror right now, she didn't look chubby. She looked good.

"You can keep that jacket," Mandy said. "I have several.

Come on. Let's go eat."

They decided to walk to the bar since it wasn't too far away. The night air was cool, but it felt good. They both agreed that spring was finally here, and hopefully it would continue to warm up. Although an April snowstorm wasn't out of the question in Minnesota.

Gallagher's was half full when they walked inside. They made their way to a table in the back where it wasn't as busy. Soon, a pretty redhead came to the table with menus.

"Hi, Debbie," the waitress said, smiling wide. "It's nice to see you again."

"Hi, Megan." She introduced Mandy to James's sister, who co-owned the bar with him. Megan was shorter, like Debbie, and had long, thick, red hair and beautiful green eyes.

"Nice to meet you, Mandy," Megan said. "What can I get you ladies?"

Debbie ordered an iced tea, and Mandy ordered a beer. When Megan left, Debbie raised her brows in question. "Beer?"

Mandy laughed. "At work, I have protein drinks and eat salads. But after a long day of spinning and doing aerobics, I'm ready for a beer."

Debbie laughed along. She would never dare drink anything with so many calories in it, especially now that she was actually losing weight, but Mandy could certainly afford the extra calories.

They both ordered and soon saw James's come in to tend the bar. He waved at them before going right to work.

"How long have you worked for Marc?" Debbie asked Mandy.

"About three years," she said. "I went to college on a basketball scholarship but was hurt after the first year and had to quit the team. Sports and exercise have always been a part of my life, so I got a degree in physical education. I wasn't sure if I'd teach in a school or do something else. Then I started working for Marc and decided this was what I wanted to do."

"It's wonderful how things always work out. You're great at what you do. It's the perfect fit."

"I think so, too. I feel lucky to have found a job there. And I'm hoping as Marc expands the business, my role will grow too," Mandy said.

Mandy asked about the bridal shop, and Debbie told her the history of it. James came with their food, and both women dug in.

"I guess I was hungrier than I'd thought," Debbie said, cutting up the chicken in her salad.

"Me, too," Mandy said. She'd ordered a burger with a side salad. "Gallagher's has the best burgers in town." She sighed after taking a bite, which made Debbie laugh.

"Marc does the same thing," Debbie said. "I have to stay away from greasy food, or I'll plump out again."

Mandy shook her head. "You weren't plump when you started coming to the gym. You probably just felt that way. I think your weight is perfect for your height. Exercising will help tighten everything."

Debbie studied her a moment. "Is that just what employees are supposed to say to make clients feel better, or do you really mean it?"

Mandy frowned. "About you being the right weight for your height? I mean it. If I had thought you were overweight, I wouldn't say a word. Instead, I'd encourage you to keep exercising. But you aren't overweight. I'm not sure who's been messing with your head, but you look great. You're built curvy. You shouldn't compare your body to someone like me who's straight up and down." She laughed. "I was a toothpick as a teenager before, thankfully, I got some curves. But you're lucky. You have curves in all the right places."

Debbie felt her face heat up. She had always been self-conscious about her body, and she hated talking about it. But she could tell Mandy was being truthful. More and more, Debbie realized that her vision of her body type was skewed. She had to change how she saw herself.

"Thanks," Debbie said. "I've always had a problem with my body image. Maybe it's time I re-evaluate the way I see myself."

Mandy took a bite of her salad. "It's tough for women. We're trained to have a certain idea of what is beautiful. I gave up a long time ago believing I'd be curvy. I'm okay with that. And you should be okay with your curves. Women have surgery to look like you. Be happy your curves are natural."

"You're right. I'll work on that," Debbie said. And she decided that she would work on her mental image of herself. She was feeling better about her body, and it was time to let go of her insecurities. Hadn't Marc said the same thing to her?

As they finished their meal, Debbie noticed two people come out from the other side of the bar and walk toward the door. The woman was tall and slender with beautiful dark skin. She was laughing at something the man beside her had said. He was tall and lean, with wavy chestnut hair. They looked like a beautiful couple, everything everyone would want to be.

"Hey, that's Marc, isn't it?" Mandy whispered. At that moment, the man looked up and waved at James before the couple walked out the door.

Debbie stared after them, stunned. It was Marc.

"Who was that woman with him?" Mandy asked. "I've never

seen her before."

Debbie shook her head. She had no idea who she was. Marc had said he had a meeting tonight. But in a bar? That didn't sound very professional to Debbie.

Her appetite now gone, Debbie pushed her plate aside. When she glanced up, she saw Mandy watching her.

"I know you said that there was nothing going on between you and Marc," Mandy said gently. "But I think there is. Or was. You like him, don't you?"

Debbie bit her lip. She couldn't tell Mandy how she felt about Marc. It was complicated. Yes, she did like him, but she was confused as to how she liked him. As a friend? Something more? Debbie had gotten a vibe from him that maybe he felt something for her too. Yet, it seemed as if he gave off that vibe to everyone. Hadn't Mandy thought he'd liked her also?

"There isn't anything going on between us," Debbie finally said. *And probably never will be.*

Mandy didn't look convinced but didn't protest. "Well, maybe that was an old friend of his," she offered. "It could have been anyone."

Debbie nodded. "Right." Although Debbie didn't believe it. To her, it had looked like he and the woman were having a night out.

They soon left Gallagher's and walked back to the gym where their cars were parked.

"That was fun. We should do it again sometime," Mandy said. "I don't have many girlfriends to hang out with. My hours are so different from everyone else since I work nights."

"I had fun too," Debbie said. "We definitely should do this again."

They exchanged phone numbers, and both drove off. Debbie

had told the truth—it had been fun being out with Mandy until she'd seen Marc. But she wasn't going to jump to any conclusions. Like Mandy had said, it could have been anyone and not necessarily a date.

At least Debbie hoped that was true.

Chapter Fourteen

Marc was happy with how the meeting had gone with Melinda Wednesday night. They were still trying to write up a contract that both agreed on. Once that was ready, he'd have to meet with the McGregory Medical Supply board of directors to discuss the plans. But as far as he could tell, it was a sure thing. He was so excited about it that he wished he could tell someone about the deal. Actually, there was only one person he wished he could share the news with—Debbie. She'd understand how important this deal was to him and would be excited for him. But he'd promised not to say anything until the deal was signed and made public. It was so hard keeping it to himself.

Mallory called him Thursday about looking at the furniture again, and he told her to come over. He called Debbie to see if she wanted to stop by for a few minutes too, since her shop wasn't far from his house. The antiques and sofas he'd purchased had arrived the day before and he wanted her to see them.

"I'm not sure I can get away," Debbie told him, sounding distant. "We're very busy putting out new merchandise."

"You have to take a lunch break though. It's the law," he said, teasing. "And I'm sure Mallory would like for you to be here."

He heard Debbie sigh on the other end, although he couldn't

tell if it was a sigh of frustration or giving in. "Fine. I'll stop by around one. But I can't stay long."

When Marc hung up, he wondered why Debbie sounded aloof. He hoped it wasn't still because of that comment Kyle had made Monday night. He had to talk with Kyle—a long talk—about the way he referred to women. It seemed that Kyle's behavior had become worse over the years. Or maybe he'd always been that way and Marc hadn't noticed before. But it had to stop.

Both Debbie and Mallory showed up precisely at one. Marc offered to get them something to drink, but both women declined.

"I brought the moving truck and two helpers," Mallory said. "I'm sure I'll want the furniture and decided there was no time like the present."

Marc laughed. "I like a woman who knows what she wants."

Debbie remained silent. Marc second-guessed what he'd said to Mallory. Did it sound like he was flirting? Cripes! He should be more careful, or he'll start sounding like Kyle.

"Would you like to see the furniture Debbie helped me pick out?" Marc asked Mallory.

Her eyes lit up. "Of course. Lead the way."

They followed him into the dining room where the new hutch stood, then to the den, where the antique desk had been placed. "It's perfect in here, isn't it?" he asked, smiling at Debbie.

She nodded. "It is. You have to get the old desk moved out of here, and we should find a rug to place under the desk."

"It's beautiful," Mallory exclaimed, running her fingertips over the polished wood. "Are you going to place glass over the top to protect that antique leather in the center?"

"I was thinking of that," Debbie said to Mallory. "It would be a shame for it to get stained or ripped."

Marc listened as the women discussed the type of rug they thought would look nice, and whether or not the draperies should be replaced. Debbie seemed comfortable discussing decorating ideas with Mallory, as if she'd been doing this her entire life. He was happy he'd asked her to help him pick furniture for his house. She was self-conscious about many things, but she was confident when it came to antiques.

He followed them into the living room where Debbie showed Mallory the new leather sofas and antique end tables.

"These are amazing," Mallory said, running her hand over the leather. "This is top grade leather. They're beautiful."

"They're going to be great for napping on," Marc said, grinning.

The women stared at him, horrified. "Napping? I'd be scared to death to sit on them," Mallory said, laughing. "But they're here to use, not to just look at."

Marc and Mallory agreed on a price for the furniture he wanted to sell, and she had the two men come inside and haul it out.

"Debbie. The items you and Marc are choosing are incredible," Mallory said. "You really are knowledgeable about antiques. You've completely impressed me."

Marc saw Debbie blush at Mallory's compliment. It was true, though. Debbie had a talent for choosing just the right pieces.

"Thanks, Mallory. But Marc chose most of the furniture; I just gave advice," Debbie said.

"That's not true," Marc piped up. "It's all Debbie. She knew exactly where to buy the right pieces and led me to all the good items. She has great taste."

Debbie shook her head but stayed silent. Marc knew she hated being praised, but he'd wanted Mallory to know the truth.

After all the furniture was loaded, Mallory headed for the door. "Thanks again, Marc. You gave me a good deal. I'll have a lot more furniture to use for high-end staging jobs now." She turned to Debbie and spoke quietly. "Think about what I said to you before. Even if we work together part-time, it would be great." The two women hugged, and Mallory left.

"Think about what?" Marc asked after Mallory had left.

"Oh, nothing," Debbie said. "I have to get back to the shop. Once school lets out, we're swamped with teenage girls buying prom dresses."

Marc studied her a moment. "Is everything okay? You're not mad at me about something, are you?"

Debbie shook her head. "No. I'm just really busy. I'm glad all your furniture came." She headed for the door with Marc right behind her. "Will I see you Friday at the gym?" she asked.

"I'll be there."

"Okay. Great. See you then." Debbie rushed out the door.

As Marc closed the front door, he wondered what was going on. The last he knew, he and Debbie were on good terms. What had happened?

Bernie came out from the direction of the kitchen, yawning. The big dog had slept through all the activity.

"You know, men came in and hauled out furniture and you didn't even bother to wake up and see what was going on," Marc told the dog. "Great watchdog you are."

Bernie didn't look too concerned. He sat and stared at Marc.

"Come on, old boy," Marc said, heading for the kitchen. "Let's have some lunch and head into work."

* * *

Friday night, Debbie made it to the gym just in time for the aerobics class. She and Lindsay had been so busy that afternoon in the shop that time had flown by. She hadn't even finished picking up before she realized she had to leave.

"Go on to your class, and I'll finish up," Lindsay had told her. "I don't mind. I don't have any plans tonight anyway."

Debbie had rushed home and fed Chloe, then changed and headed out again. She hadn't wanted to miss the class. She was slowly toning up, and she wanted to continue working at it. But since she arrived only minutes before the class started, she only had time to wave at Marc as she passed him on her way into the room.

Mandy and the new instructor, Anita, led the class. Anita was a lively young woman who was short, like Debbie, and curvy, but muscular. Her dark ponytail swung back and forth as she moved along to the music, and her energy was contagious.

Debbie did her best to keep up, but she struggled. By the time the class was over, Debbie was huffing and puffing, barely able to catch her breath.

"Debbie," Mandy called as everyone else headed out of the class. "Come and meet Anita."

Debbie walked over to the women at the front of the class. "Anita, this is Debbie. She owns a bridal shop across town."

"Nice to meet you," Anita said. "Did you enjoy the workout?"

"It's nice to meet you too," Debbie said. "I'm not sure 'enjoy' is the word I'd use after that workout." The women laughed. "But hopefully someday I'll be able to keep up and still be able to breathe afterward."

"Oh, you did fine," Anita said. "And look!" She moved up beside Debbie. "Finally, someone my own size." She chuckled. "It seems like everyone who works here is six feet tall."

Debbie nodded. "Right? I said the same thing when I started coming here."

"Anita is a kindergarten teacher during the day. She's going to work here part-time in the evenings until school lets out for the summer, then she'll work more hours," Mandy said.

"Oh. That must be fun, working with young children," Debbie said.

"It is. But it can be draining, too. I was a workout instructor all through college, so I thought it might be fun to do this part-time. I need all the energy I can get to keep up with the little ones."

Marc poked his head into the room. "Are you ready to hit the weight machine?" he asked Debbie.

Debbie rolled her eyes, and the two other women grinned. "I'm coming," she said. "It was nice meeting you, Anita. I'm sure I'll be seeing you around here."

"Nice meeting you, too," Anita said.

Debbie followed Marc out of the room and they walked to the weight machine. Debbie laid her jacket down beside the bench and sat down.

"How did you like Anita?" Marc asked.

"She's great. She has a lot of energy. Her classes should be fun if I survive them," Debbie said.

Marc chuckled. "You'll do fine." He adjusted the weights, and Debbie pulled them the way he had shown her in the past.

"Hey, you're becoming a pro at this," Marc said.

"I used the weights Wednesday night after spin class," she told him.

"That's great. Sorry I wasn't here, but I had a productive meeting."

Debbie glanced up at him to see if he was telling the truth

or lying. He seemed sincere. "Was that meeting for the deal you can't tell anyone about?"

He nodded. "I wish I could. I'm so excited about it. I promise to tell you as soon as I'm allowed."

Debbie continued pulling on the weights. Maybe the pretty woman she'd seen him with had been part of the meeting. But at Gallagher's? That seemed like a strange place to hold a business meeting. But then, what would she know? Still, they'd looked pretty friendly, like they were having a good time. Almost like a date.

"Do you already know where we're going to shop this weekend?" Marc asked as they sat on the floor to stretch.

Debbie frowned. She'd been so busy this week, she hadn't even thought about it. "No, not really. But I know a few stores we can stop at. I haven't had time to look up estate sales or auctions."

"We could skip it this weekend if that would help," Marc said. "I mean, if you need more time to work at the shop, I totally get it."

She considered that a moment. "No. We should go this weekend. I'm sure we can find some shops in St. Paul that have nice items. The next weekend is Easter, so we'll miss shopping then."

"Oh, yeah. Easter. I forgot about that." Marc stared up at the ceiling like he was contemplating something. "Do you have plans for Easter Sunday?"

"What? Easter Sunday?" Debbie was taken by surprise. "No, not really. Mallory had mentioned I should come over there, but I haven't committed to it. Since my mother died, I've kind of been tagging along with my neighbors for holidays."

"I go to my sister's house since my parents live in Florida. She's married and has a two-year-old boy, Austin." He smiled at Debbie. "Would you like to join us? She's always telling me I should bring a guest."

"Oh, well," Debbie didn't know what to say. "I couldn't barge in on your family's holiday."

"You're not barging in, silly. I'm asking you. You'll love my sister. She's very sweet and kind—nothing like me." He laughed.

Debbie wasn't sure how to answer. It would seem odd showing up at his family's holiday. But, it would be fun to spend time with him and his family. Yet, why? It wasn't like they were a couple or even dating. Wouldn't that seem weird to his sister?

"I can tell you're over-thinking it," Marc said, catching her eyes with his. "It's just dinner, nothing more. And you can bring Chloe along. I'll have Bernie with. They can sit under the table and grab anything that falls."

The idea of gigantic Bernie and little Chloe picking up scraps under the table made Debbie smile. "Are you sure your sister won't mind?"

"Absolutely. You'll see. She's great."

After stretching, Debbie stood and slipped on the jacket that Mandy had given her. Marc watched her, looking pleased.

"That looks good on you. I would have given you one, though. You didn't have to buy one," Marc said.

"I didn't buy it. Mandy gave me one of hers. I like how it fits."

Marc smiled appreciatively at her. At least, that's how Debbie interpreted his expression. It boosted her ego a bit.

"It fits you perfectly. You're really shaping up. I do good work." He grinned mischievously.

Debbie laughed. "Right. You did all the work. I'll see you on Sunday."

Marc walked with her to the door. "Ten sound good? I'll pick you up."

Debbie nodded and turned to leave. Just as the electronic glass doors began to open, she could see in the reflection a pretty brunette walking up to Marc. Debbie tried not to feel let down by the smile she saw Marc return to the woman. His job was to help everyone, not just her. But it still made her stomach twist a little. She couldn't compete with any of these gorgeous women. She didn't even know why she thought she could try.

Falling from the cloud she'd been on just moments before, Debbie drove home.

Chapter Fifteen

Marc watched as Debbie walked to the doors. She looked amazing in the form-fitting jacket instead of that big, bulky sweatshirt she usually wore. And she held herself with confidence now. Debbie wasn't slouching or trying to hide her body. It made him happy that he had a little to do with building up her self-confidence. He knew she was a great person on the inside, and maybe now, she'd feel good about her appearance as well. Just watching her made him smile.

"Hi, Marc. Can you work with me tonight?" A tall brunette in skimpy workout attire approached him just as Debbie walked out the door. Marc sighed but turned and smiled at her as she drew near. He'd rather go back to his office and do paperwork, but it was his job to work with clients.

"Sure. It's Tammi, right?" he asked. She nodded and smiled wide. "Let's review your goals and get started." He walked away with her but turned to catch one last glimpse of Debbie as she slipped into her little yellow car. The car made him smile, too. It was perfect for her.

He helped clients as they came and went, but the entire time Debbie was on his mind. When Mandy came out from her last class of the night, Marc pulled her aside.

"Would you mind picking out some workout clothes from our shop for Debbie? A couple of pants, another jacket, and tanks. She looks great in them, and it'll help build her confidence so she'll continue exercising. I'd do it myself, but I have no idea what sizes to pick."

Mandy grinned slyly. "I'd be happy to."

"Why are you grinning?" Marc asked.

"You've never given a client a bunch of workout clothes before," Mandy said. "I think you really like Debbie. Wait. No. I know you like her."

"I'm just being nice," he protested. "I want to encourage her to continue. That's all."

"Right," Mandy said.

Marc studied her a moment. "I do like Debbie. But we're just friends."

Mandy crossed her arms. "Just friends?"

He didn't know how to answer. Did he like Debbie the way Mandy thought he did? He enjoyed spending time with her, shopping for antiques. He loved teasing her and the way she gave it right back to him. And he'd actually put himself out there to help her get into shape. He'd never offered anyone a free membership before. Ever. And hadn't he just asked Debbie to his sister's house for Easter?

"Do you think Debbie likes *me* that way?" he asked Mandy.

She shrugged. "I think she does, but she claims you're just friends."

Ah. That's what he'd thought.

"Will you do me a favor, though?" Mandy asked him.

"Sure."

"Don't break her heart. She's sweet, and I think she's fragile. Strong on the outside, but fragile on the inside. So if you really think you and she are *just* friends, don't lead her on to think it's something more."

Marc's was stunned. That was exactly what Debbie had told him about Mandy. "Why would you think I'd lead Debbie on?"

Mandy gave him a small smile. "Because you do, unintentionally. You flirt and tease and women think you like them. That's the message I got from you. Debbie might think that too. Just make sure to be honest with her. She's a nice person, and I'd hate to see her hurt."

"That's the last thing I want to do," Marc said. He'd never want to hurt Debbie. He'd thought he was just being nice. "Do you think I shouldn't give Debbie the free workout clothes?"

Mandy shook her head. "No. I think you should. It's a nice gesture and she does look great in them. But if you only think of her as a *friend*, then make sure she knows that."

"Okay. Thanks." Marc wasn't quite sure what he was thanking her for. He felt like he'd just been told off, only in a nice way.

The last of the clients walked past Marc on their way out the door. One woman who'd been coming to the fitness center for about three months gave him a smile and wink as she walked past. She was probably his age, and she was single—she'd made sure he knew that. Normally, he'd have smiled back but after what Mandy had just said, he only said goodnight and turned around quickly.

Sheesh. Maybe I'm just like Kyle and I don't even know it, he thought. No wonder Kyle thought he could talk the way he did. *Am I as bad as him?*

"Going home, boss?" Kyle asked as Marc headed to his office.

"Not yet," Marc said. "Go ahead and lock up and go home. I have some paperwork to do."

"Okay. See you tomorrow." Kyle headed out.

Marc watched him as he left, noticing his cocky swagger.

Do I swagger like that? Marc walked down the hallway, trying hard not to swagger, then thought how ridiculous that was. *This is really getting to me!* He went into his office and dropped down in his chair. Maybe some paperwork would get his mind off of everything. But try as he might, all he could think about was how great Debbie had looked in the company jacket and that he couldn't wait to see her on Sunday.

* * *

Debbie awoke on Sunday feeling happy. The weather was warming up each day, and the snow had all melted. No more slush or ice covered the sidewalks and streets. She'd gone for a long walk on Saturday at lunchtime despite how busy they'd been. She realized that walking and exercising helped her manage stress as well as made her feel better.

"I should have been exercising all along," she told Chloe as she made up the little dog's breakfast. "I feel so much better."

Chloe sat and stared at her. Debbie wondered what her dog thought of the walks they were taking now. So far, Chloe hadn't been very excited about them.

After eating, Debbie dressed, feeling elated that her jeans were even looser than last week. "I'm going to need a whole new wardrobe," she said happily. Then she frowned. "Well, at least a couple of pairs of jeans. On my budget, a whole new wardrobe is out of the question." But she didn't mind. Just the feel of the clothes being looser made her happy.

There was a knock on her door, and Debbie ran to answer it. Marc stood there, a bag from Fit in 20 in his hand.

"Hi," he said. "I brought you something."

Her heart skipped unexpectedly. "Really? Come on in."

Marc walked inside and slipped off his sneakers. He followed her to the kitchen counter.

"Do you want a water or pop or something?" Debbie asked.

"No, thanks." He handed her the bag. "I hope you like these."

Debbie took the bag and peeked inside. "Workout clothes?" she asked, surprised.

Marc nodded. "Yeah. I thought you looked so good in the jacket that you'd like a few more items. I had Mandy pick them out, but if the sizes are wrong, you can exchange them."

Debbie pulled out the clothing and laid it on the counter. There was another jacket like the one she had only in a deep royal blue with a tank and yoga pants to match. Another tank and pants were in black. "I love them!" she said. "Thanks so much."

Marc beamed. "I'm glad you like them. The blue will look great with your eyes."

Debbie looked up at him. *Her eyes?*

"I mean, you know. Your eyes are blue, and the clothes are blue. I mean, you have pretty blue eyes," Marc stammered, then he sighed. "You know what I mean."

She laughed. "Yes, I do. Thank you so much. I'll get a lot of use out of these."

He looked relieved. Debbie wondered what was going on with him.

"Are you ready to go. It's another beautiful spring day out there," he said.

"Yeah. Let's head out. I was thinking instead of antiques today, we should look at rugs. Unless you'd rather have antique rugs."

His brows rose. "I have no idea which I'd rather have. You choose."

"Personally, I'd be scared to death to spend the money on antique rugs that might get ruined. They make so many beautiful new rugs these days that I think I'd buy those instead," she said.

"Then that's what we'll do."

"You know, you're really easy to please," she said.

Marc looked at her and grinned slyly. "You don't know how easy I can be." He waggled his brows.

"Oh, sheesh," she realized what she'd said. "You know what I meant."

"Come on. Let's go rug shopping."

They spent the morning going from carpet shops to large box stores looking at rugs. Debbie suggested staying in the 1920s era with small floral designs or art deco. They found a beautifully patterned rug in black and white that would look great in the dining room under the table, and a dark burgundy rug with a floral design that would brighten up all the brown in the living room. Marc also liked another black and white art deco design that he could lay on the hardwood floor beside his bed.

"Does this mean I have to replace all the draperies to match the rugs?" he asked.

Debbie shook her head. "Let's see how everything blends when we lay them down. You don't want everything to be too matchy-matchy."

He laughed. "Is that a professional decorating term? Matchy-matchy."

She smiled. "Probably not, but I say it all the time at the bridal shop."

Marc offered to buy her lunch that afternoon, so they stopped at the Olive Garden.

"You're trying to keep me fat so I'll eventually have to buy a membership," she teased as she looked at all the delicious pasta choices on the menu.

"You aren't fat," he said seriously. "Besides, you can splurge on calories once in a while. Look at all the walking we did today. Some of those stores were enormous, and the rugs were in the very back."

"You're just trying to justify the one-hundred and forty calories per breadstick here," Debbie said.

He winked. "That's right because I want to eat at least two."

They ordered their meals—Debbie had soup and salad and Marc ordered shrimp scampi—and their sodas arrived.

"How are things at the shop?" Marc asked. "Busy?"

Debbie pushed her hair back behind her shoulder. "Crazy busy. But it always is this time of year. I've even been taking home small alterations because there are too many for our sewing woman to keep up with. I can do hems and darts and fix beadwork, but I'm not good at the big projects. My mom used to do a lot of the alterations. She could fix a dress like magic."

"Really? I didn't realize women had that many alterations done. Don't they just buy a dress that fits?"

Debbie laughed. "Oh, boy. You really don't know anything about women and gowns. Wedding gowns have to be perfect, so they're almost always altered to fit right. Prom gowns, not as much, except for hems and maybe taking in the waist a little—or letting it out. Women don't pay all that money for their dresses to kind of fit."

"I had no idea," Marc said. "But then, I've never bought a gown."

"That's good to hear." Debbie grinned.

Their food came, and their easy conversation continued. Debbie was always surprised at how comfortable she was around

Marc. Maybe it was because he'd seen her at her worst—falling off a bike and lying on the ground—or because he was just a nice guy. He lived in a mansion and ran a chain of fitness centers, but you'd never guess that talking to him. He was so down-to-earth—well, besides spending money without even thinking about it—and was naturally funny. And he liked dogs. That was number one in her book.

"Hey. The other day I heard Mallory ask you if you were thinking about her offer. Can I pry and ask what that was about?" Marc looked at her curiously.

"Oh, that." Debbie felt silly even talking about it. "Well, don't laugh, but she offered for me to work alongside her, helping clients who want to find antiques for their homes."

Marc's expression grew serious. "Why would I laugh? You're incredible at choosing antiques. You're so knowledgeable about them."

"Yeah, but," Debbie said, dropping her eyes to the table. "I'm not a professional when it comes to antiques. Not enough to help a professional like Mallory decorate houses. It's silly for me to consider it."

Marc tilted his head to catch her eyes with his. "It's not silly. I'm sure your expertise would be an asset to Mallory's business. Wouldn't you like doing something like that? You said the bridal shop wasn't challenging enough for you anymore."

She looked up again, straight at Marc. "But I know my business inside and out. I know I can earn a living there, even if it isn't a lot of money. What if I tried working with Mallory, and it didn't work out? It's scary."

His expression softened. "What if you tried and it ended up being amazing? You don't know if you don't try."

She twirled her spoon around inside her soup bowl. "You

don't understand. Everything you do turns to gold."

"Are you kidding?" Marc asked. "I may be successful now, but I took a big risk when I started my first fitness center. I put every cent I had into it and borrowed money, too. I could have lost everything. And each new one I opened was a gamble too. The first few years, I was scared to death I'd lose everything. Then, it all started to click. More and more people started to join and the centers became successful. I was lucky, but I also believed in myself. Sometimes, it just takes a leap of faith—faith in yourself and your abilities."

"Faith in myself and my abilities is what I lack the most of," Debbie said softly. "You should know that about me by now."

Marc set his plate aside and moved closer to her across the table. "That isn't what I've seen. You've taken charge like a pro when we've gone furniture shopping or to auctions. You know exactly what's good and what isn't. You know a good bargain when you see it and what's overpriced. Even when you and Mallory were discussing the furniture the other day, you had the confidence to suggest what would look good in the rooms. She sees that in you, just like I do. You need to start seeing it in yourself."

Debbie nodded. She knew Marc was right. She needed to believe in herself more and stop all the self-doubt. But it was hard. Her mother had encouraged her all her life, yet she'd always second-guessed herself. She didn't know where it came from. Certainly not her mother. Gladys had always known what she wanted and had made it happen.

The waiter came at that moment and took the empty plates away. Marc paid the bill, and they headed out to his car. Just as Marc sat behind the wheel, his phone buzzed, and he glanced at it and frowned.

"Bad news?" Debbie asked, watching him.

Marc sighed. "No. The person I'm working with on this new deal wants me to meet with a few other people tomorrow at noon." He looked up at Debbie. "I'm sorry, but I'll have to miss shopping tomorrow."

"That's fine. I can do some work at the shop while it's closed. Aren't the rugs going to be delivered tomorrow at one, though?" Debbie asked.

"Oh, crap. Yeah. I'm pretty sure I won't be home in time, either."

"I could let them in, if you'd like," Debbie offered.

His face brightened. "Would you? Thanks so much." He grabbed his keys out of the ignition and slipped one off the ring. "Here's the front door key. You can keep this for a while in case you need to let anyone else in again."

Debbie looked at the key in her hand. "Are you sure you trust me with a key to your house?"

"Why wouldn't I? I'd trust you with anything," he said.

It was early evening by the time he parked in front of her house. "Thanks so much for helping me today," he said, turning toward her. "I really enjoy our shopping days." He made a face. "I never thought I'd say that I enjoyed shopping, but with you, it's fun."

"I'm enjoying it too," she said. "I'll miss it once we're done."

Marc leaned closer to her. So close, she could smell his musky aftershave, just like she had that very first day they'd met. "Then I'll just have to keep buying things so we can keep seeing each other," he said softly.

Debbie's heart pounded. He was so close, she thought he was going to kiss her. Without thinking, she backed away and pulled off her seatbelt. "Well, I'll see you at the gym tomorrow night," she said hurriedly before opening the door and practically jumping out.

As she turned to close the door, she thought she saw disappointment in Marc's eyes.

"Okay. See you tomorrow night," he said.

She waved and rushed up the sidewalk to the front door. By the time she'd stepped inside and turned, he was gone.

Chapter Sixteen

"I'm such an idiot," Debbie chastised herself for the hundredth time. She was sitting in the backroom of the quiet store, hand-stitching beads that had come loose on a dress. Chloe was lying on her little pillow beside the worktable and looked up as Debbie spoke aloud.

"I'm sure Marc was going to kiss me yesterday, and I panicked and ran away. What's wrong with me?" She stopped sewing and stared down at the little white dog. But Chloe didn't have any answers. She only stared at Debbie as if she were crazy.

"You're right. I am crazy," Debbie told Chloe. "He's a good-looking, nice guy that any woman would want to throw herself at. Yet there I sat, scared to death he'd kiss me, and I ran away." She thought about his musky cologne and how his face had been only inches from hers. She liked how the gold flecks in his brown eyes seemed to glitter when he teased her, and his silly smile and perfectly chiseled face. And he was always encouraging her, even when she didn't believe in herself. Why was she so scared?

They'd become friends, good friends, since that fateful day when she'd nearly run him over with her bike. He'd helped her lose weight and get in shape, and she was slowly helping him turn his garish mansion into a home he could feel comfortable in. Maybe that was what she was afraid of. If they took it to the next level and became involved, it might ruin their friendship. And that would be sad.

Or maybe she was scared it wouldn't last, and he'd leave her. Yet, all she could do was imagine what it would have been like if she'd let him kiss her.

"What are you doing here on your day off?" Lindsay came in from the front of the store carrying groceries. She was wearing jeans with ankle boots, a smocked black blouse, and a short jean jacket. Debbie thought she looked adorable—like a classy hippie from another era—but then, Lindsay looked cute in everything she wore.

"I need to finish some of these alterations and repairs on dresses. I figured I'd get more done if I were here instead of at home," Debbie explained.

"Aren't you supposed to be out shopping for antiques with Marc?" Lindsay asked.

"He had a meeting, so we canceled. But I'm stopping by his house in a bit to let the delivery men in. We bought some beautiful rugs yesterday that are being delivered."

"We?" Lindsay gave a sly grin.

"*He* bought the rugs. I helped him pick them out," Debbie clarified.

"And now you have a key to his house?" Lindsay asked.

"Well, yes, but someone had to let them in, and he was going to be busy," Debbie said, growing flustered.

"Oh, I see. I'm sure Marc hands out his key to just anyone."

Debbie eyed her, knowing what she was hinting at. "Don't you have groceries to put away?"

Lindsay laughed. "Yeah, I do. Then I'll come down and help

you. We could use this time to put out those new dresses that came in today."

"No, no. It's your day off," Debbie protested.

"Yeah, I know. But I'd rather do it today instead of while we're busy tomorrow." Lindsay headed upstairs to her apartment as Debbie watched her. She couldn't believe how lucky she was to have someone as dedicated as Lindsay working for her.

They worked around the shop for a time, pulling dresses from large boxes and either tagging them with prices or placing the name of the customer who'd ordered it on them. Halfway through their work, Debbie looked at the clock.

"I have to leave now, or I won't get to the house on time."

Lindsay looked up hopefully. "Can I come with you? I'd love to see the house. But only if you think Marc wouldn't mind."

Debbie didn't have to think twice. Besides, she and Lindsay could put the rugs down and surprise Marc. "Sure. Come on."

They drove in Debbie's little car and arrived at the house just as the two delivery trucks pulled up. Debbie showed the men which rooms to set the rugs in, and within minutes, the men left.

"Goodness. This place is amazing." Lindsay turned in circles in the foyer trying to take it all in. She walked into the dining room. "This table is beautiful!"

Debbie agreed. "I could pay your wages for several years with what that table and chairs cost. It's insane. But it's so beautiful."

"Geez. I guess there's a lot of money in owning fitness centers," Lindsay said. "Maybe we're in the wrong business."

"That's for sure." Debbie laughed. "Do you want to help me set these rugs down? I can't wait to see how they look."

"Sure."

They carefully moved the heavy table and chairs and rolled the black and white rug out on the wood floor, centering it under the antique chandelier. Lindsay marveled over the glittering light fixture as the crystal pendants sparkled. They moved the table back, which was no small feat, and then placed the chairs. Debbie found a large china bowl from the hutch and set it in the middle of the table. They stepped back and surveyed their work.

"I love that rug," Lindsay said. "It's perfect."

Debbie smiled. She loved it too. It warmed up the room without taking away from the beautiful table.

"He should look for black and white china, maybe with an Asian influence," Lindsay said. "It would look perfect in the hutch."

Debbie liked her suggestion. "You're right. That would be perfect. I'll mention it to him." She grinned at her friend. "You're good at this."

"It's not much different than choosing the right necklace or shoes for an evening dress," Lindsay said.

Debbie supposed she was right. Maybe that was why she and her mother had developed a good eye for antiques. It was all about style and color, just like gowns were.

They placed the burgundy rug in the living room in front of the leather sofas and set the coffee table over it. Marc had done well picking burgundy. It gave the room a dash of color. As she gazed at the white curtains hanging beside the big picture window, she decided those should be changed to burgundy too. She'd discuss that with Marc.

"The last one goes up in his bedroom," Debbie said. The delivery men had left it at the bottom of the stairs, so the two women carried it up. Luckily, it wasn't too heavy. When they walked into Marc's master suite, Lindsay whistled low.

"This is incredible," she said. "And that bed! It's amazing!"

Debbie glanced around. She'd been in here before but hadn't

given the room much thought. But Lindsay was right. The room was large with floor-to-ceiling windows across one wall and French doors on the wall that faced the back yard that opened onto a balcony. There was a tray ceiling above the bed with a lovely gold antique light fixture hanging in the center that held several glass flutes with bulbs. But the main focus was on the elegant sleigh bed made of gleaming mahogany. Unlike the modern version of a sleigh bed, this one was much different. The curved head and footboards were attached to a sleek wood frame where the mattress lay. Hand-carved designs ran along the sides of the bed as well as on the headboard and footboard. It was absolutely gorgeous.

"This is a beautiful bed," Debbie agreed. "You don't see them like this often."

"Where does the rug go?" Lindsay asked.

Debbie assumed he'd want it on the wood floor next to his side of the bed, but she had no idea which side he slept on. She glanced at the nightstands on each side. One held a clock and a small bowl with change in it. "Maybe this side?" she pointed. "It looks like he might sleep on the left side of the bed."

"You don't know?" Lindsay asked.

"How would I know? I don't sleep with him." As soon as the words left her mouth, Debbie felt her face heat up.

Lindsay laughed. "I didn't assume you do. I just thought you might know since you spend so much time with him."

Debbie shook her head. "That's one topic that hasn't come up. Let's just lay it here, and he can change it if he wants to."

They rolled it out. The black and white art deco rug looked good next to the bed. Debbie thought to suggest to Marc to find a bedspread that would blend with it. Or maybe that was too personal. She decided to let him figure it out.

As the two women were leaving the house, Debbie received a text from Marc.

"I'm sorry, but I won't be at the gym tonight. More meetings. But go and do your usual workout. You know how to run the machines now. Hopefully, I'll be there on Wednesday night. Thanks for letting the delivery men in. You're a lifesaver."

Debbie frowned. *Yeah, that's me. The little ole' lifesaver.*

"Is something wrong?" Lindsay asked.

"No. It's from Marc. He won't be at the gym tonight. He said his meeting is running long."

"That stinks." Lindsay slid into the passenger side of Debbie's car. "But you'll still go and exercise anyway, won't you?"

Debbie sighed. "Yeah. It's not as much fun without Marc there, but I will." At least she had her new workout clothes to cheer her up.

Later that evening, Debbie showed up at the gym at her regular time. She thought she'd use the elliptical machine first for twenty minutes and then the weight machine. As she walked past the desk, the guy named Kyle came around it and headed toward her.

"Hi. It's Debbie, right?" Kyle said, smiling at her.

"Yes. Hi," Debbie said. She wasn't a fan of Kyle's and didn't want to talk to him.

Kyle stopped right in front of her. "Marc's not here. He has a 'meeting' again," he said, using air quotes. He laughed tightly. "A guy like Marc has 'meetings' a lot," he added. "He's popular with the ladies if you catch my drift."

That wasn't a "drift," it was an outright tidal wave, Debbie thought. "Yes. I know Marc's not here. I'll be fine without him," she said, trying to walk around Kyle.

"I can be your trainer tonight," Kyle offered.

Debbie's skin prickled. There was something about Kyle she didn't like, besides the fact that he was always alluding to Marc having a bunch of women in his life. She didn't want him around her while she exercised. "I'll be fine," she said, again trying to go around him.

"Debbie. Hi. You're here," a woman's voice said from behind her.

Debbie turned and saw Mandy. "Hi."

"Yoga is about to start. Why don't you join us?" Mandy smiled.

Debbie frowned. Yoga? Was she kidding? But Mandy linked arms with her and practically pulled her away from Kyle toward the exercise room.

"Sorry," Mandy said softly to her as the space between them and Kyle grew wider. "I saw him bothering you and figured I should rescue you."

"Thanks," Debbie said. "He wanted to be my trainer tonight. Yuck! For some reason, that guy bothers me."

"He bothers everybody. He gives me the creeps," Mandy said. She smiled wide. "You look great in that workout wear. The color is perfect for you."

"Thanks." Debbie had worn the royal blue outfit tonight. "I love it. Thanks for picking it out."

"No problem. It was all Marc's idea. You know, I've never known him to give out free workout wear to anyone except employees." She gave Debbie a sly grin. "I think he likes you."

Debbie grew uncomfortable. Especially since she'd told Mandy that there was nothing between her and Marc, but now, she wasn't sure.

"Don't look so worried," Mandy said. "I'm okay with him liking you as long as he's honest and up front with you, so you don't get hurt. I told him that."

"You did?" Debbie was stunned. It was exactly what she'd told Marc about Mandy.

Mandy placed a hand gently on Debbie's arm. "I did. I like you. You're a nice person. You deserve only the best."

"Thank you. That's so sweet," Debbie said, her heart warmed by Mandy's words.

"And as a friend," Mandy said. "I suggest you take the yoga class instead of going into the gym and fighting off Kyle."

"Ugh! Those are my choices?"

Mandy laughed. "You'll love yoga. Come on. Try one class."

Debbie reluctantly agreed, but only because she didn't want to spend a moment with Kyle. Thirty minutes later, she was surprised at how much she'd enjoyed the yoga class. The movements weren't always easy, but she'd managed pretty well. And the music was peaceful and calming. She'd stretched muscles she hadn't known she had, but it had felt good.

"So, are you a fan of yoga now?" Mandy asked after the class.

"I never thought I'd enjoy it this much," Debbie said. "And it's a great workout."

"That's wonderful. I've converted you." Mandy laughed.

Debbie joined in. She was very surprised at herself. Over the past few weeks, she'd tried several new ways to exercise and she was enjoying it. She'd have never believed it if someone had told her this a few months ago.

That evening, as she lay in bed with Chloe sprawled out beside her, the television on low at the foot of the bed, her phone buzzed. Debbie picked it up and was pleased to see Marc was calling her.

"Hi," she answered.

"Hi." His voice was rich and husky. "I came home to a

wonderful surprise. Someone laid rugs under my furniture in the dining and living rooms. And there's a very cool rug in my bedroom as well. Any idea who did that?" he chuckled warmly.

"Must be the rug fairies," she said. "Did they guess the right side of the bed?"

"Yes, they did. All the rugs look nice. How did you do that by yourself?"

"I had some help. Lindsay came with me, so we put them down."

"Ah. Lindsay. I should have guessed. Well, it was a nice surprise to come home to after a long day. Thank you," he said.

"We were happy to do it. How did your meeting go?"

"Great. Tiring. I'm not used to spending so much time trying to impress people. I think we're almost ready to sign a deal. I hope so."

He paused, and Debbie could hear music playing it the background. Old, soft rock. Funny, but she'd never thought about the type of music he liked before. It suited him.

"How was your workout tonight? I'll bet you didn't go."

"I did go. It went well," Debbie said. "Mandy saved me from Kyle's clutches and made me take her yoga class. Surprisingly, I enjoyed it."

"That's great. But what's this about Kyle? Did he bother you?" Marc's voice had turned serious. Debbie could picture a crease forming between his brows.

"No. He just offered to be my trainer for the night since you were 'air quotes at a meeting.' He loves his air quotes and inuendoes, doesn't he?" It was silent on the other end of the line except for Marc's breathing growing heavier. Debbie wondered if she shouldn't have told him about Kyle.

"I'll tell him to leave you alone when I'm not there," Marc

finally said. "He's always saying stuff he shouldn't." He took a deep breath, and his voice grew calmer. "I'm glad you did yoga instead. And here you thought you weren't coordinated enough for it."

Debbie was relieved he'd gone back to teasing. "I'm not that coordinated, but Mandy is a good teacher. It was relaxing but challenging. I think I'll continue taking that class on Mondays for a while if that's all right."

"Of course, it's fine. We can do the weight machine and stretches afterward when I'm there. I tell you, I can't wait until this deal is final, even though it'll mean more work for me after we sign. But it will be a big boost for the business."

Debbie could hear the excitement in his voice, and it made her excited for him. "I hope it goes well. Will you be at the gym Wednesday night?"

"As far as I know, I will be." He paused. "And don't forget about Easter. I'll pick you up around noon if that's okay."

"I'll be ready. Can you ask your sister if I could bring something?" Debbie asked. She'd been taught by her mother the number one Minnesotan rule of being a guest—never go to a dinner empty-handed.

"She said just to bring yourself. She's excited to meet you."

"I'm looking forward to meeting her too."

He yawned on the other end of the line. Debbie laughed. "Am I boring you?"

"Never. I'm ready to go to sleep. I'll see you on Wednesday," he said, sounding sleepy.

"Okay. Goodnight."

"And Debbie?"

"Yes."

"Thank you for turning my house into a home. I really love

how everything looks."

Her heart did a flip. She loved that he loved it. "You're welcome."

"Goodnight."

"Goodnight," she said softly before hanging up.

Long after she'd turned out the light, Debbie thought about Marc and how easy their friendship felt. She wondered if it could turn into something more. Or if she wanted it to. All she knew for sure was she enjoyed Marc's company, even though women seemed to flirt endlessly with him. What she didn't know for certain was if she could trust him completely with her heart.

But then, she'd never know unless she tried.

Chapter Seventeen

Marc showed up at Debbie's door exactly at noon on Easter Sunday. She answered wearing a deep blue floral print dress that had a fitted top and full skirt. It looked great on her, especially the color since it accentuated her beautiful eyes. Her curly hair was half up, half down and tumbled around her shoulders. He wondered if her hair felt as silky as it looked but refrained from touching a rogue curl with his fingers.

That would be weird, right? he thought. *Yeah, definitely weird.* And the last thing he wanted was to act like Kyle. His manager wouldn't even hesitate to touch someone's hair without asking. Just the thought of Kyle made him angry. The day after Marc's conversation with Debbie, he'd stormed into work and had Kyle follow him into the office where he'd told Kyle in no uncertain terms to never speak to Debbie in any way, shape, or form. And to also watch his mouth around the women who came into the gym.

"Cripes. What's gotten into you?" Kyle had asked. "I only offered to help her work out."

"Yeah, and I also know that you insinuated all kinds of things that are inappropriate. Like saying I'm in a 'meeting' and making air quotes like I'm actually out with a woman instead.

You have no idea what I do on my own time, so stop making it sound like I'm out with a new girl every night." Marc's anger had increased as he spoke.

"Well, you used to be out every night with a different girl," Kyle had said defensively. "And you used to be a lot nicer, too. I didn't know you had a thing for Debbie. It's not like she's your type."

"How do you know what my type is?" Marc had asked, incensed. "And why is it any of your business? Just leave her alone, watch how you talk to women, and stop making shit up, okay?"

Kyle had angrily left the room, muttering something about how he could get a job somewhere else if he wanted to. Marc wished he would. Kyle had worked for him a long time, but he'd changed into a jerk over the years. He'd be thrilled if Kyle left.

"Earth to Marc," Debbie said, staring at him strangely. "What are you spacing out about?"

Marc refocused his attention on Debbie. "Sorry. I was lost a moment. You look great. Are you ready to go?"

"Yes. Just give me a moment to pack up Chloe," she said.

"Pack up Chloe? In a suitcase?" Marc followed her into the house and closed the door.

She laughed. "Sort of." She picked up a cloth carrier and set Chloe inside, partially zipping up the top. Chloe popped her head out but didn't try to wriggle out completely. "She's safer in this, and if she gets anxious at your sister's house, she'll feel more relaxed in her own little space."

Marc chuckled. "I'm sure she'll love being at the house. And Bernie will be there to help her feel safe."

Debbie smiled over at Marc. "Is that what Bernie does? Makes girl dogs feel safe?"

He couldn't help but smile. He loved it when they teased each other. "Isn't that what any self-respecting male should do?"

She rolled her eyes. "Sweet, but very archaic, don't you think?"

Marc shrugged. "Probably. But I'd like to think that you feel safe with me."

Debbie cocked her head. "Am I? Safe with you, I mean?"

Marc studied her, wondering if she was teasing or serious. It was sometimes hard to tell. "Of course."

She just smiled, and her blue eyes twinkled. "Chloe and I are ready. Lead the way."

Marc offered to carry Chloe's bag, and they walked out to his SUV. Bernie was in the very back, lying down, so Marc set Chloe's bag on the back seat and ran the seatbelt through the strap. Then they headed out.

"You know, you've never told me anything about your sister other than she's married and has a two-year-old," Debbie said as she smoothed out her skirt.

"Her name is Dawn, and her husband is Craig. She's four years younger than me, but you wouldn't know it by the way she bosses me around." He chuckled. "Of course, I let her because she's my baby sister."

"Does she work?" Debbie asked.

"She did until Austin was born. She was a veterinary technician. She loves animals, but strangely enough, they don't have any. Craig is a pharmacist at a clinic not far from their home. They have a very nice house in Eden Prairie."

"What suburb did you grow up in?" Debbie asked.

"I was afraid you'd ask that." Marc weaved in and out of traffic on the freeway. "Don't hold it against me, but I grew up in Edina."

"Ah. So you were a rich kid who grew up to be a rich adult, huh?" She gave him a teasing smile.

"Not exactly a rich kid. We lived a very middle-class lifestyle. My dad was a lawyer and my mom was a grade-school teacher. I never really fit in with the rich kids in school. My friends were more down to earth."

"That's interesting," Debbie said. "I had you pegged as the high-school football star or at least the star basketball player. Prom king, too."

Marc snorted. "Boy, did you have me pegged wrong. I was in the Chess club and on the school newspaper. You can't get much nerdier than that."

She glanced over at him as if trying to figure out if he was telling the truth, but didn't say anything. Marc maneuvered through the traffic, and soon the sign for Eden Prairie appeared.

"Be prepared to go off your diet and gain five pounds today," Marc said. "My sister will put on the works—lots of food and cookies and cake. I'd weigh a ton if I ate there all the time. I don't know how she stays so slender."

"She runs around after a toddler all day." She smiled, and her eyes looked dreamy.

"What were you just thinking?" Marc asked, glancing over at her.

"Oh, nothing. It's just that everyone in my neighborhood has little children, and they're all so adorable. I wonder what it's like, having a little person to take care of. I'm sure it's a lot of work, but so rewarding to raise a child, too."

"So, how many children do you want?" Marc asked.

Debbie looked up at him, startled. "How many? I was thinking of only one. I can't imagine having a whole brood."

"I think two is good. One of each—a boy and a girl. Of

course, you can't plan it that way, but that would be perfect."

Marc felt Debbie's eyes on him, but he kept his on the road. He'd never opened up about having children with anyone before, not even Alyssa. He'd known all along that Alyssa hadn't wanted children, which had been disappointing to him.

"A miniature Marc," Debbie said. "Hmm. I suppose he'd have wavy hair and wear workout clothes all the time." She grinned.

"Yep. And a little Debbie with long curly blond hair and big blue eyes that all the boys will fall in love with. I'll be beating them off with a stick," he said.

Her brows lifted. "You?"

"Oh, well, uh, we were just pretending, right?" He couldn't believe he'd said that out loud. But in truth, he liked the idea of a little girl like Debbie. She'd be adorable, just like her mom.

Marc finally exited the freeway and pulled off into a neighborhood of lovely homes that weren't exactly new but not old either. He stopped in front of a tan, two-story house with brown trim and shutters and a beautiful large oak tree in the front yard.

"Here we are," he announced as Debbie studied the house out her window. "Ready to meet the troops?"

"As ready as I'll ever be," she said.

He let Bernie out of the back of the SUV and then lifted Chloe's carrier. Bernie ran ahead to the front door, definitely not a stranger to the house. Dawn was standing at the door with Austin in her arms, waiting for them.

"Bernie!" Dawn said, greeting the dog. Bernie ran past her and right to the living room where he found a cushy rug to lay on. "And you must be Debbie," Dawn said. She reached out and gave her a one-armed hug, which looked like it took Debbie by surprise. "It's so great to meet you." She was taller than Debbie and had a slender build with shoulder-length blond hair and hazel-blue eyes.

Debbie smiled warmly. "I'm happy to meet you, too. This must be Austin."

"It is. Can you say hi to Uncle Marc's friend?" Dawn asked Austin.

The little boy dropped his head into his mother's shoulder. "He's usually shy around new people," Dawn explained. "But he'll warm up to you soon."

"What about me? Is anyone going to notice I'm standing here?" Marc said with a smirk.

"Hello, big brother." Dawn gave him a side hug too. "Did you bring your overnight bag?" She pointed to Chloe's floral carrier.

"Very funny," Marc said. "This is her royal princess, Chloe. She came to visit for the day."

Austin lifted his head and smiled wide at his uncle. "Uncle Marc!" he said, reaching for him.

Debbie took the carrier from Marc so he could hold his nephew. He lifted him up and stepped deeper inside the entryway, spinning the boy around in circles. The little boy squealed with laughter.

"Don't make him sick before dinner," Dawn said. She turned to Debbie. "Come in. Make yourself at home. I'm sure Chloe would like to get out and investigate."

Debbie walked in, and Dawn took her jacket and Marc's as well. They stepped into a large living room that had a vaulted ceiling and was open into the kitchen. Debbie brought Chloe to the kitchen to let her out on the tile floor.

"Puppy!" Austin yelled with delight when he saw the little white dog. Marc had set Austin down, and the little boy ran to touch the dog.

"Careful, Austin," Dawn cautioned. "The doggie doesn't know you yet. Don't just grab at her."

Debbie knelt next to Chloe as Austin approached. "She's pretty mild with new people," she said. "I have her in the shop with me all the time. Strangers are always petting her."

Austin reached out and touched the dog, then giggled. "Soft," he said. He sat on the floor next to Chloe and ran his hand up and down her back.

"Good job, Austin," Marc said. "Pet her nice, and she'll be you're best friend."

Bernie came into the kitchen to see what was going on. Austin grabbed Bernie's head and pulled the dog to him. "Bernie!"

Debbie laughed. "I guess Bernie is used to playing with Austin."

"Bernie is a big old softy," Marc said. He looked slyly over at Debbie. "And you thought he'd eat Chloe when we first met," he teased.

Debbie reddened. "Don't remind me."

"Oh, I have to hear that story," Dawn said. "As soon as I check on the food. You two go into the living room and get comfortable. I'll be right in." She turned toward the back of the house. "Craig! Everyone's here."

Craig walked in from somewhere in the back of the house. "Sorry. I was just getting some beer out of the fridge in the back porch," he said, smiling. He was a good-looking, tall man with sandy hair and blue eyes. He set the bottles of beer on the counter and walked over to Debbie. "Hi. It's nice to meet you finally."

He and Debbie shook hands as she gave Marc a side-glance and mouthed the word *finally?* "Nice to meet you, too," she told Craig.

He greeted Marc, then asked, "Who wants a beer?"

Marc took one, but Debbie declined.

"Water or soda?" Dawn asked her. Debbie chose water, and they all went into the living room to sit down. Chloe followed Debbie, and Austin did also so he could sit by the small dog.

"Marc told me you own a bridal shop," Dawn said to Debbie. "That must be fun, being around all those beautiful gowns and helping women with their dream wedding."

"It is," Debbie said, nodding. "It's work, though, too. Especially now, when prom and wedding season collide. Once we get through the middle of May, it'll be a little easier to manage when prom is over."

"I didn't think of prom, too," Dawn said. "That would be crazy."

The conversation flowed between the two couples, and in-between, Austin climbed all over Marc, and the two rolled around on the floor, making Debbie laugh. Chloe and Bernie found a corner together where they would be safe and promptly fell asleep. It was the perfect family gathering, and Marc was enjoying every minute of it. It was the first time in years he'd brought someone who actually seemed to be enjoying herself. Alyssa had always complained about having to spend time with his "boring" sister, and that had caused a few fights between them. But Debbie seemed to get along with Dawn quite well and the two women talked about many things that interested them.

Soon, the food was ready, and Debbie and Marc helped Dawn bring the food to the table while Craig poured drinks and set Austin in his high-chair. They sat down to a meal of ham, mashed potatoes, yams, green beans, coleslaw, and biscuits as well as a plate of raw vegetables and dip. Just as Marc had warned Debbie, it was a lot of food, but it all looked delicious.

Once everyone had filled their plates, Dawn said, "Tell me how you two met. Marc said it was comical, so I want to hear every detail."

Debbie looked at Marc. "You tell it."

"Okay. Well, it was early March and there was still ice on the pathways around Lake Harriet. I was running with Bernie and not paying attention to where I was going, and suddenly I looked up, and there was a bundled-up person on a bike heading right at me. I jumped out of the way and pulled Bernie with me and the next thing I saw was the bundle of clothes on the ground."

"Bundle of clothes?" Debbie said, frowning. "Is that how you thought of me that first day?"

"Well, you did have a big heavy coat on and a cap and scarf. All I saw when you looked up at me were your big blue eyes."

"I sound like a crazy cartoon character," Debbie said, but she couldn't help but laugh along with everyone else. "And I'm sure I looked like one," she agreed.

Marc smiled at her. "No, you didn't. I felt terrible. I tried to help you up, but then Bernie came running toward you to help, too, and scared you to death. You fell down again, remember? You asked if Bernie was a bear."

Dawn laughed so hard, she nearly choked on her food. "He looks like a bear, so I don't blame you a bit."

"Thank you," Debbie said. She turned to Marc. "Then, that's when I realized Chloe was missing from the basket on my bike and I freaked out."

"Oh, no! Poor Chloe. Was she okay?" Dawn asked.

"She was fine," Marc answered. "She'd hid in a bush, and Debbie freaked out when Bernie started sniffing around looking for Chloe. What did you say? 'Your monster dog is eating my dog!'"

"I didn't say that." Debbie playfully hit his arm. "I said your dog was attacking poor Chloe. And if I remember right, you called my dog a 'puffball' and said she wasn't a dog. You pointed to Bernie and said, 'That's a dog.'"

By now, everyone at the table was laughing hysterically. "I can hear him saying that," Dawn said. "He thinks his dog is a normal-sized dog. But as sweet as Bernie is, he is a monster."

"He's a gentle giant," Marc said, defending his dog. But he was laughing too. Thinking back to that first day he met Debbie made him feel warm inside. It was one of the best things that had ever happened to him.

"So how did you go from arguing over the size of your dogs to Debbie decorating your house?" Craig asked. "If I'd been her, I wouldn't have ever talked to you again."

Marc looked over at Debbie and raised his brows in question. She shrugged, so he took it as she didn't mind his telling the whole story. "Debbie was trying to exercise to tone up that day, so I invited her to visit the gym and try it. After I saw the antique display cabinets in her bridal shop, I took her to my house to show her how it looked and asked if she could help me pick out antique furniture. So, we're helping each other. I'm her trainer and she's my decorator."

Dawn smiled. "I love stories like that. It's adorable how you two met. What a great way to start a relationship." She sighed dreamily.

Debbie turned to Marc, looking startled. It was his turn to shrug. He'd told his sister before that they weren't in a relationship, but she hadn't believed him. "We're not in a relationship," he protested. "We're just friends."

"Of course you're in a relationship," Dawn said. "You see each other practically every day, and you're shopping together to make your house a home. That sounds like a relationship to me."

Marc tried to ignore the stunned look on Debbie's face. It was no use arguing with his sister, and to tell the truth, he liked the idea of being in a relationship with Debbie. He wasn't so sure she liked that idea, though.

Chapter Eighteen

Debbie helped Dawn clear the table while Marc and Craig took Austin outside to the back yard to play with Bernie and Chloe. Debbie watched as Marc ran around with the little boy and then lifted him in the air and spun him around in circles until he squealed. Marc was really good with children, and that both surprised her and warmed her heart. But then, he got along with everyone, so she shouldn't be surprised he'd be good with children too.

"He's a great guy," Dawn said, following her gaze to Marc. "I'm glad he's found you. You two are perfect for each other."

Once again, Debbie was shocked by Dawn's remark. "Uh, I'm not sure what Marc has told you, but we aren't a couple. We're just friends."

Dawn smiled knowingly. "Right. Marc said that too. But his eyes light up when he talks about you, and I've been to his house and have seen the beautiful things you've helped him pick out. You have amazing taste, by the way. He also talks about you all the time. That sounds like more than friends to me."

Debbie was surprised to hear that Marc had talked about her with his sister. Yet, it secretly made her happy, too.

"And I hear he's attending a wedding with you in the

Bahamas. That sounds magical. It seems to me that you don't go all the way to the Bahamas just for a *friend*." Dawn winked conspiratorially at her, and Debbie felt her face flush. It was hard to argue with that logic. Debbie didn't want to ruin Dawn's fun by telling her that the Bahama trip was part of the deal between them.

Debbie helped scoop leftovers into Tupperware bowls and place dishes in the dishwasher. She then pulled down the dessert plates while Dawn cut Angel food cake and set out the strawberries and whipped cream. Everything looked delicious.

"You know," Dawn said, turning serious. "You're the only woman Marc has talked about or brought to a family dinner since Alyssa. He may not know it yet, or you either, but he's serious about you. I hope you are about him, too. I'd hate to see his heart get broken again."

"I wouldn't do that to him," Debbie said, and Dawn smiled and nodded.

As Dawn moved around the kitchen, Debbie walked into the attached family room where the French doors led to the deck outside. She saw family pictures on a side table and went to look at them. There were ones of Craig, Dawn, and Austin, and plenty of Austin from the past two years. Next to those was an older, slightly faded picture of a little blond girl next to a chubby brown-haired boy. Another larger photo showed parents with the same two children. She realized that it must be Marc's parents with him and Dawn as kids.

Dawn came over to Debbie. "Cute, huh? That's us with our parents a long time ago. Back when Marc was a chub." She laughed.

"Must have been before he became health-conscious," Debbie said lightly.

"Way before. Poor guy. He was overweight all through school and didn't even go to the senior prom. I don't think he had one date in high school."

Debbie turned to Dawn, completely stunned. "Marc? Really? He said he was in Chess club, but I thought he was kidding."

Dawn shook her head. "Nope. It's true. Here, look." She opened the cabinet underneath the table and pulled out a framed picture. "I had this out until Marc told me to hide it. It's his high school graduation picture." She handed it to Debbie.

The boy she saw in the photo looked nothing like the man he'd become. He was quite chubby and had hair down to his shoulders. But his eyes were the same with that familiar twinkle in them. She looked at Dawn. "When did he become the fitness king?"

"In college. He started running in freshman year and lost weight. He was even recruited by the coach for the track team." She grinned. "And he finally had his first date."

Debbie gazed down at the photo of him again. She could relate to how he'd felt. She hadn't dated in high school either. Her whole perspective on who she'd thought Marc was suddenly changed.

Dawn took the photo and placed it back inside the cabinet. "Don't tell Marc I showed you that picture. He'd have a fit." She smiled. "But then, that's what little sisters are for."

Debbie laughed. She really liked Dawn. She was as nice and as full of mischief as Marc.

That evening as they rode back to Debbie's house with the dogs all snuggled up in the back, Debbie spoke up. "I like your sister. She's great. She and Craig are down-to-earth like the couples in my neighborhood."

"She is great," Marc said. "And isn't Austin adorable? I have so much fun with him."

She smiled. "I saw you acting like a two-year-old outside. Yes, he's a sweetie. You have a wonderful family."

"I knew you'd like them. They like you, too." Marc grew more serious. "And about that stuff my sister said. About us being a couple? I never told her we were. Not that it would be a bad thing," he added hastily, looking in her direction.

"That's okay. I can see why she thinks it. We do spend a lot of time together, and she even knows you're going to the Bahamas with me. I guess it would sound like we're dating."

"As I said," he added, his voice husky. "It wouldn't be a bad thing, us being a couple."

Debbie could feel the heat rising to her face. She swallowed hard. She had no idea how to respond to that. *Why do I always get tongue-tied in times like this?* It drove her crazy.

Marc pulled his car up in front of Debbie's house, and they sat in silence a moment. Finally, she turned to him. "I get it now why you tell me not to call myself fat or put myself down," she said softly. "You understand how it feels to be self-conscious about how you look."

Marc grimaced. "Dawn showed you my high school graduation picture, didn't she? Ugh!" Then he smiled. "Yes, I know how it feels. I wasn't lying when I said I was in Chess club in high school and on the school newspaper. I was the smart best friend, but never the boyfriend. I learned to be funny and extra nice to cover for how I felt about myself. In many ways, I'm still like that. That's probably why I'm nice to the women who flirt with me at the fitness center and I can't seem to separate being nice from flirting. I've been working on it, though."

"Even after all you've accomplished, you still feel self-conscious sometimes?" Debbie asked, stunned by his admission.

"Sometimes. I think we always carry that lost teenager inside us no matter how many years have gone by and no matter who we become. But I've worked hard to build up my confidence, just as you have, too. I've seen you change over the past few weeks. And even though I liked you before, I think you like yourself a lot more now. Am I right?" He looked at her expectantly.

He was right, Debbie knew that. She did feel better about herself and more confident, but getting in shape wasn't the only reason. It was because she'd found out she was capable of doing so much more than she'd realized before. "I do feel better about myself," she admitted. "And I've grown as a person. I guess I needed that one person to encourage me."

"Happy to help," he said, his eyes twinkling.

They sat in the dark car with only the dome light on, gazing into each other's eyes. Debbie's heart skipped as Marc drew nearer. He was going to kiss her, and she wanted him to. Just as he was only inches from her face, Bernie let out a loud, deep bark. They both startled and moved apart quickly.

Debbie looked out the window and saw Lisa and Avery walking past with Abby bundled up in her wagon. She quickly rolled it down.

"Sorry," Lisa said. "We were going home after having Easter dinner at Kristen and Ryan's house. We didn't mean to startle the dog."

"No, that's fine," Debbie said, her heart still pounding from Bernie scaring her. "Did you have a nice dinner?"

"Yes. It was fun. How about you?" She bent down to see who Debbie was with. "Did you two have a good time?"

Debbie introduced Lisa and Avery to Marc. "We did. His family is wonderful. And his sister is a great cook. It was a nice day."

"That's wonderful. Well, you two go back to what you were

doing. Goodnight." Lisa hurried off as Avery chuckled.

Debbie shook her head. "My neighbors can be nosy sometimes. But it's a good nosy."

"They seemed nice. It's good to have people like them around you. Are they the ones getting married soon?"

Debbie nodded. "If you'd like to come to the wedding, you can go with me. James and Mallory and the whole neighborhood will be there." She held her breath. It wasn't like her to invite men on dates, especially to someone's wedding. Well, except for the one in the Bahamas.

"I think that would be fun. Count me in," he said, smiling.

"Okay, but you've been warned. Once you get wrapped up in this neighborhood, they may never let you go."

"I can't think of anything better," he said.

Debbie's heart gave a little thud.

"Are we still on for shopping tomorrow?" Marc asked.

"Sure. We'll wander a few antique stores and see what we can find. Lindsay came up with a good idea for a china pattern. We'll see if we can find something nice."

"I'm game," he said. They both got out, and Marc carried Chloe to the door. The entire time, Debbie wondered if he'd try to kiss her again. But unfortunately, he didn't.

"See you tomorrow," he said once she'd stepped inside the house.

"Goodnight." She watched Marc walk back to the car, then closed the door. Letting Chloe out of her carrier, Debbie picked up the dog and hugged her. So much had happened that day that Debbie could barely wrap her head around it. After learning more about Marc's past, she felt closer to him. And she no longer resented his telling her to be easy on herself. He understood her. Not even her mother, who she'd loved dearly, had understood

Debbie's lack of confidence. But Marc did, and it felt wonderful to be understood.

"A snack for you, then bed," Debbie told Chloe. It had been a long day, and she was exhausted. But it was a good exhausted. She smiled to herself as she carried Chloe to the kitchen to feed her.

* * *

The next morning, Marc's spirits were high the entire time he was running through the park with Bernie. His earbuds were on, and high energy music was playing but he barely noticed it. All he kept thinking about was Debbie.

He was happy he'd invited her to his sister's for Easter, despite Dawn showing Debbie his high school photo. Debbie and Dawn had gotten along well, and they'd all had a great time. That was important to Marc. Alyssa had never enjoyed family get-togethers, and that had always been a bone of contention between them. But Debbie fit right in and seemed comfortable with everyone. It was just one more thing that made him like her even more.

Like? Or Love? He nearly tripped over his feet when that thought popped into his head. Over the past few weeks, the word *love* had come into his mind when he thought of Debbie. He *loved* going antique shopping with her. He also *loved* it when she teased him, which she did quite often. He *loved* it when she smiled at him and her blue eyes sparkled or when he embarrassed her and she blushed. No one blushed anymore, except Debbie. Just thinking about it made him smile.

He had strong feelings for Debbie, that was for certain, but was it love? The word warmed his heart and scared him to death all at the same time.

Marc and Bernie headed home, and he showered before leaving to pick Debbie up. As he sat in his car, he remembered last night, and his goofy smile returned. He'd almost kissed her—they were so close—until Bernie barked and startled them. Would he have regretted the kiss? Marc hoped not. Because he really wanted to kiss Debbie. But it had to be the right moment. And it had to be serious. Debbie wasn't the type of girl you just flirted with. She was the real deal and if he kissed her, it would be because he was all in.

He couldn't remember when he'd felt this serious about anyone. That had been one of the problems with his relationship with Alyssa. They'd never been serious. Everything had been fun and games and playing house. He no longer wanted to play house. He wanted a long-term commitment with someone he could love forever.

Could that someone be Debbie?

It was drizzling outside when he met her at the door. She smiled sweetly and looked adorable in her jeans, light sweater, and red spring jacket. Her hair was pulled back in a French braid. She grabbed a red umbrella from the stand next to the door.

"My hair frizzes like crazy in the rain," she said, grimacing. "But, I'll risk it for you." She grinned, and he couldn't help but smile back.

"Let's go," he said, and they both ran out to the car.

They spent the morning browsing antique shops. Cute little items caught their eye as well as funny things.

"How about this suit of armor," Marc said, looking serious.

Debbie's brows shot up, but she stayed calm. "Do you have a castle somewhere that I'm not aware of?"

"No. But we could put it in the entryway. What do you think?"

"Great idea," she said. "I'll go tell the clerk you want it." She headed away, and Marc laughed, taking ahold of her arm and gently swinging her around to face him.

"Okay. You called my bluff. But it is cool, isn't it?"

Debbie laughed. "For a twelve-year-old boy or a king, maybe."

As they stepped into a shop filled with cabinets of antique china, Marc's phone buzzed. He pulled it out of his pocket and glanced at the screen. Seeing it was from Melinda, he told Debbie he had to take it and walked outside, under the awning.

"Hi, Melinda. What's up?" he asked, hoping that she was finally going to tell him that their fitness plan for McGregory Medical Supply was a go.

"Something's happened, I'm afraid," Melinda said. "Now the board wants to look at a bid by another local fitness company. I don't know how this happened since we were keeping this under wraps. Somehow, this other company heard about our offer to you and complained to a board member that it's only fair they get to bid too. Now the board is afraid of being sued if they don't at least look at it. I'm so sorry, Marc."

Marc stood there, stunned, as the rain droplets fell off the awning in front of him. "How could this have happened? I thought you came to me exclusively because you liked my idea of the twenty-minute fitness plan. I never said a word to anyone. Could a board member have sabotaged this?"

"I'm not sure, but I don't think a board member would have," Melinda said. "They all seemed to like your ideas. If I find out anything about how this happened, I'll let you know. Until then, our contract is on hold until the board hears ideas from the other company. I'm sorry. Hopefully, they will see fit to go with your company in the end."

"All right. Thank you, Melinda. Please keep me in the loop." Marc shut off the call and slid his phone back into his pocket. He had no idea how this could have happened. But somehow, word had leaked out. And now, he might lose the bid on this project. Sighing, he turned and walked back inside the store. He saw Debbie at the other end, waving him over, so he headed that way.

"Look at what I've found!" she said excitedly. "This china would be perfect for your dining room." She pointed to the open hutch where the dishes sat. They were white, trimmed in black, and had a gold design swirling over the black. "They're masculine yet elegant. What do you think?" She looked up at him expectantly, but her smile faded when she saw his face.

"Oh. You don't like them," she said.

"No. I do like the dishes. You're right; they'd look wonderful in the dining room. And they have an art deco flair to them, so they'd go well with the period." He tried to sound upbeat, but his mind was on only one thing—the botched deal.

Debbie cocked her head and studied him. "Did something happen? Was it the call you just answered?"

Marc wanted nothing more than to confide in Debbie and tell her what had happened, but he couldn't tell her everything. And definitely not here. "I'll tell you about it later," he said. "Maybe we can grab a bite to eat somewhere."

Debbie looked at her watch. "It's already one. Let's go now. I saw a little café down the street."

"What about the china?"

"It'll be here another day. Or we'll find it somewhere else. Right now, whatever is upsetting you is more important than china," Debbie said matter-of-factly. She linked her arm through his and smiled up at him. "Let's have lunch. You're buying."

Marc grinned. The rain had stopped, so they walked down

the street to the café without the umbrella. Once they were tucked away in a corner booth and had ordered drinks and sandwiches, Debbie leaned in close.

"Tell me what's bothering you."

"That call was from the lead on the project I was working on. Somehow, another fitness company heard about the deal we were discussing and asked to be allowed to place a bid too. The board decided that they would let them, even though they had approached me exclusively. Now, after all the time I've put into this, I could lose it."

Debbie's face softened. "I'm so sorry. I know you've been working hard on it. It's weird, though, that another company heard about the deal. Who would have told them?"

He shook his head. "I have no idea. It wasn't me, that's for sure. I haven't told a soul what is going on except you, and I never gave any details. I wouldn't be surprised if a board member mentioned it to someone. That happens. But I guess it doesn't matter now. All I can do is hope they vote to choose my company."

She reached across the table and took his hands. "They will choose you. I have no doubt. They came to you first, so there was something they liked specifically about your company. In the end, they won't be able to resist you or your business." She grinned.

"Oh, so I'm irresistible?" he asked, waggling his eyebrows.

"Sure, you are. Sometimes." She laughed.

By the time their meals had arrived, Marc felt a little better. Debbie was right. They'd approached him first, so why would they go with the other company? And, if they did, well, it wasn't the end of the world. He had a good business with or without their offer.

"Thanks for making me feel better," he said after they'd

eaten and left the café. "I'm not going to worry about it. What happens happens."

"That's a great attitude," she said. "But they'll choose you. You wait and see."

Marc reached for her hand as they walked to the car. "Look at you, being all confident about the future. I appreciate the pep talk. I needed it."

Debbie grinned. "It's easy to be positive when I'm with you. I guess you've been rubbing off on me."

Again, his brows shot up comically. "Rubbing?"

Debbie's face turned a deep shade of pink. "You're incorrigible. You've been hanging around Kyle too long."

As he slid behind the wheel, a thought hit him. Kyle? He tried to think if he'd said anything to Kyle about the deal, but he absolutely hadn't talked to anyone about it. Still, Kyle's name sat on the edge of his mind.

Chapter Nineteen

The next week flew by for Debbie. She and Lindsay were in the thick of prom season, and women were coming for their second and third fittings for bridal gowns. Debbie attended yoga class on Monday night again and enjoyed it. Marc teased her mercilessly about her initially stating she hated yoga. "See what happens when you try something new?" he said. She didn't mind his teasing. She was toning up and that made her happy. Every day as she dressed for work, her clothes were a little looser. She'd have to start taking pants and skirts in, and even though she hated doing alterations, she was thrilled to do it for her own clothes.

Marc missed Wednesday and Friday nights at the gym because of more meetings. He'd told her that a few of the board members wanted to speak with him in a casual setting outside the board room. Debbie thought that was a good sign. It meant they were still interested.

On Sunday, they returned to the antique china shop and bought the entire set of black and white place settings. "I'm not sure when I'll ever use them," he said, "but they'll look great in the hutch."

Debbie laughed. "That's an awful lot of money to spend on dust collectors for the hutch. Maybe you can invite your sister and her family over for dinner sometime."

"Are you going to cook?" he asked. "Because no one wants to eat what I make."

"We'll see," she said slyly.

Marc wasn't able to go shopping on Monday because he had to deal with issues at one of his fitness centers. A manager had insulted a client, and Marc fired him. So he spent the day there, sorting things out for the new manager to step in. Debbie went into her shop that day and worked on easy alterations again. Lindsay worked at Gallagher's that day, so Debbie had the shop all to herself.

As she sat in the back room, she thought a lot about her mother and the memories of watching Gladys doing this very same thing—sewing and repairing dresses. Debbie had so many good memories of her mother and the shop, but as she expertly ran the needle through the filmy fabric, she realized she didn't want to do this for the rest of her life. More and more, Mallory's offer of working alongside her in her design and staging business sounded more enticing. Debbie had even gone so far as to ask Mallory how they would manage it if she were to join her. The two had discussed the business for two hours and had come up with a workable plan—that is, if Debbie decided to take the plunge. Debbie could start by working with Mallory two days a week to see how it went. If it worked out well, she could come in full-time as a partial partner. Mallory's younger sister, Amber, also worked in the business, and Debbie got along well with her. She just had to make the decision to do it. But that was the hardest part. Debbie hoped to discuss her concerns with Marc the next time she saw him. He had a level head about business, and she respected his opinion.

After spin class on Wednesday, Debbie sought out Marc

and found him helping an older woman learn to operate the treadmill. She smiled as she watched him. He was so patient and kind, and the woman looked grateful for his help. That's what made his business so successful. No one felt like a newbie when they came here—they were treated with kindness and respect.

"Ready for the weight machine?" Marc asked after he had finished helping the woman. Debbie nodded, and they walked past the older woman to get to the machine.

"Your boyfriend is the nicest person," the woman said to Debbie. "He's a keeper."

Debbie stopped short. *Boyfriend?* She caught herself and smiled at the woman, then went to where Marc was waiting.

"I hear I'm a keeper," Marc said when Debbie sat on the weight bench.

She looked at him with wide eyes. "Did you tell her you were my boyfriend?"

"No," he chuckled. "But she's been in here before, and I suppose she's seen me working with you. She just assumed we were together. She was telling me how cute you were and how I'd better not let you get away."

Debbie laughed. "Oh, my goodness. We're the talk of the gym."

Marc set up the machine, and Debbie began pulling. It was harder tonight, but she was able to lift the weights without straining. "You must have added more weight," she said after a time.

"I've been adding weight all along," he said. "I just never told you because I figured you'd think you couldn't do it."

"Really?" Debbie was surprised. "No wonder it's a lot easier when I set the machine."

After they were done with the weights and stretching, Debbie asked if he had a few minutes to talk.

"Sure. Let's go to my office."

Bernie raised his head when they entered, and Debbie pet him behind the ears. "Hey, Bernie. You should be out on the floor, helping people."

"Scaring people would be more like it," Marc said. "Like he scared you that first time." Marc grabbed two bottles of water from his refrigerator and handed her one. She drank it thirstily.

"Those look good on you," he said, nodding to the blue workout outfit she'd worn. "I think you need a couple of more sets."

She grinned. "Thanks, but you can't keep giving me free clothes. What will the staff think?"

"Probably that I like you." He winked.

"Stop being silly. I have something serious to discuss," Debbie said, but she smiled. She liked it when he flirted with her.

"I'm all ears."

"I had a long conversation with Mallory about the possibility of working with her in her business. She really believes there's a niche for me helping clients shop for antiques to decorate their homes. I'd love to do it, but I'm still not completely sure. What do you think?"

"I think it's worth trying," he said. "You're knowledgeable about antiques, and you love doing it. It's a no-brainer."

"Yeah, but what if I can't make enough money or I run out of clients?"

"Couldn't you also help with regular decorating clients too? I thought Mallory said she was super busy and had to turn away clients."

Debbie bit her lip. "I could. But I don't feel as confident about that as I do with antiques."

Marc leaned back against his desk and nodded for Debbie to

sit down. "Isn't that what you do at the bridal shop? Match the women with the style of dress they want? Or the right color for the person? That's a thing, right? Where people look better in some colors than others?"

Debbie gave a small laugh. "Yes, that's a thing. But I've been doing that forever. It's second nature to me."

"I think matching furniture styles and colors with clients would be similar."

"I don't know," Debbie said. "Mallory suggested I work a couple of days a week, and we can see how much business we draw in. I could manage that by hiring another worker at the shop and letting Lindsay manage the store when I'm not there. But to sell my shop and do it full-time scares me."

Marc smiled warmly. "Then that's what you should do. You can build up your clientele slowly and see how it goes. I have a feeling that most people won't be like me and want to buy all their antiques at once. You'll probably have clients who'll keep coming back for help finding a piece here and there as well as those looking for many pieces. You might be surprised just how busy you'll be after a few months."

She nodded. It was what she'd been thinking too. She just had to make herself take that first step.

"So? What are you thinking?" he asked.

Her eyes met his. "I'm going to try working part-time. I have to try at least. If it flops, then I'll still have the shop."

"And if it's a success, you'll be doing something you love."

"Think positive, right?" she said, standing up. She felt like a weight had been dropped off her shoulders. She'd finally decided to try, and she was excited about it.

"Yes. Think positive." Marc took a step toward her.

"Thank you. Your belief in me helped me make the decision.

I don't think I would ever have tried this if I hadn't met you and you hadn't encouraged me every step of the way." Without even thinking twice about it, Debbie reached out and hugged Marc. His arms encircled her, too, and she fit up against his shoulder perfectly. She could smell his musky cologne and the light scent of his shampoo. She liked being in his arms. It felt good.

"You're welcome," he whispered into her ear. "I'll do anything for a hug."

Debbie pulled away and laughed nervously. She wasn't sure what was going on between them, but she wouldn't have minded if they became more than just friends. In the short time she'd known Marc, she'd grown to depend on him and trust him. And that was saying a lot for her.

As her eyes dropped to his desk, her smile suddenly faded.

"Oh, oh. What now? Did I say something wrong?" Marc asked, looking distressed.

"No, not at all. I was just looking at your desk. I see you have file folders lying open. It made me wonder, do you lock your office when you're not in here?"

Marc shook his head. "No. Sometimes Kyle or Mandy needs to come in here to get change for the register or put the money in the safe at night. Why?"

Debbie looked up at Marc. "I don't want to blame anyone, but is there a chance someone here saw the proposal on your desk and read it?"

He glanced at his desk as if trying to remember. "I thought I put it away when I wasn't here. But I can't be one hundred percent certain. Even if I closed the file, someone could have dug through it and read it." His eyes returned to Debbie. "Do you think one of them would really do that? Crap! I always thought I could trust my employees."

"I don't know," Debbie said, feeling sick at the thought of someone close to Marc cheating him like that. "It's something to think about. I can't even imagine Mandy would do such a thing."

Marc's expression turned hard. "Yeah, but I can imagine Kyle doing it."

"You can't say anything to him without proof, though."

"No, I can't. But from now on, I'm locking up everything in my desk."

"I'm sorry. Maybe I shouldn't have said anything," Debbie said, worried now that she might have upset Marc over nothing. "It may not have been either of them."

"No. I'm glad you did mention it. I've been too trusting of everyone. I have to stop that. When it comes to business, you can't be too careful. It's sad, though."

Marc walked Debbie out to her car. "I'll see you Friday night," he said. She drove off as he headed back inside. Debbie hoped it wasn't Kyle or Mandy who'd sabotaged Marc's deal. She really couldn't believe that Mandy would do it. But Kyle? Well, she wouldn't put it past him.

She pushed those thoughts aside as she drove home and instead focused on her future. She was excited to start working with Mallory. She couldn't wait to call her.

* * *

Debbie brought up the subject of her working with Mallory to Lindsay in the shop on Tuesday morning.

"So you've finally decided? That's wonderful!" Lindsay said. Then her excitement faded. "Are you going to sell the shop?"

Debbie shook her head. "No, not for a while. Probably not

for a long time. Maybe never. I have to see how it works out with Mallory. This is all so new that even she isn't one hundred percent certain it can be a full-time job."

Lindsay looked relieved. "What are you thinking, then? Would we need to hire a part-time worker or would I run the shop alone on days you aren't here?"

"Mallory is going to put out some feelers and advertise the new service to see what kind of response she gets. We're thinking about two days a week. And I probably wouldn't get started until June or July. So I'm hoping we can hold off on hiring someone until fall. Unless things take off quickly."

Lindsay's face lit up. "I'm so happy for you. I really am. I'm just a little scared of losing this job, but I'm sure we can manage somehow." She pulled Debbie into a hug. "I know you're going to be successful at your new job. It's perfect for you."

Debbie's heart warmed at Lindsay's excitement for her, and it was contagious. She also was suddenly excited about her new opportunity. She studied her employee who she'd known for over ten years. Lindsay looked carefree with her bobbed hair, dangling earrings, and bohemian style of dressing, but the truth was she was always dependable and a good worker. Even at twenty-eight, Debbie would trust her with entirely running the shop.

"Lindsay, have you ever thought of possibly buying this shop if I end up leaving? Would you even consider it?"

"I would love to, but I'm not sure I could manage it. I've saved some money, but not enough by any means to buy the building and business. Although," she wrinkled her nose adorably. "My father once told me he'd be willing to help me go into business if I ever wanted to. I'd hate to borrow from my parents, but it's an idea."

"Well, we'll cross that bridge when we come to it. I mean, I could always try to keep the shop and have you manage it too. Or you and I could be part-owners later on. We'll see how this goes and what happens."

Lindsay beamed and went back to unpacking the dresses that had come in. Debbie's mind was in a whirl. So many ideas were swimming through her head. She had to take things one step at a time and see what happened.

But she was thrilled that she now had options for her future.

Chapter Twenty

On the last day of April, Marc came into the shop with an excited look on his face. Debbie had been helping a woman with wedding dresses, and Lindsay was bagging bridesmaid dresses for a customer.

Debbie excused herself from the customer and walked over to Marc. "What's up?"

He smiled wide. "You have to come with me right now! I need to show you something."

She frowned as she stared at him. What on earth could be so important that she had to drop everything and leave? "Is this about the bedroom set you bought on Monday?" she asked. She knew they were delivering it today, and she wondered if something had happened. He'd spent a hefty sum on the guest room bed, dresser, and nightstands. Hopefully, they hadn't scratched them.

"No. They're fine. Just come with me, okay? I want to show you something."

Debbie glanced behind her and saw the customer beckoning her to come over. "I can't leave right now," she whispered, pulling Marc farther from the dressing rooms. "I'm helping a customer."

Disappointment fell over Marc's face. He looked around,

spotted Chloe in her favorite tufted chair, and walked over there. Picking up the dog, Marc sat and set Chloe in his lap. "Okay. I'll wait right here. But hurry, please?"

Debbie sighed and shook her head. She had no idea what was going on with Marc.

Lindsay waved to Marc and told Debbie she could take over for a while. "The customer won't mind. She's at the beginning stages of looking for a dress. She could be here all afternoon," Lindsay whispered.

Debbie knew that Lindsay was right. "Well, okay. I hate leaving a customer, though. Tell her I had an emergency, so it doesn't sound like I'm just abandoning her."

Lindsay laughed. "Yes. A Marc emergency."

"Okay," Debbie said, approaching Marc. "Let's go see what this emergency is all about."

He set Chloe back on the chair, and they left the store with his arm around her waist. Debbie had worn a blouse and skirt with very high heels today. She'd been pleased when she'd had to pin the skirt to fit her waist this morning. They walked out into the sunshine and got into Marc's SUV.

"Where are we going?" Debbie asked, putting on her seatbelt.

"My house," he said.

"Does this have anything to do with the project you're working on? Did it go through?" she asked, growing excited.

"It's not about that. I wish it were. But it's something you're going to like," he said.

"Are you going to tell me what's going on?"

"Nope. I'll show you when we get there." He turned and winked. She sighed, realizing this wasn't going to be a serious emergency.

They finally parked on the street in front of his house and he ran around the car and offered his hand to help her down.

"Such a gentleman," she said, teasing. To her surprise, he continued to hold her hand as they walked up the steps and down the sidewalk to his door. He opened it, and they went inside.

"Are you going to show me how the guest bedroom turned out?" she asked.

"Not yet. Come on."

Bernie came running when he heard them and followed the couple to the kitchen in the back of the house.

"Okay. You have to close your eyes," Marc said.

"What?"

"Please? Just close your eyes. You'll see why in a moment."

Debbie reluctantly did as he asked. "It's a good thing I trust you," she muttered, which only made him laugh. He led her through the kitchen, and she heard the back door open. Soon, her heels were clicking on the back deck.

"Can I open my eyes?" she asked.

"Not yet."

He led her carefully down the steps and then a little way into the yard. Finally, he said, "Open your eyes."

Debbie did. It took a moment for her eyes to adjust to the light, but when they did, she was standing under an extraordinary canopy of pink and white. Crabapple flowers bloomed everywhere, filling the air with sweetness and the yard with color.

"Oh, my goodness!" She spun around to take it all in. Soft pink, bright pink, and white petals filled the sky. "It's so beautiful!" she exclaimed. She turned and looked up at Marc, who was smiling down at her, obviously thrilled by her reaction.

"I told you it was amazing when they bloomed. And when they start to fall, it rains pink and white petals. It's gorgeous."

His eyes met hers. "Like you."

She smiled up at him, the sweet scent of the blossoms intoxicating. It felt like she was somewhere magical, like a fairyland far, far away. And as Marc gazed down into her eyes, she knew it was the right moment. The perfect moment. He wrapped his arms around her and dropped his lips to hers.

* * *

Feeling Debbie's lips on his was the most magical thing of all for Marc as they stood under the sweet petals and held each other tight. He'd known the minute she'd looked up at him, those big, blue eyes wide with amazement meeting his. If he were ever going to kiss her, it had to be now, under the apple blossoms.

After their first kiss, they parted for only a moment, smiled at each other, then kissed again, this time more passionately. Heat rushed through Marc as he held her closer, wanting, needing to feel her against him. He'd thought about this moment many times but hadn't realized how emotional it would be for him. He was falling completely for Debbie, in a way he'd never fallen for any other woman.

Reluctantly, they parted, and he watched her blush as pink as the blossoms, suddenly turning shy. But he wasn't sorry in the least. He wanted to kiss her a hundred more times, no a thousand. The way he felt right this moment, he knew he never wanted to kiss anyone else but her.

He reached for her and hugged her tight, breathing in the scent of the blooms along with her sweet scent. He'd forever remember this day, the fragrant air and the warmth of her body in his arms, for as long as he lived.

Debbie finally pulled back and gazed tenderly up at him.

"Is this what you've planned all along? To seduce me under the apple blossoms?"

He let out a soft laugh. "No. But then again, yes." He laughed again. "I couldn't help myself. I've wanted to kiss you for a long time, and this seemed right."

She took a breath as if stunned by his words.

"You can't be too surprised that I have feelings for you, can you?" he asked.

She pulled away and walked a few steps away from him before turning around. Bernie was sitting in the grass, watching them with curious eyes. Marc suddenly worried if he'd gone too far too fast. Even Bernie seemed nervous for him.

Debbie looked at him seriously and asked, "Are you teasing me?"

He shook his head. "No. This is real. I feel closer to you than anyone I've ever known." He paused and stepped closer to her. "Is there any chance you have feelings for me too?"

Tears filled her eyes as she whispered, "Yes. I do. I just hadn't allowed myself to believe you felt the same way."

Marc's smile grew wide as he picked her up and swung her in a circle, laughing. She squealed with delight and laughed too, and when he set her down, he kissed her again. A sweet, slow kiss that he felt throughout his entire body.

After a time, they walked hand-in-hand inside with Bernie following behind them.

"I'm so happy you made me come here today," Debbie said, giving him a teasing smile. "The apple blossoms are beautiful."

"I'm glad I made you come over too," he said, kissing the tip of her nose. "Would you like to go out on a real dinner date tonight? I'll call in sick to work."

She chuckled. "Yes. I'd like that. But you'd better take me

back to my shop, or poor Lindsay will go crazy. The last-minute prom girls will be in after three o'clock and it gets busy."

"Okay. If I have to." He pulled her close again and kissed her. He loved kissing her.

Marc drove her back to the shop. "I'll pick you up at seven if that works for you," he said.

"That'll be fine. See you then."

He watched her walk inside, a big smile on his face. A goofy grin, he was sure, but he didn't care. His whole world had changed the second he'd kissed Debbie, and he was thrilled about it. Marc headed to the gym to do some paperwork, and then he'd pick her up tonight. He could hardly wait.

Chapter Twenty-One

Marc picked Debbie up right on time, and she walked out to his car. She'd changed into a deep blue dress with black heels and had a cream sweater slung over her arm for when it became chilly later in the evening.

"You look beautiful," he said, giving her a sweet kiss on the lips. He drove them to an impressive restaurant downtown that sat on the tenth floor of a high-rise building. They were shown to a table beside one of the floor-to-ceiling windows where there was a view of the city, river, and the many bridges that crossed it.

After ordering their drinks, a beer for him and wine for her, the waiter left them to peruse the menu.

"You go all out when you invite a woman to dinner," she said, giving him a mischievous smile. "No little corner pub tonight."

He chuckled. "Only the best for you."

For once, Marc was wearing dress slacks and a button-up shirt and tie instead of his usual workout clothes. She'd only seen him one other time in regular clothes at Easter. He looked handsome dressed up, but she actually preferred the casual Marc. It suited him better.

"I told Lindsay about the apple blossoms in your back yard," Debbie said. "She wants pictures. She even suggested we should take photos of models in wedding gowns in your yard before the blooms fade away. We could blow the pictures up and hang them on the wall or use them in displays every spring."

"That's a good idea. Feel free to come and do that anytime, but you should do it before next week. If we get a windstorm, that will be the end of the petals. They'll be all over the yard."

"That would be great," Debbie said, growing excited. "I know an amateur photographer who'd be willing, and I know the perfect women to ask to model the dresses—Lisa, Kristen, and Mallory. Lindsay too. They would all look beautiful."

"And you," he said. "You'd look lovely in a wedding gown." The flecks in his eyes twinkled.

"Thanks," she said, feeling her face heat up. "But I'm too short. I can supervise instead."

Marc's brows rose. "Too short? Not in heels. You'd look beautiful."

Her eyes dropped to the menu, and she was saved from a response by the waiter. He took their order and left again, and luckily, Marc changed the subject.

"Did you tell Lindsay what you were doing under the apple blossoms?"

"Heavens no!" she said, looking shocked. "I don't kiss and tell."

They spent the evening talking over their delicious dinner and watched the sunset spread golden hues over the city. They touched on every subject from their jobs to their hopes for the future. Debbie told Marc about Lisa's upcoming bridal shower on Saturday and invited him to the groom's dinner a week from Friday. They talked about the week they'd be spending at the resort in Nassau and how they both were looking forward to it.

"And I still have to pay you back for the tickets and room," he reminded her. She said she'd let him know how much as soon as her credit card bill came.

They were so comfortable together and had such a good time that it grew late before they realized it. Finally, they left the restaurant and Marc drove her home.

Marc walked her to her door, and she unlocked it, inviting him in. Debbie was a little nervous he'd think it was an invitation for more than just saying goodbye, but she didn't want to stand on the porch outside for all the neighbors to see.

Marc, however, seemed able to read her thoughts. "It's late," he said, standing in the entryway. "I'll say goodnight here so you can get some sleep."

Debbie was grateful he hadn't asked to stay longer. Not waiting for him to make the first move, she drew closer, and he wrapped his arms around her. "I hope you'll understand if I want to take things slowly," she said, feeling silly about sounding so old-fashioned, yet wanting to be upfront with him.

"I do understand," he said gently. "And I agree. You've been burned before, and you need time to make sure this is the real deal." He smiled. "I do too. I don't want to ruin what we have right now by rushing. We have all the time in the world." He kissed her softly, and she rose up on tiptoe to reach him. She loved his kisses. They were gentle, yet passionate, and her body responded in kind. It was difficult pulling away because she didn't want the kiss to stop.

"Although," he said playfully. "I'm not against kissing you over and over again."

She laughed lightly. "Me either."

"Goodnight," he said, looking cute and rakish all at once.

"Goodnight." She watched him walk down the sidewalk and drive away. After locking the door, she turned to find Chloe sitting there, staring at her.

"Goodness. Have you been watching us this whole time?" She picked the dog up and hugged her tight. "I'm falling fast for Marc," she whispered to Chloe. "I hope you approve."

The dog gave no opinion on the matter.

* * *

The next week flew by for Debbie. She felt lighter than air and happier than she'd ever been before. Marc had waited for her at the gym on Friday night and escorted her to the aerobics class, even though it had been unnecessary and silly. But she didn't mind. She'd found it romantic. Afterward, they'd stretched and talked a bit before he secretly kissed her goodbye behind a tall plant near the locker rooms.

"I don't want everyone to gossip," he said, which made her laugh.

Saturday afternoon, all the women in the neighborhood, along with a few of Lisa's friends, attended a bridal shower for Lisa at Kristen's house. The three little girls, Marie, Abby, and Shannon, were there too. Kristen's husband, Ryan, had taken baby Joshua, now seven weeks old, upstairs to sleep. Debbie noticed that Kristen looked tired but happy.

"I don't know how you managed to put on a shower for Lisa only a few weeks after having Joshua," Debbie told her. "You're definitely a supermom."

Kristen laughed. "I'm no supermom. I could fall asleep in the corner right now. But I love doing this for Lisa. She deserves all the happiness in the world."

Debbie agreed. Lisa had been through a tough time after her first husband left her, but she'd pulled through and now had Avery by her side.

After presents and cake and a lot of silly laughter and fun, Debbie asked her friends if they'd be willing to take part in a quick photo shoot on Sunday for the shop. She told them about Marc's magical back yard and they instantly agreed.

"I have to see those trees," Lisa said. "Count me in."

"I'll have everything ready at his house, and all you have to do is come and put on the dresses. I already know your sizes, so it shouldn't take too long," Debbie said. "And bring the girls. They'll look adorable in little dresses."

They agreed to meet the next day. Debbie had already set a time for the photographer to come, and Lindsay was available too.

On the day of the photoshoot, Marc left the house to the women and went into work. Lindsay and Debbie had brought over several wedding dresses and tiny dresses for the little girls in colors of lilac, pink, and purple. They put everything in the family room in the kitchen so they could change in there. Each of the women had done their makeup and hair, and they all looked gorgeous.

"I hope a dress fits me," Kristen said, looking uncertain. "I just had a baby, after all. My body is a mess."

"You look amazing," Debbie told her. "Staying in shape before you were pregnant helped you a lot. I need to remember that."

Kristen's brows rose. "Are you planning on having a baby anytime soon?"

All eyes turned to Debbie, and she felt her face flush. "No. I meant that I need to continue with my exercising if I ever decide to have a baby," she said clumsily.

Lindsay laughed. "It's a big secret, but she's dating Marc," she told the group.

"Lindsay!" Debbie hadn't told her they were dating.

"Oh, come on, Deb," Lindsay said. "It's so obvious. Share the good news. Don't keep it a secret."

"Oh, my goodness!" Mallory exclaimed, coming over to hug her friend. "I'm so excited for you! A new career and a new relationship. Your life is so exciting!"

"A new career?" Lisa asked. "Tell us everything."

As they dressed, Debbie explained to everyone how she and Mallory were going to be working together and giving it a try. "And don't say anything to Marc about us dating," Debbie begged. "It's new. I don't want to scare him away."

"Is there going to be another wedding in the future?" Kristen asked, looking hopeful.

"Oh, goodness." Debbie couldn't believe her friends. "No wedding. We're just dating."

The women laughed, and the little girls giggled along, and soon they were all in their dresses and heading for the back door. Jade, the photographer, had already set up her equipment and followed them out. All the women stopped and stared in wonder as they stood under the blossoms. The day was sunny, and there was a light breeze, but nothing that would ruin the photos. A few petals had fallen, which added to the color on the grass, and occasionally a petal or two would drop.

"This is magical," Mallory said in a whisper as if in awe. "Wouldn't this make a beautiful setting for a wedding?"

Debbie agreed. Secretly, she knew it was the perfect place for a first kiss, too.

The photoshoot went well. The women stood in varying spots on the lawn or sat in the decorative chairs that had been placed around. They interacted with the little girls, who looked like sweet fairies in their lacy dresses and Mary Janes.

"Debbie. You need to get a dress on and join us," Lindsay said. "Come on. I'll help you change."

Debbie looked panicked. "I didn't bring one for me."

"I did," Lindsay said, her eyes twinkling. She took Debbie's arm and pulled her inside, then lifted up a dress that had been lying over the back of the sofa. "Put this on. It'll look gorgeous on you."

Debbie scowled at her friend but quickly did as she asked. The dress was made of satin with a sheer netting overlay that had tiny seed pearls all over it. The skirt wasn't too full, and it had a fitted bodice with cap sleeves.

"I'm going to look like a short puffball next to the taller women," Debbie grumbled as Lindsay buttoned the back.

"Here. Slip on these gloves, and I brought shoes for you too," Lindsay said, ignoring Debbie's complaining.

Debbie pulled on the elbow-length white gloves and stepped into the lace-covered, high-heeled pumps. Lindsay turned her to face the full-length mirror they'd brought along.

"See. You look beautiful."

Debbie gazed at herself in disbelief. "This dress looks good on me." She turned to Lindsay. "How did you know it would? I would never have chosen this for me."

Lindsay smiled proudly. "Because I see you as you actually are, curvy and beautiful. I knew it would look good on you. I've been doing this for a long time, you know."

Debbie smiled. "Yes, you have. And you do a wonderful job."

"Here. There's one last thing." Lindsay pulled a short veil out of a box and attached the comb in Debbie's hair. It hung to her shoulders with tiny beads trimming the hem, sparkling in the light. "Perfect," Lindsay said.

"It is perfect," Debbie said softly. "Thank you." She took a deep breath. "Let's join the others."

Everyone clapped and exclaimed delight when Debbie walked into the yard.

"You make a gorgeous bride," Lisa said.

"You look beautiful!" Mallory said excitedly.

Jade arranged the women in several different poses but told them to move slowly and naturally for each shot. "Just look like you're talking to each other," she said.

The women did as they were told, as the little girls danced around them or sat on the grass and gazed up at the canopy of flowers. Debbie was having so much fun that the time slipped by, and soon Jade announced, "One last shot."

She arranged the women standing in a line with their arms around each other's waists and the little girls sitting on the grass in front of them. They all smiled and giggled and had a lovely time. It had been such a delight, spending time with the women, that Debbie was sad when it was over.

They went inside and changed back into their clothes while Jade loaded the photos on her laptop. Then Debbie took her neighbors on a tour of the house and showed them the furniture she'd helped Marc pick out.

"Everything is so elegant," Lisa remarked as they stood in the dining room. "And I love this china. Debbie, you have a great eye for antiques."

Debbie smiled her appreciation. "I only guided Marc by telling him what would fit the style of the house, and if the price was good. He picked out the pieces he liked best."

"But that's what a good designer does," Mallory said. "Inform the client and guide them, but let them pick their style."

"That's what we do with dresses," Lindsay said. "We can lead a customer to the styles that would look good on her figure, but it's up to her to decide what she loves."

Debbie knew they were right, but she wasn't comfortable with their praise. She'd never been good at taking a compliment, and that was something she knew she needed to work on. She found that funny—a couple of months ago, Debbie would never have encouraged herself to work on changing her attitude about herself. But since meeting Marc, she'd learned that she didn't have to stay the same as she'd always been. She could work on changing the aspects of her personality that she wasn't comfortable with, so she would feel better about herself. She'd been changing her outside appearance with exercise and eating healthier, so why not change her attitude too?

After the tour, they all went back into the kitchen to carry the dresses out to Debbie and Lindsay's cars. Jade was still there, putting her equipment away.

"Come here a moment," she said, beckoning Debbie and the other women to look at her computer screen. "I think this was the best shot of the day." She opened one of the last photos she'd taken of the group standing together and laughing.

Debbie moved in closer to study it. The picture was beautiful in every way. They looked like a close-knit group of friends, in a fairyland setting, enjoying being together. Every face glowed with happiness, and much to her surprise, she looked joyful too. These women were her friends, her neighbors, her tribe. They were the women she'd shared laughter and tears with through the years, as well as joy and sorrow. They'd been there for her when her mother died, and she'd been there for them on their most blissful days when they married or celebrated the birth of their children.

Tears filled her eyes as she realized she was not alone in this world, nor friendless, as she'd always felt. She had these amazing women by her side.

"It's beautiful," she said, wiping the tears that had fallen down her cheeks. As she gazed around, Debbie realized the other women were wiping away tears too. What they had as a group of long-time neighbors and friends was more special than any of them had realized, and the photo reflected that.

"I love it," Lisa said. "It's us. It's who we are when we're all together."

Everyone agreed, and tissues were passed around as they sniffled and wiped tears and laughed at themselves for crying. The little girls stared at the grown women, looking confused by their tears. But they were happy tears. It was a moment none of them would ever forget.

After packing up the cars with the dresses and waving good-bye to the other women, Debbie stood by her car with Mallory and Lindsay, who'd stayed behind. Jade had packed up also and left, promising to send the link to the picture file to Debbie in a couple of days.

"It's amazing, isn't it?" Mallory asked as Lake Harriet sparkled in the sunlight across the street. "That a fun day like this could end up being so emotional."

Debbie nodded. "That picture of all of us told me more than I'd ever realized. Since my mom's passing, I've felt all alone in the world. I knew I had you in my life, Lindsay," she smiled at her friend, "and I had my amazing neighbors, but I never realized what our friendships meant to me. I do have friends. Close friends. People I can count on and who can count on me. It's like that photo opened my eyes."

Mallory hugged Debbie. "We've always been here for you, sweetie. You've never been alone. I know you've always thought you were on the sidelines, but you've been an important part of all of our lives from the beginning. That photo proves just how close we all are."

Lindsay hugged her, too, and Debbie's heart filled with love for her friends. Maybe she'd been afraid all these years to let anyone in, even them. Now, she couldn't imagine living without all these incredible people in her life."

As she drove back to the shop to put the dresses away, Debbie realized that she was changing and growing as a person and that Marc had a large part in that growth. He'd encouraged her to be the best version of herself. To apply herself, try new things, and become a stronger, more confident person. His belief in her had given her the strength to do it all.

At that moment, her heart opened up to him in a way it hadn't before. She knew right then that she was truly falling in love with him. Her heart was full.

Chapter Twenty-Two

Wednesday evening, Marc sat at his desk looking over his proposal for the McGregory project for the hundredth time. He couldn't lower the cost any further. He wanted the best workout equipment and the prices were the lowest he could get. Marc also refused to skimp on paying the trainers they'd need to hire. He had only the best at his gyms and he refused to cut corners if he put studios in their office buildings. He'd rather lose the deal than risk the excellent reputation he'd built through the years.

Marc had sat in a meeting with Melinda and one of the board members for two hours on Monday, missing out on shopping with Debbie. If the deal weren't so important to growing his business, he'd have happily told them to reschedule and spend the day in antique shops with Debbie instead. They'd just wanted to rehash everything over and over again, but Marc had stood firm. If they were more worried about the money instead of giving their employees the best workout experience, then they could hire the competition.

But it still irked Marc that word had gotten out about the project in the first place. Now, a second fitness chain had approached the McGregory group. Marc had no idea how these other chains had learned about the deal. The idea that one of his employees had possibly been snooping in his office and may have spread the word made him bristle. He couldn't imagine Mandy doing that, but Kyle? Maybe. The guy had been angry at Marc for reprimanding him about his behavior. Had Kyle been mad enough to stab Marc in the back? That thought didn't settle well with Marc. He'd known Kyle for years, and that was why he'd made him the manager of this location. Now, he didn't know if he could trust the guy to come into his office. But since he had no proof, he also couldn't fire him. That would be grounds for a lawsuit, and Marc didn't want that either.

Sighing, he locked the papers away in his desk and stood, walking over to where Bernie was lying on the floor. He kneeled and petted his best friend. "At least I know I can trust you, Bernie old pal," he said.

Of course, Bernie didn't reply. He only gave him a look that said, "Well, duh!"

Marc headed out to the main floor, happy he'd get to see Debbie tonight. He'd missed Monday night, so he wanted to escort her to spin class and then help her on the weight machine afterward. He knew it was silly to "escort" her, but he liked doing it. Any time with Debbie was better than no time around her. She always brightened his day.

After spin class, Debbie filled him in on the photoshoot at his house and the beautiful pictures that were taken.

"Wait until you see them," she said, her eyes lighting up with excitement. "The yard is so gorgeous, and the photos are amazing. I'm going to have a few blown up and hang them in the shop, and use even larger, poster-style ones for a spring and summer display in the window. Everyone will want to rent your yard for a wedding."

He laughed. "Wouldn't that be crazy? I guess I could rent out the yard and house for weddings and receptions. Wouldn't my neighbors love that?"

She laughed too. "And talking about weddings, do you still want to come to Lisa and Avery's groom's dinner Friday and wedding on Saturday? I won't hold you to it if you'd rather not."

"Are you kidding? Miss going out with you to two events in a row? I'm definitely coming," he said. "Just tell me when to pick you up and what to wear, and I'll be there."

Friday night, precisely at six, Marc arrived at Debbie's house dressed in a navy suit. When she opened the door, he gasped in delight. "You look beautiful!"

Debbie blushed, which Marc found adorable. She wore a one-shoulder strap turquoise satin dress that hugged her trimmed-down waist and flared out slightly to just above her knees.

"It isn't too much?" she asked nervously. "Lindsay talked me into this dress for tonight, and I thought I could also wear it in the Bahamas for the groom's dinner. But I'm still not sure about it."

"What aren't you sure of?" he asked. Moving in closer, he kissed her softly on the lips so as not to smear her rose-colored lipstick. "You look incredible in that dress. All your hard work at the gym is paying off. Look how toned you are. And those arms! I'd better watch out or you'll be able to wrestle me to the ground."

"I hope not," she said, looking aghast. "I don't want to look like a weight-lifter."

He smiled. "You don't. You look like a beautiful woman."

She retrieved her small purse and wrap, and they left for the restaurant. The dinner was being held in the banquet room of an upscale hotel downtown where many of the wedding guests and family were staying. All the women looked lovely in their evening dresses and best jewelry, and the men were handsome in their suits. Debbie introduced Marc to the groom, Avery, and to Kristen's husband, Ryan, who he hadn't met yet. Marc congratulated the couple on their upcoming wedding and Lisa complimented Marc on his beautiful house.

"It's gorgeous," she said. "And that yard! It's a fairyland. We had so much fun at the photoshoot there."

"Thank you," Marc said, genuinely pleased that Debbie's friends liked his house. "It wouldn't look as nice without Debbie's help. You should have seen the décor before she helped me change it. It was atrocious."

Lisa laughed. "Debbie told us about the leopard rug in the entryway. Very creative."

Marc liked all of Debbie's friends from her neighborhood. Each couple came to greet them and they were all so warm and kind. He barely knew his neighbors after living there for nearly five years. Marc had thought that was how neighborhoods were these days. But Debbie's neighbors were different. They genuinely cared about each other and it showed.

They had a delicious dinner, and there were speeches from Avery's parents and Lisa's father, who had flown in for the wedding. It was after ten by the time everyone began to leave. After saying their goodbyes, Marc drove Debbie home.

"What a great group of friends you have," Marc said as they rode along. "I wish my neighborhood was like that. But everyone stays to themselves."

"It's a special neighborhood, that's for certain," Debbie said. "When Avery first moved in across the street from Lisa, she called him a hermit. He didn't talk to anyone or join in on any of our neighborhood activities for the first year. But that all changed and now they're getting married. It's funny how life turns out."

Marc glanced over at Debbie, knowing how it felt for things to change quickly. "It is, isn't it?" he said.

She grinned back.

When they arrived at her house, he walked her to the door as he always did. "What's the plan for tomorrow?" he asked.

"The wedding is at the church on the corner at two o'clock, and then the reception is across the street at Lisa and Avery's new house. I thought you could bring Bernie to my house for the day, and that way one of us could run over and feed them dinner. I hate thinking of poor Bernie missing a meal because you were gone all day."

"That's a good idea." He bent down and brushed his lips on hers. "And it's nice of you to think of Bernie. He'll love spending the day with Chloe."

Debbie laughed. "And I'll enjoy spending the day with you."

He kissed her again and reluctantly said goodnight. As he drove away from her house, he smiled. He hadn't been this happy in a long time. The funny thing was, he hadn't been unhappy or lonely before he'd met Debbie, but now, he realized he'd just been going through the motions of life. Working, running, home. He now realized his life had been empty without her in it. After only a few weeks, he couldn't imagine life without her sweet smile or beautiful eyes. It was a thought that made him very happy.

* * *

Debbie spent a couple of hours the next morning helping Lisa do last minute set-ups in their back yard for the reception and making sure there were no issues with the wedding dress and

Abby's little dress. Kristen was there too, helping out, and would be there right before the wedding to help with any last-minute details since she was the matron-of-honor.

"Thank you both, ladies," Lisa said, looking a bit harried. "I couldn't have finished everything without your help. I'm a nervous wreck!"

"Don't be," Kristen told her firmly, then laughed. "You're marrying an amazing man who loves you. It doesn't matter what goes right or wrong today, because in the end, it'll be perfect."

Debbie left soon after that and took her time getting ready. She left her hair down, taming the natural waves and curls as best she could. She carefully applied her make-up then dressed in an azure blue, A-line dress that was sleeveless with a scoop neck. She was thankful she could buy dresses at cost since she was attending so many weddings this year. She slipped on a pair of nude pumps and grabbed a dressy, waist-length cardigan out of her closet just as her doorbell rang. Marc was standing on her stoop, waiting for her, looking handsome in a dark suit. Bernie sat there, too, wearing a bow-tie.

Debbie laughed out loud. "Is Bernie coming to the wedding?"

"No. He just wanted to impress his lady-friend," Marc said. He walked inside and kissed her lightly on the cheek, as Bernie came in too and sought out Chloe. The little white dog was lying on the sofa, looking unconcerned and unimpressed by the dog in the bow-tie.

"Poor Bernie," Debbie said. "He has competition, you know. Brewster is in love with her."

"Bernie will have to learn to fight for his woman," Marc said jokingly. He moved closer to Debbie and kissed her again, their bodies touching. "Do I have to fight anyone for you?" he asked when he pulled away.

Debbie laughed. "No, I'm afraid not. Does that make me any less desirable?"

"Not in the least. In fact, it's a relief because I'd probably lose a fight."

They finally pulled apart, and Marc took off Bernie's bow-tie and put his water bowl in the kitchen while Debbie fixed her lipstick in the hallway mirror.

"You look amazing," Marc said, coming up behind her.

"Thanks to you helping me with my workouts," she said.

"No. You were beautiful before, and you're beautiful now."

"And you're too sweet," she said.

It was a lovely day, warmer than normal for so early in the spring. They walked the short distance to the church and found a spot to sit next to Mallory, James, and little Shannon. The elegant old church was filled with friends and family and hushed whispers of conversation until the organist started to play. Soon, Avery stood in front with his best man, Ryan, awaiting his bride.

As everyone watched, Kristen led little Abby up the aisle as the youngster dropped pink and white rose petals along the way. When the music swelled, everyone stood, and there were gasps of delight when Lisa walked down the aisle on her father's arm.

Debbie's heart warmed as she watched her friend float by in her wedding dress. Lisa was absolutely stunning, and Debbie was proud to have had a hand in helping her choose the gown.

As the vows were exchanged, Marc reached for Debbie's hand and smiled over at her. She felt so lucky to be sitting here with him. Only weeks before, she'd thought she would never meet someone to share her life with. And although she wasn't sure how their relationship would turn out, she was happy to be here with him now, with all her friends, celebrating Lisa and Avery's special day.

Afterward, everyone crossed the street to the lovely old Victorian house that Lisa and Avery now called home. Lisa planned to quit her job as a school nurse in May and run a daycare on the bottom floor of their home so she could be home with her daughter. Avery, a romance writer, had turned the attic into his office so he could work undisturbed during the day.

Now, though, the crowd went to the back yard where tables were set up and a caterer had placed a long table of food for the luncheon. Strings of lights were strung overhead through the old oaks and elms and along the fence line. Music played from a stereo set in the corner of the yard. Bailey and Maddie, Lisa and Avery's dogs, mingled with the guests hoping to catch food as it fell off plates. It was elegant yet casual, and everyone enjoyed themselves as they congratulated the newlyweds and sat down to a nice lunch.

As the champagne was passed around, Marc hesitated a moment before taking a second glass.

"Go ahead. Enjoy," Debbie told him. "We're only steps away from my house."

"But I still have to drive home," he said.

"Or sleep in the guest room," she offered, feeling the beginning of a blush warm her cheeks.

He waggled his brows at her and took the glass. Rarely did either of them let loose and have fun since both of them owned their own businesses and always worked. Debbie didn't feel guilty at all about taking a second glass as well.

The party went on into the early evening, and since most of the neighborhood was in attendance, there was no one to complain about the noise. Around five, Marc went next door to Debbie's to feed the dogs their dinner, then returned to the party. A small area on the cement patio was cleared and the bride and groom danced their first dance, then the parents danced also. Soon, the area filled with couples dancing as a cousin of Lisa's took on the duties of a D.J., choosing the music.

"Shall we dance?" Marc asked, standing up and offering his hand to Debbie. She loved how sweet he was and nodded, taking his hand and heading to the dance floor. A slow song was playing, and Marc took Debbie into his arms and glided her around the small space.

"I didn't know you could dance," Debbie said, surprised that this late-blooming fitness instructor could move so smoothly.

"Sixth-grade gym class," he said. "We had dance lessons for a six-week session. I was petrified when we started, but I took to it pretty well. By the end of the six weeks, the girls all wanted to dance with me—the pudgy non-athletic guy—because I didn't step on their toes."

Debbie laughed. "You learned well. You should have known then that you were coordinated enough to be in sports."

"I had no interest," he said. "Running around a basketball court, or getting tackled on a football field sounded terrible to me. And don't even get me started on hockey. I did six months of peewee hockey and begged my parents to quit. Even at that age, the boys were aggressive."

"Well, everything worked out for you," Debbie said. "Quite well, I'd say."

He gazed down into her eyes, and she saw them sparkle. "Yes. Quite well is right."

They danced and drank and ate well into the evening until one by one, the couples began to leave. Those with children left first, carrying out sleepy little angels in pretty dresses. Soon everyone was saying goodnight, congratulating the couple one last time before heading home.

"You were gorgeous," Debbie told Lisa before they left.

"Thanks to you," she replied with a grin. "Thank you for all the help."

"Anytime." Debbie hugged her and Avery, and soon she and Marc were walking, hand-in-hand, next door to her house. They were greeted at the door by Bernie and Chloe, and Marc took them out. Debbie filled their bowls for a late snack and then slipped off her heels and nearly fell onto the sofa, laughing. Marc joined her.

"What's so funny?" he asked.

"I don't think I've danced as much in my entire life as I did tonight."

He slid his arm around her shoulders, and she snuggled in closer to him. "But you had fun, right? I didn't see you complaining."

"Yes. I had fun. More fun than I've had in a long time."

He smiled down at her. Chloe had made herself comfortable in a chair while Bernie had fallen fast asleep on the living room carpet. Marc gestured to the dogs. "They look comfortable."

"They do. I'm comfortable too. It's going to take a crane to get me off this sofa."

Marc gave her a mischievous grin. "I could carry you to bed and tuck you in."

Debbie looked up into his handsome face. She'd had such a wonderful time tonight that she hated for it to end. Marc was everything she'd ever wanted in a man, maybe even more than she'd ever hoped for. And he cared about her. It was easy being around him and they fit so well together. She didn't know if it was the lovely day, the wedding, the dancing, or the champagne that gave her the courage to say what she said next, but she knew what she wanted.

"Or you could carry me to bed and stay," she said softly.

He bent low and kissed her more passionately than he'd ever kissed her before. Her arms rose up around his neck, and his wrapped around her waist. His kiss was warm and inviting and brought out emotions in her that had long been dormant. She wanted nothing more than to lie in his arms and hold him close.

Marc pulled away slightly and looked at her seriously. "Is that what you really want, or is it the champagne talking?"

"It's what I want," she said. "If it's what you want."

He stood and scooped her up into his arms in one smooth motion, making her laugh out loud. "You don't have to ask me twice," he said, dropping a kiss on her lips. He carried her to her bed, kicking the door shut with his foot, and laid her gently on the comforter. "There is nothing I'd like better than to stay," he said sweetly, sitting down beside her. And when he kissed her again, she knew it was right.

Chapter Twenty-Three

Marc was the happiest he'd been in years and the most content. And it was all because of Debbie. Their first night together had been pure bliss. He'd already adored everything about her and now, he adored her even more.

That Sunday, they'd gone shopping for antiques as usual, but it had felt different. It was better. They'd laughed and joked and held hands the entire time. Debbie had seemed more relaxed in his company, and he was pleased with that. He'd been afraid she'd be shy or have second thoughts after they'd been intimate, but instead, she'd opened up and completely let him in. He'd always known she was amazing, but now, he thought she was even more incredible. He wanted nothing more than to do whatever made her happy because that would make him happy too.

They spent every night together that next week. Marc was at the gym to greet Debbie on her workout nights, and even though she took the various classes, he made sure he was available afterward to work with her. Then, they'd go home together, to her place, and spend their nights in each other's arms. He loved falling asleep next to her and waking up feeling her warmth beside him. It felt right—as if they'd been together for years—but it was also new and exciting. He couldn't explain it properly. It was as if they'd always been meant to be together.

The next week, unfortunately, life got in the way. He had more meetings with Melinda and various board members as they tried to compare what Marc was offering against what the other companies had bid. Marc was getting tired of continually defending his offer. After three more meetings, he told Melinda he was through trying to set up a deal. The board had to decide one way or another, and he wasn't going to change his proposal because they'd started looking at other fitness chains.

"You came to me first," he told Melinda. "And I appreciated it. But I can't spend another minute of my time trying to persuade the board. Tell them I'm serious about working with your company, but I will not change my costs. I've given them the best price I can."

Melinda told him she understood—it had dragged on long enough. She said she'd let him know the minute the board decided.

Marc knew it would be an incredible deal if he got it, but enough was enough. He happily spent his time with Debbie instead, and at work, running his chain of centers.

"Are you sure giving them an ultimatum was a good idea?" Debbie asked Marc after her Monday yoga class. "What if they think you're giving up?"

Marc shrugged. "Then they can give it to someone else. I have a good business, and I'll expand on my own at some point anyway. If they think being cheap is the way to go, then fine."

"So, you're a tough guy now, huh?" she asked, her eyes glittering with humor.

He leaned over her on the weight machine bench and brushed her lips with his. "No. I'm a marshmallow in the right hands."

"Geez, you two, get a room," Mandy said jokingly as she

walked over to them. "If the other female clients see you two, they're going to insist on a trainer with benefits too."

Marc laughed. Mandy needed him at the desk, so he said he'd be back in a minute. "Keep working out," he told Debbie. "I'll be back."

* * *

Debbie continued using the weight machine in Marc's absence. She was used to using it alone, so it wasn't a problem. To her dismay, Kyle headed directly toward her.

"Do you want any assistance since Marc is busy?" Kyle asked.

That was the last thing Debbie wanted. "No, thank you. I can finish on my own."

Kyle nodded but didn't leave. "I'm sorry if I said anything in the past that upset you. Marc was pretty mad at me for something a while back, and try as I might, I'm not sure what I said wrong. But please accept my apologies."

Debbie stopped pulling on the weights, stunned by his words. "Thank you. But I wasn't the one who was upset. He was angry over something else you'd said."

Kyle shrugged. "He's been pretty touchy lately. I'm not sure why. I thought it might be over that secret deal he was working on. Do you know anything about that?"

Debbie frowned. Was this guy fishing for information from her? "No. It's a secret from me, too."

"Huh. Well, that's not unusual. Marc likes his secrets. Like all his meetings with that pretty woman. He claims they're about business, but that seems odd to me. He's always been popular with the ladies if you know what I mean," he said, winking at Debbie.

She bristled at his words. What was he doing? Was he trying to make Debbie angry at him, or Marc? "I wouldn't know anything about that," she finally said. She worked the weights again, aggressively. Kyle stood there another minute, then left. She guessed he'd gotten the hint to leave.

When Marc returned to do stretches with her, he never asked what Kyle had said to her, so she figured he hadn't seen him there. She just let it go, not wanting to start anything more between Marc and his employee. Kyle was just a jerk, so he wasn't worth mentioning.

Marc finally had to give in and stay at his place that night. "I have laundry to do, and I'm sure Bernie has forgotten we still live there," he said. "You can always come to my place and try out the new bed."

Debbie chuckled. "While that is a tempting offer, I'd better stay home, too. Work is still crazy, and I need to get things in order before leaving for the Bahamas. We have less than two weeks before we go. I'm getting excited."

"I can't wait," he said. "It'll be nice to relax for a few days."

They planned to meet up for dinner the next night as Marc walked her to her car. He kissed her sweetly. "I hate saying goodbye."

"It's just one night," she said. "I think you'll survive."

"Are you sure?" They kissed again, both realizing how much they'd miss the other. Finally, she pulled away and slipped into her car.

"I'll see you tomorrow night," she said, then waved and drove away.

* * *

Debbie was busy the next day at work, organizing more new shipments, calling clients to let them know their dresses were in, and organizing the dresses going to the alterations woman. Both she and Lindsay were knee-deep in poufy gowns and boxes in the back room when suddenly Lindsay exclaimed, "Here it is!"

Startled, Debbie looked up. "Here is what?" she asked.

Lindsay pulled a dress out of the box and carefully took off the plastic covering. She held it up on the hanger for Debbie to see. It was a beautiful aqua-blue satin dress with off-the-shoulder straps and a draped scooped neck. The bodice was form-fitting with a sash at the waist, then the skirt fell straight to the knees. "Isn't it beautiful?" Lindsay asked excitedly.

Debbie looked at it as she would any dress that came in. "Yes. It is. But why is it so special?"

Lindsay's lips lifted into a sly grin. "Because you're going to wear this dress at Felicia's groom's dinner in the Bahamas."

Debbie frowned. "I didn't order this dress. I already have a dress to wear."

"Yes, I know. But Marc has already seen you in the other dress. This one is perfect for the Bahamas. You'll look gorgeous in this one."

"What am I? A celebrity? Who cares if he's seen me in the other dress before?"

"I care. Besides, when I saw this, I knew it would be perfect for you. You have to try it on," Lindsay urged.

"You ordered it for me?" Debbie asked.

Lindsay shook her head slowly. "No, I didn't. A girl ordered it as a prom dress, then asked if she could cancel it. I let her once I had a good look at it. I knew this would be perfect for you instead."

Debbie sighed. She walked closer and inspected the dress.

It was beautiful, and the color was perfect for an island vacation. But she really couldn't afford to shell out money for another dress when she already had a perfectly good one. "I don't know," she said.

"At least try it on. If you hate it, we'll return it. Please?"

Debbie rolled her eyes. "Fine." She took the dress, then saw the size marked on the inside. "Are you crazy? I can't fit into this size."

"You can now," Lindsay said. "Try it on. You'll see."

Reluctantly, Debbie went to the dressing rooms and slipped off her skirt and blouse. This morning she'd pinned the waistband of her skirt even tighter, and she knew she had to make time to alter some of her clothes. While her weight hadn't changed too much, her body had from exercising. Her waist had trimmed down, and her arms and legs were more muscular and less flabby. Clothes looked better on her now, and fit differently. She liked that she didn't look dumpy in her clothes anymore.

Debbie slipped on the dress and had to contort herself to zip up the back. When she turned and looked in the mirror, she was stunned. The dress not only fit her, but it also looked good. She loved the color and cut of the dress and the feel of the fabric.

"How does it look?" Lindsay asked from the other side of the curtain.

Debbie opened it up and stepped out. "I love it."

Her friend's eyes lit up. "It's perfect for you. Just as I thought it would be. You have to buy that dress."

"I'd like to, but I really shouldn't spend the money on it when I have a perfectly good dress already."

Lindsay opened her mouth to protest but was interrupted by the bell on the door. Both women turned to see who'd entered. To Debbie's horror, Felicia stood there, staring at her.

"Hi, Felicia," Debbie said, wishing she wasn't wearing this dress right at this moment. "What can we do for you?"

Felicia sauntered over and studied Debbie. "You didn't wear that to work today, did you?" she asked, frowning.

Debbie laughed. "No. Of course not. I was trying it on. Lindsay thought I should."

"Why?" Felicia asked.

Debbie's mouth nearly dropped open, but she refrained from doing so. Lindsay's face, however, twisted up with anger, and Debbie was thankful Lindsay was standing behind Felicia.

"Because she thought it would be a nice dress for the Bahamas," Debbie answered quickly before Lindsay exploded.

"Really?" Felicia's brows drew together. "Well. I suppose. It's not really your style, dear. Or your color. But of course, you should wear whatever you want."

Anger bubbled up inside Debbie, but she did her best not to burst. She knew the dress looked good on her and didn't care what Felicia said. "Did you come in for a reason?" she asked as politely as possible.

"Oh, yes. I came to pick up one of the bridesmaid dresses. Your assistant called to say it was ready."

Again, Debbie saw Lindsay's eyes pop out at being called the "assistant" by Felicia. This time, Debbie wanted to laugh. "Wonderful. *Lindsay* will help you with that while I change."

Lindsay glared at Debbie over Felicia's shoulder, then smiled when the woman turned toward her and led her to the counter. Debbie went back into the dressing room, muffling the laughter that had replaced her anger.

She stared at her reflection in the mirror again and liked what she saw. A month ago, she would have cringed at Felicia's withering look and comments, but now, she knew that Felicia was wrong. Maybe even jealous. Because Debbie looked good in this dress and Felicia didn't like it.

"I guess I'll be buying a new dress," Debbie said to her reflection. Now more than ever, she wanted it. Not only to spite Felicia but also to see Marc's reaction when he saw it on her. She smiled. She couldn't wait to go to the Bahamas.

Chapter Twenty-Four

The week before their Bahama trip went by quickly. Marc was busy making visits to all his centers to ensure all was well, and also had the monthly managers meeting. He trusted all his managers and made sure he was always available to them. Except for Kyle, he'd never had any issues with his current managers, and he hoped it would stay that way.

The last weekend in May, he spent a happy, relaxing time with Debbie at his house. She'd brought along Chloe, who seemed to enjoy staying at the larger home. They did a little antique shopping but mainly spent time together, binge-watching shows, eating out, and cuddling in bed. He couldn't remember having a more relaxing weekend.

Marc hadn't heard yet from the McGregory group, and he figured he probably wouldn't. He thought they'd chosen a cheaper bid, and that was fine with him. He wanted to maintain the integrity of his fitness centers, and that would apply to the smaller business models as well. It was McGregory's loss as far as he was concerned.

Debbie, however, had good news from Mallory that week. "She called to say she had two people express interest in working with an antique specialist to find pieces for their homes," she told Marc on Friday when they'd met at his house for dinner. "As soon as I come back from the Bahamas, I'm going to set up meetings with them. It's so exciting!"

Marc was happy for her. This was a new venture for Debbie, and he knew she'd be excellent at it. After all, she'd helped him redecorate his house with antiques and he loved all his new furniture.

On Monday, as he sat in his office, he received a call from Melinda.

"The board would like to meet with you one last time," she said. "They were wondering if you could come to the downtown offices on Tuesday."

Marc frowned. He had packing to finish before leaving Wednesday morning with Debbie, and the last thing he wanted to do was spend hours in another of their board meetings. "To tell the truth, Melinda, I'm leaving on Wednesday and will be busy Tuesday. I'm not sure I can go downtown that day to meet."

She hesitated on the other end of the line. "Is there somewhere near you that we could all meet?" she asked.

Marc perked up. Maybe this was good news. "Why don't they come to my house? I have a room big enough for everyone to gather."

"Done," she said. "Text me your address, and we'll see you there around two in the afternoon."

Marc was surprised. He hadn't expected them to come to him. "I'll see you then," he said before hanging up.

At the gym that night, Marc didn't mention the meeting to Debbie. He still wasn't sure if they had chosen him or were going to let him down in person politely. Until he knew for sure, he didn't want to ruin Debbie's excitement about the trip with his news.

She worked out as usual in the yoga class, and he helped her with the weight machine.

"You're not going to give up on exercise the minute the trip is over, are you?" Marc asked, teasing her. "I remember how hesitant you were to come in here in the first place."

She laughed. "No. I'm serious about staying in shape now. I love how healthy I feel. And I never want to embarrass myself again by falling off a bike in front of a handsome man and his dog." Her eyes twinkled as she spoke.

"I don't ever want you to fall in front of a handsome guy either. He might take you away from me."

"Never," she said.

They both laughed as they stretched. Marc could hardly believe she was the same woman he'd met a few months earlier, bundled up and peeking out from under a stocking cap with those big, beautiful eyes. She was more confident now than when he'd met her, and much more open with him. The day Debbie fell in front of him was the best day of his life. And he was going to make sure she knew that while they were in the Bahamas.

"What a difference a few weeks can make," he said, giving her a sweet kiss.

She beamed up at him. "One more day and we'll be on a plane to paradise. I can hardly wait."

"Me too," he said. No truer words had ever come out of his mouth.

* * *

Debbie flew around the shop on Tuesday, tying up as many loose ends as possible so she didn't leave a mess for Lindsay.

"Don't work yourself into a frenzy," Lindsay said. "I'll be fine.

I don't want you to leave tomorrow all worn out from today."

"My head is spinning," Debbie told her. "I'm thinking about all I have to pack, about what needs to get done here, and also about how I'm going to balance working with Mallory and running this shop when I get back. It's all too much at once."

Lindsay walked over to her and placed a calming hand on her shoulder. "The shop will be fine, your packing will get done, and you'll manage perfectly working both here and with Mallory. All you need to focus on is you and Marc spending six days in paradise together. Minus having to attend the evil woman's wedding."

Debbie chuckled. "Felicia isn't that evil. She invited me to be in her wedding, didn't she?"

"Yeah, but only because you gave her a big discount on dresses. But forget her. Focus on you and Marc on a beautiful beach drinking Hurricanes. Or margaritas, or whatever you want to drink."

Debbie smiled gratefully at her friend. "You're right. That's what I'll do. It's going to be fun. And I couldn't do it if it wasn't for you taking care of the shop. I hope you know that I appreciate you very much."

Lindsay nodded. "I know. But thanks for saying it."

Debbie worked until a little after two, and Lindsay finally shooed her out. "Go pack," she told Debbie. "The shop will be fine."

Debbie agreed. "I'll go." She stopped a moment to try to call Marc again. She'd tried several times that morning, but he hadn't answered. She wanted to give him the flight numbers and times because they wouldn't be riding together to the airport since they had to be there so early in the morning.

"What's wrong?" Lindsay asked.

"Marc hasn't answered his phone. He must be busy, too. I need to get this flight information to him."

"Text it," Lindsay suggested.

"It's a lot to text. Maybe I'll print it and drop it in his mailbox."

"You'd better set it inside his house where he'll find it," Lindsay suggested. "He may have already checked his mail. You still have a key, don't you?"

Debbie nodded. "I guess I can do that." She sent the information to her printer and grabbed the sheets once they were ready. Hugging Lindsay goodbye, she left and drove to Marc's place first.

There were several cars parked on the street, but Debbie didn't see Marc's. That didn't mean he wasn't home, though, because there was a back alley that led to his garage. She had to park a block away and walk to his house. It was a gray day with dark clouds rolling in, threatening rain. She hoped it didn't rain in the morning when their plane took off. She wasn't a nervous flyer, but she didn't like flying in bad weather.

Debbie finally reached his door and hesitated a moment. She hated walking into his house uninvited, but she wanted to make sure he had the flight information. After she dropped it off, she'd text him where he could find it.

Debbie opened the door and stepped inside. She set the papers on the table by the door, so he would see them. Just as she was about to leave, Debbie thought she heard music coming from the back of the house. Hesitantly, she walked toward the kitchen, and the music grew louder. Halfway there, Bernie came running to her, and she bent to pet the dog. "Marc must be home if you're here," she said.

Taking a few more steps, she halted. Around the corner, she

caught a glimpse of Marc and the woman she'd seen him with at Gallagher's. They were both holding champagne flutes and smiling and laughing. Debbie frowned as she watched. They looked like they were extremely familiar with each other. In the moment that Debbie hesitated, the woman and Marc hugged. That was all she needed to see. Debbie spun on her heel and ran toward the front door.

Tears filled her eyes as she shut the door and ran from the house, stumbling on the steps that led to the street. She hurried to her car and got inside as the tears ran down her cheeks.

She should have known that woman wasn't a business associate. She was tall and beautiful—just his type. How on earth could Debbie have ever thought that Marc would fall in love with her when so many gorgeous women were flirting with him daily? Once again, she'd been a fool.

Wiping the tears from her eyes, Debbie pulled out onto the street and hurried the few blocks home. As she drove, Kyle's words came back to her loud and clear. *Marc likes his secrets. He's always been pretty popular with the ladies if you know what I mean.* Well, maybe Kyle wasn't as off the mark as she'd thought. Or as Marc would have her believe. Maybe Marc was the one who'd been lying to her all along.

Her heart ached as she pulled into her driveway and put the car in park. How could she have been so stupid? Why hadn't she seen this coming? She'd believed in Marc. Tears continued to flow, and she dropped her head in her hands. She'd thought Marc was the one. It tore her apart.

A tapping came on the window beside her, and Debbie looked up into Mallory's concerned face.

"Debbie? What's wrong?" her neighbor asked.

Shame washed over Debbie. How could she tell her friend

and neighbor that she'd screwed up and trusted the wrong man? It made her sound like an idiot.

Mallory ran around the car and got in the passenger side. "Debbie? Tell me what happened? Let me help," she said, sounding desperate to comfort her friend.

The story of finding Marc with the other woman tumbled from Debbie's lips. How she'd seen him with the woman before when he was supposed to be at a meeting and how his manager at the fitness center had insinuated that Marc was a player. "I saw it with my own eyes," Debbie said through her sobs. "He's been playing me the entire time."

Mallory looked shocked. "I believe that's what you saw, but are you absolutely sure he was cheating on you? Could there be another explanation?" she asked hopefully.

"I know he was seeing this woman. He didn't answer my calls all day, and he never told me he had a meeting with anyone today. He was at his home with her, and they were drinking champagne. What other reason could there be?" Debbie asked, wiping away her tears. "I trusted him. I believed in him. I can't believe I was so stupid."

"You're not stupid," Mallory insisted. "You let him into your life in good faith. I'm so sorry it turned out this way. He seemed like a great guy. He had us all fooled."

Mallory walked Debbie inside and had her sit down while she made her a cup of tea. Chloe jumped up on Debbie's lap, and she hugged her tight. "We were both fooled," she told the little dog.

"We were all fooled," Mallory said, bringing Debbie her tea. "He seemed so sincere. So real. I can't believe he'd do that to you."

Debbie nodded. Her tears had abated, and she felt weary. "I

don't even want to go on this trip now. I can't go alone and have Felicia throw it in my face that I don't have a date after all."

"You have to go," Mallory insisted. "Go and have a great time and forget about Marc. Who cares what this Felicia thinks? You can relax and dance with anyone you like and have fun. Don't let Marc or anyone else ruin your vacation."

Debbie thought about it for a moment. Mallory was right. She'd go, and she'd try to have fun. But forget about Marc? That was impossible. She sighed. "You're right. I need to pack and get ready and go tomorrow as planned."

"I'll help you," Mallory said, rising. "Come on. Let's get you ready for a great vacation. You worked hard and look amazing. It's time you enjoyed yourself."

With great effort, Debbie pulled herself up and led the way to her bedroom, where her suitcase awaited. Mallory was right. She'd go and do her best to have fun. But it would take more than a week in the Bahamas to fix the hole in her heart that Marc had caused.

Chapter Twenty-Five

Marc was so excited that he couldn't wait to tell Debbie the good news. It was after five in the evening by the time the last of the board members from the McGregory group had left his house. He tried calling Debbie, but she didn't answer. Disappointed, he left a message on her voicemail.

He'd really wanted Debbie to hear the news first, but he'd have to wait to tell her. He knew she was busy getting ready for the trip. Marc decided he'd run over to the fitness center and tell Kyle and Mandy the news, then drop by Debbie's house. He was so happy, he thought he'd burst if he didn't tell someone.

On his way out the back to his garage, his phone rang. He looked at it eagerly, hoping it was Debbie, but it wasn't. "Hello?"

"Marc Bennett?" the male voice asked.

"Yes. Who is this?"

"I'm Arnie Sundahl from Forever Fitness. I know we've never met, but I thought I'd give you a call and congratulate you on winning the McGregory project."

Marc's brows shot up. So this was the fitness place bidding against him. "Well, that's very nice of you. Thank you."

"I'm just happy that they kept it local. They could have picked a company anywhere in the U.S. Glad they picked one here in Minneapolis."

"Me too," Marc said.

"I was talking with another friend of mine, Kevin Chase of Chase Fitness. I guess he put in a bid, too. Do you know him?"

"No, I don't," Marc said. "I'm curious, though. How did you and Kevin hear about this project? I was told it was confidential when they approached me."

There was a pause, and Arnie cleared his throat. "I suppose it would be remiss of me not to tell you. We were both approached by an employee of yours. Kyle Giffard. He said he'd let me in on a good deal if I would promise to hire him if I won the contract. Well, I can't say no to a good deal, right? So he told me about it and I threw in my bid. I guess he did the same with Kevin Chase, too. That employee of yours is a pretty shady character."

Marc sucked in his breath when he heard Kyle's name. So, he had been snooping through his paperwork, just as Debbie suspected. His blood boiled with anger. "Thanks for telling me," he told Arnie. "I'm curious. Would you have hired him if you'd been awarded the contract?"

"No way," Arnie said. "I wouldn't have a turncoat like him on my payroll. If he'd do that to you, he'd do it to me too. Of course, he didn't know that."

Marc thanked him for calling, and after he hung up, he got in his car. "I have a few words for Kyle," he said aloud as he put the car in gear.

* * *

Marc strode into Fit in 20 and headed for the desk. As usual, Kyle was there.

"Hey, boss. What's up? You ready for that fancy Bahama vacation?"

"Stay here a moment, I need to get Mandy," he told Kyle, holding in his anger. He would have loved to punch the guy right then and there, but all that would get him was a lawsuit. He went to the classroom and waved Mandy over. Luckily, their new instructor, Anita, was leading the class too.

"What's up?" Mandy asked, catching her breath.

"Can you join me at the desk? I have good news," Marc said. She followed him over.

"As you both know, I was working on a project that would increase business for Fit in 20. I haven't shared any of the details because it was supposed to be confidential until we worked out a contract. I'm happy to announce that I just signed the contract."

"Hey, that's great!" Kyle said.

"Congratulations," Mandy added. "I'm so happy for you."

"Thank you," Marc said. "I was going to move some of my top employees up to help run this project. And then I received a call from an owner of another fitness center who'd bid on the project too." His stare turned to Kyle. "It seems we have a mole here. Someone who'd sell out a friend to move up the ranks."

Kyle's face dropped, and Mandy looked stunned.

"Arnie Sundahl told me you tried to make a deal with him, Kyle. You dug through my papers and gave him confidential information. Unluckily for you, I won the contract anyway."

Kyle glared at Marc. "You were such a jerk to me. I was only looking for a better opportunity."

"You're free to pursue any opportunity you want," Marc said. "Although, if I were you, I wouldn't go to Forever Fit or Chase Fitness. They don't want you. And neither do I. You're fired, Kyle."

Kyle's face turned bright red. "You can't fire me! I'm your right-hand man. I've been here since the beginning. You can't prove I did anything. I'll sue!"

"Go ahead. Sue. I have two men who'll say you tried to cheat me. Now get out of here and don't come into any of my fitness centers again."

Kyle grabbed his keys and headed for the door.

"Hey! Leave the key to this place here," Marc said.

Kyle stopped, pulled the key off his ring, and threw it at Marc. "You'll hear from my lawyer!" he yelled before retreating out to the parking lot.

Marc sighed and picked up the key. Mandy's eyes were wide.

"Good riddance," Marc said. He took a breath and then held out the key to Mandy. "Would you be interested in becoming the new manager of this location?"

Her eyes lit up. "Are you kidding? I'd love to be the manager." She accepted the key from him. "Thank you, Marc."

"You're welcome. But we'll have to give you a crash course on what you need to learn right now because I'm leaving for the Bahamas tomorrow, and there's no way I'm going to miss that flight."

Mandy nodded as they headed into his back office. Marc felt one-hundred percent safe leaving the center in Mandy's hands.

* * *

In-between showing Mandy her new work duties, Marc tried calling Debbie several times. Each time, it went directly to voice mail. He figured she was busy packing and getting ready for the trip, but by eight o'clock, when he hadn't heard from her, he started to worry. On his way home from the center, he drove past Debbie's house. It was completely dark. Had she gone to bed already? He stopped in front and wondered if he should knock on her door. He hated to wake her since their flight was so early. But he really wanted to tell her the good news about being awarded the project. In the end, he decided to let her sleep. He'd catch up with Debbie at the airport and tell her his good news then. He could hardly wait.

Once home, Marc parked out front and went inside the house. Immediately, he noticed the sheets of paper on the entryway table. He wondered when Debbie had dropped them off. Maybe while he was at Fit in 20. He smiled. At least he had his ticket information in case he didn't catch her before going through security. He'd see her in the boarding area for sure tomorrow. First, he had to drop Bernie off at his sister's house before heading to the airport. Debbie had booked a ride to the airport so she wouldn't have to drive there. He knew that Mallory was taking Chloe for the week.

Knowing that everything was set, he relaxed. He just had to pack his bag, and he'd be ready to go. Marc couldn't wait to spend a week with Debbie in paradise.

Chapter Twenty-Six

Debbie arrived at the airport by six a.m., checked in, and checked her bag. She went through security fairly quickly since it was so early and walked the long distance to where her plane would take off. As she waited to board, her heart still ached over what she'd seen yesterday. She'd been looking forward to this trip with Marc and now, here she was, going to a wedding alone again. Was that going to be the story of her life?

Debbie pulled out her phone and scrolled through her recent calls. Marc had tried to call her several times last night, and she'd finally turned off her phone. It didn't matter what he had to say to her. She couldn't bear to hear his lies or excuses. It would only hurt more.

Finally, the flight attendant announced that the plane was boarding. Debbie stood and walked to the line. She would go and try to have a good time. She had to forget Marc—forget all the good times they'd shared and the feelings she'd had for him. It was going to be hard, but she had no choice. Letting out a small sigh, she gave the attendant her ticket to be scanned, then boarded the plane.

* * *

Marc rushed into the terminal and waited impatiently for a kiosk to become available to key in his flight information. The morning had gone badly from the moment he woke up an hour late to the traffic driving into the airport. He should have been here an hour ago, but if he could get through the line here and through security quickly, he might still make his flight.

He finally got to an open ticket kiosk and started entering the flight information. The machine buzzed and rejected his numbers. He tried again. Rejected! *What the hell?*

Frantic now, Marc stood in line so an airport employee could check his information. When he finally got to the counter, he explained that his tickets wouldn't print.

"I'll check it for you," the woman in the blue uniform said. But after she entered the information, she frowned. "The computer is rejecting this information."

"Why?" Marc asked. "This is my flight information. I'm already late, and I have to get on that plane. Can you find what the problem is?"

The woman sighed and clicked the keys of her computer. "Ah, here it is. This ticket was canceled. Yesterday. It's no longer valid."

He stood there, stunned. "What? Are you sure? I don't understand."

The woman looked up from the computer. "It's been canceled. I'm sorry. It's no longer valid."

Marc panicked. "But you don't understand. I need to get on that flight. Can I book another ticket at this counter?"

The woman entered more information. "I'm sorry, but that flight is leaving in ten minutes. You'd never make it." Her face softened. "I'm very sorry."

Mark moved out of line and pulled out his phone. He

tried calling Debbie, but there was no answer. She was probably already on the plane, sitting alone, wondering what had happened to him. But his ticket had been canceled. Had she canceled it? Why? He quickly texted her and waited, hoping she'd be able to reply.

Finally, he saw the three dots that signified she was texting him. He waited for what felt like hours for it to turn into text. But when it did come through, his heart dropped.

"I canceled the tickets. I didn't want you to feel obligated to come. It's fine. We both held up our end of the bargain, and now you can go on with your life."

Marc stared at the text, dumfounded. What on earth did she mean? Why had she canceled the tickets? He was missing something and had no idea what it was. He looked at the time and realized the plane would be leaving right now. As he glanced around him, he had no idea what to do. Get on another flight or go home? He was at a complete loss.

* * *

Thursday evening, Debbie stood on the outside patio where the wedding party was enjoying drinks before heading inside for the groom's dinner. It was a gorgeous evening; the air was warm, and the palm trees swayed in the breeze. Hibiscus and orchids of varying colors decorated the thick shrubbery. Debbie wore the aqua-blue dress and felt as if she blended in with the landscape. She knew Felicia hated the dress—which gave Debbie a little pleasure. Even now, Felicia shot her a disparaging look but hadn't said a word.

When Debbie arrived yesterday afternoon, she'd run into Felicia in the hotel hallway and had to admit that her date hadn't come after all. By the look in Felicia's eyes, she could tell the woman was thrilled that Debbie had come alone, although Felicia pretended to sympathize with her and even said that Debbie was sure to meet a nice man here on the island. But that was the last thing Debbie wanted to do. No more men. She would enjoy her solitude here and relax once the wedding festivities were over.

Now, as she sipped her wine and glanced around, she tried to ignore Dave, the groomsman she'd been paired with. Felicia had whispered to her earlier at the rehearsal that Dave was single as if that would entice Debbie to be interested. She wasn't. Just standing next to him for that few minutes with his bad breath and sweaty underarms had been enough for Debbie. She couldn't wait for this party, and the wedding, to be over.

Debbie turned away from Dave's stare, and that's when she saw him. He was walking toward her, looking incredibly handsome in a three-piece suit, smiling wide. He stopped only inches from her and gazed down at her with those warm brown eyes that held sparkling golden flecks. "Marc."

"Hi, Debbie," he said softly. "I hope I'm not too late."

She wanted to be angry with him and tell him to go away, but she couldn't. Not because everyone was staring at them, and not because she didn't want to make a scene. She didn't want to tell him to leave because she really wanted him to stay. She'd missed him.

"How?" she asked. "I canceled the ticket."

"It wasn't easy," he said, grinning. "That's why I wasn't here earlier. My flight cut it so close, I had to dress on the plane." He stepped nearer, so close she could smell his musky cologne. It was a scent she knew well.

"I didn't want to let you down," Marc said. "I don't know what happened, but there was no way I was going back on my promise. I want to be here with you."

Debbie's heart swelled. She wanted to believe him, but she knew what she'd seen, and she couldn't forget it.

"So, who is this gentleman?" Felicia asked, sidling up to Debbie and Marc.

Debbie put on a smile and turned to Felicia. "This is my boyfriend, Marc," she said proudly. Marc slipped his arm around her waist to emphasize the boyfriend part.

"Oh, *this* is your date?" Felicia asked, looking stunned. "Well, I would have never guessed. I'm glad you were able to come after all."

Marc gave Felicia his most charming smile, then said, "Will you excuse us?" He linked arms with Debbie and escorted her away from the group.

Debbie did her best not to laugh at the insulted look on Felicia's face.

When they were alone, he looked at her with questions in his eyes. "I don't understand what happened. Why did you cancel my ticket? Did I do something wrong?"

She dropped her eyes, but he touched her chin with his fingertips and lifted her eyes to his.

"I saw you," she said. "I saw you at your house with that woman."

Marc's brows furrowed. "What woman?"

"The woman you were at Gallagher's with that one night. I saw you two together at the house, and you were drinking champagne and looking like you were..." she halted, unable to go on. Tears formed in her eyes, and she didn't want him to see how hurt she'd been.

"Wait? You saw us at the house? With champagne? Debbie. It wasn't what you thought. That was Melinda, the woman I've been working with on the fitness deal. There wasn't anything going on between us."

"Why was she at your house? Why were you hugging her?" Debbie asked.

"Oh, no. Is that what you saw? Didn't you see the other people there too?"

Debbie frowned. "What other people? I just saw the two of you."

Marc gave a relieved sigh. "I was hugging her because we'd just signed the contract. She and I had put a lot of work into that deal. It was a relief. And the entire board was there, too. We'd opened champagne for everyone and celebrated."

Debbie thought about what she'd seen and realized he was telling the truth. She'd misunderstood it. "So, nothing is going on between you and her?"

Marc gently placed his hands on her arms. "Not a thing. The only person I have anything going on with is you." He drew her into a hug and placed a warm kiss on her cheek.

Debbie sighed.

"I'm so sorry," she said softly. "I should have confronted you, but that's not something I'd ever do. I could have saved myself a lot of heartache if I'd just asked."

"Don't apologize. It wasn't your fault. I can understand why you thought what you did. But you have to believe me when I say there is no one else in my life except you." He pulled away and looked into her eyes. "I love you, Debbie. You. Only you."

Tears pooled in her eyes, and she trembled as she spoke. "I love you, too. Only you."

He kissed her, wrapping his arms tightly around her. Her heart swelled with love for him. She was so happy he was here, and they were together again.

Finally, reluctantly, he pulled away.

"Congratulations on your deal," she said, smiling up at him. "You're going to be a very rich man."

He chuckled. "You're all I need. Well, you, Bernie, and Chloe."

She laughed. "How did you get here? Did you get on another flight?"

"Not exactly. I hired a private plane that took me to Atlanta, and then another smaller plane to Nassau. I would have never made it here by tonight if I'd waited for a seat to open on a commercial flight."

"And you did all that for me?" she asked.

"Only for you," he said, grinning. "I only have one problem."

"What's that?" She couldn't imagine what it could be.

"You canceled my room, too. You wouldn't know of a room I could stay in, would you?" he waggled his brows at her.

"I think we can arrange something."

Marc nodded toward the wedding group that was so obviously staring at them. "Should we rejoin them? They look like they're bursting with curiosity."

"Not quite yet," Debbie said, raising on tip-toe toward his lips. "Let's just have another moment alone."

Marc happily obliged with one more kiss.

Epilogue

One Year Later

Debbie stood in Marc's kitchen with her neighborhood friends, gazing out at the back yard and the many guests sitting in chairs, waiting for the spectacle to begin. Music was playing softly in the background as the canopy of pink and white blossoms swayed gently in the breeze. It was a lovely sight, but Debbie was shaking like a leaf.

"You're going to be fine," Lindsay said, turning Debbie away from the window. She fussed with Debbie's gown and checked her veil. "You look as pretty as a princess," Lindsay said, smiling wide.

"Thanks to you and your expertise," Debbie told her friend. Lindsay had been the one to help her choose her wedding dress, and she'd done a wonderful job. The satin and lace dress fit her to perfection, and she did feel like royalty in it.

Mallory, Lisa, and Kristen all stood in the kitchen wearing beautiful dresses they'd bought at the bridal shop while their little girls, Marie, Abby, and Shannon fidgeted in their adorable dresses of lavender, pink, and sage. Just as they had looked a year ago when they'd had the photoshoot, the girls were like pretty little fairies ready to soar. But today they had a different job. Today they were Debbie's flower girls and ring bearer.

"You look beautiful," Lisa said, smiling at Debbie. Lisa's hand went unconsciously to the small bump on her belly. Lisa and Avery were expecting a baby in five months, and she barely showed yet. Debbie was thrilled for the couple and knew that little Abby was going to love having a new little brother or sister.

"Thanks, Lisa," Debbie said, hugging her carefully so as not to pull on her veil.

"I can't believe this day is already here," Kristen said, hugging her also. "Marie has been asking me every day when she gets to wear the pretty dress and carry the ring on the tiny pillow." She laughed.

"I saw her practicing earlier, carrying the pillow so carefully," Debbie said, chuckling. "She looked adorable."

Mallory came over and hugged her too. "I'm so happy for you. You and Marc are going to have an amazing life."

Tears threatened to fill Debbie's eyes. Mallory knew how heartbroken Debbie had been when she'd thought Marc was cheating on her, and Mallory also knew how happy this day made her, too. After Marc had explained what had happened, they'd enjoyed their time in the Bahamas together and hadn't been apart since. Debbie had begun working with Mallory, and things progressed very quickly. Before she knew it, she had so many clients wanting her decorating advice for both antiques and new furniture that she no longer had time for the bridal shop. It was then that Lindsay stepped up and offered to buy it from her.

"My father said he'd loan me some of the money, and I think I can swing the rest," Lindsay had told her the day she'd offered to purchase the Victorian house and the business. "I can't picture myself doing anything else."

Debbie had been thrilled for her. She knew Lindsay was capable of running the business, and might even have fresh ideas on how to make it grow. Debbie knew the day they'd closed on the sale that her mother would have been pleased with Lindsay owning it too. It helped Debbie move on, without guilt, to her new career, which she was loving.

And then Marc had proposed, and her life had changed again. There wasn't anyone else Debbie would have wanted to spend her life with. He was everything she'd always hoped to find in a man, and she knew they'd be happy together. It was his encouragement that had helped to build up her confidence in not only herself but in her business abilities. He'd been nothing but positive about her new career every step of the way. She hadn't needed a man to make her feel whole—she'd needed a partner who loved her and to build a life with. And he was the perfect partner for her.

Ryan came into the kitchen, carrying one-year-old Joshua. "Are you ready to walk down that aisle?" he asked Debbie, handing Joshua over to Kristen. Debbie had known Ryan the longest since he'd lived in the neighborhood before any of the others, and she'd asked him to walk her down the aisle. He'd been honored that she'd asked.

Debbie took a deep breath. "It's now or never, I guess."

The women in the room laughed. "Everyone out there is someone who loves or cares about you," Mallory said. "There's no need to be nervous."

"Just lock eyes with Marc, and you'll be fine," Lindsay told her.

Debbie walked to the window again and saw Marc standing beside the minister in front of the crowd. Craig, his brother-in-law, was standing beside him as the best man. Marc looked so handsome in his black tux that her heart melted. She couldn't believe this adorable, sweet, kind, and successful man wanted to spend his life with her. She felt like the luckiest woman on earth.

Finally, the wedding march swelled through the fragrant air, and the women urged the girls out with their baskets of rose petals while Marie held the pillow with the rings. Lindsay turned and winked encouragingly at Debbie, then walked behind the girls, down the aisle.

Debbie took another deep breath. Ryan offered his arm, and they stepped out the door and down the aisle. Debbie smiled when she saw Bernie in his bow-tie sitting in the front next to Marc's father, and Chloe wearing a tiara, sitting on a tufted pillow in a chair. When Debbie raised her eyes, she saw those warm brown eyes that had first caught her attention over a year ago, with those twinkling gold flecks in that handsome face. She held her gaze with Marc as he reached for her hands, and they proclaimed their love for each other under the apple blossoms.

-End-

About the Author

Deanna Lynn Sletten is the author of THE WOMEN OF GREAT HERON LAKE, MISS ETTA, MAGGIE'S TURN, FINDING LIBBIE, THE LAKE HARRIET SERIES, and several other titles. She writes heartwarming women's fiction, historical fiction, and romance novels with unforgettable characters. She has also written one middle-grade novel that takes you on the adventure of a lifetime.

Deanna is married and has two grown children. When not writing, she enjoys walking the wooded trails around her home with her beautiful Australian Shepherd, traveling, and relaxing on the lake.

Deanna loves hearing from her readers. Connect with her on her website at: deannalsletten.com